EXCUSE ME
I'M NOT DEAD YET

EXCUSE ME
I'M NOT DEAD YET

The secret of staying young is
to live honestly, eat slowly and
lie about your age.

— LUCILLE BALL

Nola Rocco

EXCUSE ME I'M NOT DEAD YET

Engaging Books For The Fifty+ Woman
Northport House, New York

Contact information: excusemeimnotdeadyet.com

Excuse Me...I'm Not Dead Yet!: novel/Nola Rocco
First Edition 2013
Second Edition 2018

The Library of Congress Cataloging-in-Publication Data
Subjects: 1- fiction/relationships 2- fiction/self-empowerment 3- fiction/romance
4- fiction/humor 5-fiction/transgender
ISBN-13: 978-0-692-18738-8

Cover Photo: Kelli Udall
Cover Design: Shark Adelic
Interior Design: Amnet

Printed in the United States of America

Introduction

Excuse me...I'm Not Dead Yet! is for the reluctant aging baby boomer who navigates dating after fifty or who gave up and started wearing pajamas to the supermarket.

Prologue

The birth of the problem began in the parking garage across from the beauty salon. Scrunching her mousy wet strands in the rearview mirror, Suzanne struggled to convince herself. "It'll be better after it dries."

She inhaled, started the Volvo and with pursed lips exhaled releasing a sigh of relief as the engine turned over…a technique she performed in childbirth. She shifted into reverse. Still scrunching the hair, the car rolled backwards.

But Suzanne couldn't stop thinking; she knew women in their fifties were having sex regularly. Divorced and contented with her opinionated, reclusive, tightly choreographed routine, pampering for Suzanne meant going to the dentist. Independence ranked of prime importance, finding a man was not—she owned an electric blanket. Suzanne liked it that way.

Then she slammed on the brakes.

CHAPTER 1

Sixty Days Before B'Day

"I'm going to freeze myself at 59 + 364 forever. After all, *one* day does not make me a different person." Suzanne mumbled, as she was about to leave behind another monochromatic, mundane, prosaic, repetitious, droning, unremarkable and...sexually stale year. "Turning sixty...is the new fifty," she told herself.

Falling into a self-dialogue being self-contradictory opened both sides of the brain making her see things more clearly. It began when Lucy, Suzanne's daughter, afraid her birthday gift wouldn't arrive in time sent it early—eighty-nine days pre-mature to be exact. When the package arrived, Suzanne unwrapped it. Lucy won a doctorial internship to an exploration project cruising the sea floor off Greece searching for sunken ships and ancient treasures. But surprisingly, the gift was purchased on Amazon and not an old crusted gold coin.

"Yes I got it," Suzanne emailed her. "Just wonder why you sent it early since you purchased it online?"

"Mom, I rarely get Wi-Fi." Lucy emailed back.

The gift was a small plastic disc on a thin metal chain accented with a bright red button. Suzanne's thumb fit perfectly in its grove. Fortunately the necklace had a long chain.

"I love it...promise to always wear it." Suzanne emailed her...millennium kids need reinforcement. Although Suzanne lived alone, she believed any sort of medical alert—unless you were ill—seemed a bit much, especially for someone like herself. Suzanne's lifestyle was deliberately well choreographed.

"OK, boring, flat, monotonous, sexually stale, but happy."

That was until she received Lucy's birthday gift and almost ran into the man in the jeep. Alone at home that night, her well choreographed, single life of twenty-seven years felt like a thread from a beautiful sweater had been pulled, and like the sweater her life began to unravel.

As most single divorced women, she did fine...maybe not great if you left your unemployed husband back when the divorce laws were in favor of the working partner.

"A meager $200 a month barely covered childcare." Suzanne complained to the judge, but like most young women, got a better job and got into the swing of being a single parent. Weighing the degrees of mental and physical abuse against the stigma of being divorced, divorce looked good. She went for it. Now years later, her daughter was soon to get her doctorate, and a *job*. Having married young, Suzanne was finally experiencing freedom.

Many of Suzanne's girlfriends became very wealthy hanging in there waiting until the financials were better. She chose a better life without abuse. And like most single mothers dated at first. But Suzanne stopped when she saw how the new boyfriend's kids were spoiled, or his career came first leaving dirty dishes, childcare and carpooling for her. She pictured herself a housekeeper...that would never work. But then Suzanne, thirty-two at the time, met this successful Palo Alto orthopedic surgeon whose kids were out of the house. A widower. He was financially successful, well established—she Googled him.

"Older is better, right?" after all twenty years difference was no big deal. Upscale foodie hangouts, wine tastings and season theater tickets, she loved dressing up like a princess. Even the thought of him excited her. Being cautious, she didn't rush into anything, yet she didn't want to lose him either. So the invitation for a long weekend in Hawaii sounded perfect.

It was a warm, breezy evening in Maui and a night Suzanne never forgot. Her body was draped in a tight Ralph Lauren periwinkle blue, silk slip dress—*sexy*. Excited, she felt incredible.

They dined under the palms of a five-star resort overlooking the ocean while drinking Whispering Angel, an expensive French rosé. Not only were there hundreds of stars in the sky, there were twinkles in Suzanne's starry-eyes. Newly divorced she didn't want to seem needy and then too, having a small child at home she had been holding back. She had all she could do not to have an orgasm on the plane sitting close let him reach down between her legs. Sex was definitely on Suzanne's mind. After all isn't that what Hawaii was about—sun, sand, Mai Tai's and sex?

The first night they were deep in conversation and Suzanne encouraged the doctor to talk about his past wife…they would get to this sooner or later. And she didn't want a ghost hanging around.

"…Nancy had terminal breast cancer." The doctor said with sincerity. "We had ten wonderful years, but with three kids I was anxious to find a new wife. It's faster if I help her along," he said point blank. "Get it over with and move on. Right?"

His frankness and angry undertone startled Suzanne, as if the wife's cancer was her fault. But then surprise—the doc was a widower twice. Suzanne listened becoming uncomfortable as more slime oozed with additional scary details. Facts she would never have known until it was too late. And what was really interesting, he had no problems sharing this information.

"My second wife had a brain tumor. Yep, Jamie was terminal. The kids were in high school then. And you know *me*…I'm not a man who likes to be alone. Nothing's wrong with putting her down? She's dying anyway. I'm a doctor…" taking a sip of the pricey rosé, smiling at her, he justifies his actions "…we need to think of those still living. You, me right?"

Really—*dying anyway*? His words turned Suzanne off.

That night, it didn't take long for the Whispering Angel to shout loud and clear, Suzanne's starry eyes opened. She saw buttons on his pajama shirt pulling on the buttonholes, and ugly gray hairs peeking through. The little openings tugged against his belly fat. As he undressed, her no longer blind eyes saw more belly fat generously pouring over super hung genitals.

Does he think because he had money and two dead wives, he can let himself become one big ball of excessive hanging skin with enormous swaying genitalia? He was thinking sex. But Suzanne was elsewhere. — *It's impossible for our bodies to meet. And if they did, I would be dead wife number three smothered by belly-fat.*

Besides, Suzanne noticed he had an unpleasant smell—an old man's smell. Life was all about him. His wants, his needs. He couldn't wait. Well neither could Suzanne. Livid, she boiled in anger. The next day while the doctor was on the Maui golf course, she packed all her things and flew back to San Francisco. Divorced men wanted younger women. Widowers were needy.

There seemed always a reason for Suzanne not to develop a serious relationship. In time, the extra twenty pounds put Suzanne into a less attractive bracket. Of course she did Pilates and yoga, working her body like a circus performer—all good stuff. But she *hated* it. Only now she accepted herself…bumps, lumps and quirks…having no problem wearing pajamas to the supermarket, bunny slippers to work and Uggs even when it's eighty degrees. At 59 + 304 days, Suzanne felt two-thirds of her life was over.

"Not to worry. I have no ticking clock—I have a kid." She reminded herself every time she felt guilty or worse, thought of being "never married". Purchasing a small cottage with a San Francisco city view and having a profession you quit only when you have died gave Suzanne independence and security.

But the emotional reaction to the medical alert tag, lead to a hideous nightmare. When it developed into recurring nightmares with panic attacks, Suzanne's life became a disaster zone. Lack of sleep left her exhausted, especially since she had to get up at 4:00 a.m. At first, she tried to knock herself out with a glass or two or three of wine…even switched to double, extra dry martinis. When the martinis failed, she knew it was time to see a psychiatrist.

CHAPTER 2

The Panic Attack

––––––––––

"**W**hat triggered the panic attack?" Dr. Markowitz asked.

"B'day is coming up? I'll be...sixty. It's no big deal," Suzanne assured her.

"Yes, you told me." Dr. Markowitz gave her *a let's move on*, look.

Fidgeting with her ring, Suzanne realized she'd been repeating herself.

Dr. Markowitz opened a large Pellegrino, poured it into a tall, thin glass. She offered it to Suzanne. Jessica Markowitz had rich auburn hair. It was natural. She wore it shoulder length, professional, but sexy. And it had a shine you didn't get from any man-made product. In her mid-fifties, her porcelain skin showed no trace of Botox or facial filler. Her lips were outlined with a thin tattoo. Suzanne studied every tiny detail of her face, because she was *jealous!* The woman, slim at five-nine, was intense with a haughty look you see on the cover of expensive women's magazines. No one dared challenge this woman. Talented, she had a gift for this with no time for trivial or frivolous cases. In fact, Dr. Markowitz only agreed to see Suzanne because Paige asked.

Paige, the co-host at the radio station and Suzanne's BFF, was Dr. Markowitz's long-standing client. Suzanne thought for sure she wasn't high profile enough. But that wasn't the problem. Suzanne's type of anxiety was not Dr. Markowitz's specialty. A panic attack for Markowitz equaled a headache for a brain surgeon. But when Paige got

Suzanne the appointment, she grabbed the opportunity. If this was what it took—she was into it.

"There was knocking at my front door." Picking up where she left off.

"Your nightmare begins with this knocking. Who's knocking?" Markowitz asked.

"It's more like a pounding...yep, definitely a *pounding* by two policemen. It was loud."

"Names?" Markowitz wanted more. "Know these policemen?"

"Irish, I think...." Suzanne paused. "Maybe, Kelly and O'Connor? I've seen them hanging out at the Starbucks at the corner of Princess and Bridgeway. But no, I don't *know* these guys."

"Go on."

"When no one answered they try to open the front door, but it's locked. So the Kelly guy goes to the trunk of the police car, gets an ax..." Suzanne gasped, "...that front door is special."

"It's still the middle of the night?" Markowitz clarified.

"Four. Paige and I have to be at the radio station by five and...."

The good doctor gave her another look—rambling, again.

"So Kelly gets the ax." Markowitz repeated. "Go on."

"Dr. Markowitz...this front door is one-hundred-years old." Suzanne took a deep breath. "I painfully scrubbed the old brass hardware with a lethal chemical, sanded, and glued this door back together...all by herself I gave it a second life. The etched glass panels are original with the house. When these policemen break the glass to get in...I *scream!*"

Markowitz took notes. "OK. Go on. The dream comes back?"

"Not that night, a few nights later." Suzanne felt hot, but worse her sweaty body smelled. She couldn't remember if she used deodorant that morning. And she was nauseous. "It's as if this terrible dream is telling me something bad is about to happen...a warning!"

"Did you feel threatened by these men?"

"Why were they breaking into my house? Dr. Markowitz, I was home."

"In the dream, you were *home*?"

"Yes, upstairs sleeping."

Suzanne caught Markowitz checking her watch. She picked up the pace not wanting to leave the session with only half a story.

"A couple nights later the same nightmare comes back. My heart races, but I watch the dream as if it's a TV show."

"O'Connor and Kelly?"

Who else but O'Connor and Kelly? Is she listening?

"Yes, but now they're in my bedroom. Under the amber reading light I'm in bed with a book…by the way, it's the perfect bedside lamp for my shabby-chic look." —*Why do I always have to set the scene?*

Quickly not to loose her attention, Suzanne continued, "Kelly throws back the drapes and the street light pours in."

"OK, OK, I get the picture," Markowitz interrupted, rolling her hand to move the conversation forward. "What happens?"

"O'Connor and Kelly walk smack into rows and rows of tiny cobwebs. Millions of them…like no one had been in that room for weeks." Using swim-like arm gestures, Suzanne developed another scene, "Cobwebs spread from the book, to the reading lamp to the headboard, to the windows…" and with even more exaggerated arm gestures, "…the policemen swim, clawing their way, spitting out cobwebs O'Conner and Kelly finally reach me…."

Holding up her hand, Suzanne stopped Markowitz from cutting in. —*No, not now!*

"…O'Connor leans over and *gently* takes the book out of my hands."

Demonstrating, Suzanne picked up one of the books from the table holding it between her two fingers, showed how motionless the move was. "Although he's careful, it upsets the delicate balance, I gradually fall forward."

Before Suzanne could finish she took another deep breath, and quietly exhaling, "Dr. Markowitz—I'm *d-e-a-d*!"

"What makes you think you're dead?"

"My face is a *ghastly* decaying blue. *Disgusting!* The dried skin on this haunting face shrank onto its facial structure as if glued to the cheekbones."

"But wait…wait. How do you know it's…*you*?"

"I'm wearing the exact same pink striped pajamas as the dead woman."

Taking another long deep yoga breath, then with pursed lips Suzanne slowly blows it out, counting in her head. Her heart raced. Pressing both hands against her chest, she applied pressure.

"I've been dead in bed, for God knows how long. Days? Maybe a week?"

Markowitz glanced at her watch, again.

Standing up Suzanne's hands shook. "Oh my GOD! It's a sign I'm going to die! OK, OK, I'm not dying at this exact moment, but I know one thing, I'm going to puke!"

Markowitz handed her the wastebasket just in time.

"Suzanne Robins, you have thanatophobia."

"What? What the hell is thanatophobia?"

CHAPTER 3

Bob

———

Suzanne hustled through her morning routine—brush hair, clamp, brush teeth, floss—then rinsed the dental floss under hot water, shaking it, and hanging it over the towel rack. It was tough stuff so a second use was acceptable. Actually, so tough Suzanne thought about squeezing in a third run. But it was the scent of the French Lavender gel that drew her into the shower. She focused on that—the smell of lavender and a new day.

If only Suzanne had time for a good soak in the tub, but then again she'd probably fall asleep and drown. In reality she's still totally exhausted and wants only to go back to bed.

"How many more days can I hang on?" she dialogued with the image in the mirror. "Is there an individual in the Guinness World Book of Records who has gone the longest without sleep? I think that would be classified as torture!"

She couldn't linger. Without a good night's sleep, dragging, Suzanne threw on old sweats and stained Uggs then headed downstairs.

Bob watched.

"OK. Who are you, the fashion police?" she said to his quizzical stare. "Hey, I do radio, remember? I'm *invisible*. I don't dress for success, I dress for comfort!" —*Bob's judging me. Yet I wonder if he really cares what I'm wearing.*

Suzanne questioned if he really understood, after all he knew a few words like *dinner* and *ball*. She occasionally commented on people who conversed with their dogs. These people who talked to pets she concluded were lonely. Now Suzanne found herself sharing thoughts and feelings with Bob, often going as far as telling him stories about stuff that happened at the radio station. "Would you believe Bob, this dumb little Smart Car holds up the Bay Bridge for hours. They dropped a mechanic by helicopter. Don't ask why the helicopter didn't pick up the little car and airlift it off the bridge."

The words had no meaning, but the attention he loved. And more important, as a listener he was great.

"Go do your thing, Bobby Boy! I'll call you when *dinner* is ready." Opening the back door, Suzanne let Bob out. Why she said *dinner* for breakfast, she didn't know nor did she think it mattered to Bob. *Dinner* sounded more special.

In any case Suzanne perfected multitasking. She grabbed the day old bagel as it popped from the toaster, smearing it with cream cheese. Then added flax, powdered protein and green algae into the pre-poured juice sitting in the fridge, downing the juice with pre-counted vitamins from one of the pre-counted plastic zip bags stashed in the lower cabinet draw—the draw closest to the fridge. Time: 180 seconds. She made a point to avoid the glass front of the upper cabinets—God forbid she'd catch her reflection. The coffee was already brewed set on a timer that beeped reminding Suzanne it was time to let Bob inside. She still had to heat the milk and froth it, which she did with this gadget that worked on two AA batteries. It whipped perfectly as the coffee dripped through its filter a second time—making it strong.

Suzanne's choreographed routine worked without fail. No fuss. No mess. She usually grabbed something from the fridge like a non-fat yogurt...more likely the one with strawberries on the bottom throwing it into her large canvas bag. She liked having something to snack on. It was security—*What if my car breaks down? Do I sound like my mother?*

"Bobby Boy, come in!"

Bob sprints straight to his bowl. Yummy stuff! At least he seemed to think so. Suzanne must not forget to unlock the doggy door, dog freedom to run into the back yard. She never worried about the doggy door until a skunk invaded her neighbor's kitchen when she watched TV…about ten when the creature came scavenging via the doggy door. The dog got its scent and attacked. No need to say more.

The only times Suzanne smelled skunk was when the neighbor down hill smoked weed. She'd sit on the back step and inhale. Not only skunks, raccoons, but even deer munched on her flowers. Only three miles from the San Francisco city limits and the Golden Gate Bridge, who would believe…one hundred percent country, and exactly why Suzanne lived there.

Suzanne balanced the bagel in her mouth and coffee in one hand. Grabbing her safari jacket and stained canvas bag filled with snacks, purse, and iPhone, she still managed to reach down like a multi-jointed circus performer to grab the newspaper from the driveway…a feat she perfected with only a few disasters.

The Volvo needed time to warm up. Running the engine, the heater blast felt good on her legs. No matter what season in the bay area, it was cold at 4:40 in the morning. Then Suzanne dashed from Sausalito over the ever-awesome Golden Gate Bridge to the KABC Radio Station in downtown San Francisco. Suzanne *loved* this drive!

CHAPTER 4

KABC Traffic and Weather

Posted in black and white letters on the backside of every MUNI bus—SUZANNE ROBINS—took up the whole back view. But unlike the TV Carrie Bradshaw character, it was not a sexy visual. To the everyday early-morning San Francisco commuter, the traffic and weather were crucial. Listeners may not remember the name or recognize the face, but as for the traffic report the commuters tuned in from the time they woke up until the minute they parked their car. Suzanne ran their life.

"KABC traffic and weather, every ten minutes."

That radio voice was heard before their wife's, lover's, kids screaming, dog barking, or neighbor's whose driveway they may have blocked. A voice buried into their morning brain, even more delicious than their latte. After eighteen years, Suzanne's words delivered information with a twist of quirky humor. It became recognizable. Well, not as recognizable as Terry Gross on NPR's *Fresh Air*...her hero. Still, she liked to think her personalized chitchats with the early commuters—the bridge and tunnel people of San Francisco—were famous.

Over the years, traffic apps became indispensable and more accurate, but they didn't tell *why* there was a problem. And for some reason, knowing the *why* made sitting in traffic almost bearable.

"Stuck in traffic? *It sucks!*"

Boy that made you feel better at 6:00 a.m. Traffic alerts sounded like teenage warnings: "Potholes yawning at the Pacifica Exit. The road zombies haven't forgotten, just partied too hard over the weekend." At least you felt someone out there cared.

Then Suzanne preached her morning mantra—"Keep your eyes on the road. Don't you dare think about texting. Keep that hot coffee capped and not in your lap!"

She followed it without a hesitation—"Call and tell us the *hot* spot." She encouraged all listeners to report, hands free, any traffic issues they encountered en route to work. And if carpooling, reminded them to wait until they unloaded the kids.

Call-in conversations heard over the radio often warned other morning commuters before the app showed the data. Like the day a Loomis armored truck got stuck in the Golden Gate tollgate during the early morning traffic rush. What was the driver thinking using the narrow tollgate rather than the wider one especially designed for such vehicles? Was he asleep at the wheel? It took police ten minutes to arrive. No one stopped. Fortunately, traffic avoided that gate. Think…what if the truck had been loaded with money and this accident was planned?

Actually next to Suzanne's ex-husband, she considered herself one of the luckiest people in the world. Unlike a TV news personality who worried about every line on her face, weight fluctuation, gray hair and the never-ending stress of competition, no one ever saw her. Over eighteen years, Suzanne had gone from "acceptably attractive" to "plain Jane." Pampering for Suzanne meant going to the dentist—she was fine with that.

But lately an inner anxiety of leaving her fifties was taking a toll on her well-choreographed life.

Suzanne's tired body worked its way into the radio station at the dawn breaking time of 4:58 looking like a hangover.

Paige, filed her nails, and waited.

The broadcast warning light blinked red, ready to go green.

Suzanne burst into the sound booth, catching the engineer as he checked the clock. Grabbing the fresh coffee Paige handed her, she let her take the half-eaten bagel out of her mouth. They've been doing this routine for the past few weeks.

Paige stared at Suzanne saying without words—Casual...*again?*

"Hey! Who's here to impress?" Deliberately glancing around the glass both.

Paige's two thumbs pointed to herself.

One of the beauties of this job was the fact they were in a glass sound booth. Co-workers may or may not know your life, as there was little time between reports to talk. It was through personal tidbits over the radio they would learn about each other. Suzanne liked that. Being a private person she didn't air dirty laundry...so to speak. The radio listeners were her family, and her job was to get them to work on time. They counted on her.

Starting in radio for Suzanne was easy being a morning person. She looked forward to driving from Sausalito into the city making her way over the Golden Gate Bridge in the fog...the day before light breaks, before the sunrise. Dark and cold, she got to fight the fog ghosts who drifted across the bridge and tightly circled her car. So thick the Volvo's headlights bounced off reflecting their image back. Rumor had it that the Portuguese fishermen who settled Sausalito, came back to their boats early in the mornings just the way they did when they lived here. Suzanne believed she saw them...she drove carefully.

The drawback to an early morning job was how it killed your social life. Having been divorced for some twenty-seven years, Suzanne had given up on having a relationship.

"Men don't like going to bed with the six o'clock news and waking up hours before the crack of dawn," she'd defend her position to Lucy.

But Lucy rebutted warning her, "Mom, you're going to die alone."

Finding a boyfriend with similar hours was short-lived. When the weekends came, sleep was the only thing on Suzanne's mind. With no biological clock to worry about, she believed Mr. Right...if there were a Mr. Right...would somehow drop into her life. Hating the dating scene left it to fate. Finding a man was not her priority—Suzanne owned an electric blanket.

"I'm growing old naturally," she muttered as each wrinkle appeared.

Independence spoiled her, along with privacy and a great job. Suzanne was confident even if the producers didn't know her name or recognize her face they liked what she said and how she said it. Personal chats with callers made traffic interesting, keeping ratings up…high ratings were good. The producers often referred to Suzanne as "Traffic" and Paige as "Weather", like when she'd grab coffee at the snack bar— "Good Morning, Traffic." Neither Paige nor Suzanne cared; the low profile suited them, even if for different reasons.

As a single mom, Suzanne was proud of her daughter. She reasoned this had lots to do with settling in Marin County, some ten miles from downtown San Francisco, living in the country, yet city inches away. Narrow tree-lined streets curved displaying glorified Victorians. At the time it was the rage for young couples to buy and restore to their turn-of-the-century original beauty. Suzanne got a bonus—a view of the San Francisco skyline.

"It's a good investment," she convinced herself pouring more money into the house year after year.

"With those city lights, you will never get lonely. You need to think about retirement," Lucy reminded her…a thought very unlike a millennium kid. "People love Sausalito. What a great B&B the place would make." And rubbed in, "…and you could take the ferry when you can't drive."

Suzanne got the point—she wanted the basement!

Delighted in fixing the house to her unique, eclectic style, Suzanne copied ideas from the shabby-chic store on Fillmore Street. It was soft, comfortable, lots of white—a woman's house. And, of course, she loved finding little treasures at flea markets to add to the look. Well, not when Lucy was home.

"Antiquing happens only in Greece or China." Lucy lectured, "That stuff is junk!"

The quirkiness of the house appealed to Suzanne. The uneven hardwood floors sloping south made leveling all the furniture legs a carpenter's nightmare. After spending a small fortune refinishing the redwood paneling, Suzanne painted it white.

"It wasn't a mistake!" she insisted. "It's a learning experience, like going to college," determined to restore the house the way she wanted it.

"Yes. I can do it alone! A man only complains about cost, anyway!" she ragged further.

So it was understandable in the nightmare, Suzanne went bananas when the front door was being smashed. She saved the door almost destroying her hands sanding and scrubbing the etched glass panels, which had become extremely fragile with age.

As the panic attacks became more frequent, she was glad to be seeing Markowitz. Without Paige's insistence, she might have gotten into a serious depression. Paige was her BFF and has always been there for her.

CHAPTER 5

Peter

———

Peter Miller did the weather, a serious meteorologist. Suzanne did the traffic report, but unlike Paige was a college graduate with no training in broadcasting getting the job only because she read well and had a great voice. They offered her a two-week trial covering for the regular guy retiring ahead of schedule. The first week she did pretty normal readings from the monitor...word for word. By the second week Suzanne was bored out of her mind, she couldn't help herself...tidbits of humor popped out.

"I have this chip in my brain and can't control my tongue." She vented to Paige.

But she didn't get bumped! Somehow the listeners related to her frustrations, callers jammed the station, and the producers were over joyed when the ratings soared! So, Suzanne stayed. That was eighteen years ago.

Peter was thirty at the time. They hit it off immediately. Over time they became best friends. He had gone to one of those prep schools back East and married his college sweetheart. Super social, Peter loved to party, even Burning Man. He'd run off to a charity gala in a heartbeat, hobnobbing with the San Francisco social A-list—museum fundraisers, art openings and foodie functions. He wasn't ever crazy-in-love with his wife, but he did love her and never strayed.

Nothing romantic ever developed between Suzanne and Peter. As the years rolled on and as truly good friends, it didn't surprise Suzanne when Peter wanted to move on with his life. She had been in those shoes. When Peter got his divorce papers, she was there one hundred percent.

"Martinis on me!"

Because of the strong bond, Peter told her everything. "I'm going to be *Paige*, Suzanne."

Suzanne didn't see it coming. She had encountered Peter's feminine qualities—softer and more sensitive than most men.

Going to lunch they would pass the Cole Haan store window on Union Square, Peter lagged behind studying the women's shoes, especially the boots. Suzanne could tell he wanted to touch the soft leather and try them on.

"Forget it! They don't have size twelve," she'd tease.

Peter loved clothes especially upscale labels—Ralph Lauren, Hermés, Gucci. He'd arrive at work at five a walking Polo ad—cabled cashmere sweaters, pleated khakis, alligator belts, and wonderful casual English leather shoes. He wore brown and dark green tones, maybe a touch of pale pink or peach. Yet, lots of men used those colors.

"You, a woman?" Suzanne's mouth hung open—*Does Peter mean he's going to arrive in drag? Was he saying he's becoming a transvestite, sneaking around as a woman?*

Suzanne was confused. The only time a man surprised her was when she waited at the plastic surgeon's office to get her ears pinned back and sat next to a guy dressed in a business suit...you seldom see men in plastic surgery offices. She didn't have to ask. He read her curiosity.

"Breast augmentation." The guy beamed.

So when Peter told Suzanne he's becoming Paige, she didn't know exactly he was talking about—*How much of a woman?*

"I've wanted to tell you for a long time. But had to be sure."

"You're referring to a *real* woman? Boobs...and all?" Catching her breath, she needed to get her right and left-brain on the same page.

Peter had been on hormone treatments for a number of years, and in analysis for a long time. Now that he mentioned it, she had noticed his facial hair getting finer and finer down to almost nothing, and then it was completely gone. Yet she didn't think much of it as it happened so slowly over time. Even the breast augmentation was unnoticeable under a jacket or bulky sweater.

Now, Peter's has been waiting for the final step. He must be certain he wants surgery to remove his male genitalia.

"Does Sasha know?" Suzanne asked.

"It's killing her."

How do you tell a child at twelve your dad is going to become your mother? Do you have Biological Mom #1 and Biological Mom #2? What if you are all dressed up in your stilettos, and she still called you *Dad*? How does that work? Suzanne didn't know just how far to go with questions having many, but did know Peter needed her. So typically Suzanne, kept it light.

"When do I start calling you Paige?"

"You'll know."

"Hey, we'll get through this!" Suzanne remembered saying, although she wasn't quite sure how this would work out.

Born Peter J. Miller, Jr., Peter always believed he was in the wrong body. Ever since he could remember, he felt he was a girl. He loved the feel of silk and in awe of lace. Pink, lavender, and all pastels were colors of choice. Loving makeup...lipstick was delicious. As a small boy, he gravitated towards dolls. When caught touching his sister's doll, he was teased.

"Only pansies play with dolls!" his father yelled. Then he'd throw Peter a football. Which Peter would drop, crying.

Peter never dated as a teenager and when he met his college sweetheart, he thought maybe he was normal. Happily, he tried. Delighted to be a father, yet he never felt right, and couldn't figure it out. He knew he wasn't gay. He knew he wasn't a man either. Peter knew one thing, he felt he was a woman and it had been haunting him. He hid this inside his heart and mind; spending the last ten in Dr. Markowitz's care gradually making the physical gender changes. He believed in his soul, he was born a woman. He was sure of it. No matter the cost—his marriage, his job, friends—he was going to make the outside like the inside deciding to change his gender. His biggest hurdle was not losing his daughter.

The morning came some two years ago. Peter, now forty-six, arrived in a tight skirt, sweater, stilettos and a sleek ponytail. First Suzanne thought Peter was just too busy to get a haircut, but then it made sense.

Peter had been dreaming of his *coming out* day, envisioning it many times—preparing himself, practicing makeup and learning to walk in heels. Peter was six-feet plus, slender and worked out almost every day…a great body and beautiful facial bone structure. Peter was almost free. Being true to his new self, was ready for the final surgery. Then one morning Peter arrived at the station, Suzanne was shocked.

"Oh my God! Good-bye, Peter. Hello, *Paige*!"

And Paige was anxious to start dating—men.

CHAPTER 6

Bonding

———

Suzanne hesitated, but she knew she needed to return to Markowitz, even after puking on her collector Oriental rug…in some ways Suzanne thought they were bonding. On second thought, could her hesitation have anything to do with the fact that her ex-husband was a psychotherapist?

Married as students Suzanne worked while getting her undergraduate degree, to pay for his doctorate program at UCLA. This was after he blew his family's three hundred-year-old Mayflower Trust fund on LSD. His tendency to join Big Sur orgies and screw around with his female students did not sit well with her. Then came the night when Suzanne's class got canceled and she returned home early to find the house all lit up, "Hello". There was no one to be found except a sleeping child—good news. Then finally she discovered a sleeping husband and babysitter—bad news. Babysitter was fourteen—really bad news!

After weighing his good points: six-foot-three with perfect posture, against the bad points: drugs and under aged sex, Suzanne packed up Lucy and left. The court gave the daughter to Suzanne. He got Sigmund Freud, the German shepherd puppy.

Moving to San Francisco, Suzanne changed back to her maiden name for fear the ex would be plastered all over the news. Instead, she soon discovered he had published a study on deviant sexual behaviors based on first-hand experiences. Somehow, he managed to join the Peace Corps and got out of the country. Upon his return, he married the babysitter—a different one. She might have been young, but Suzanne was much better looking!

The ex managed to get away with everything, including a free college education. Thanks to Suzanne—this was the luckiest man on earth.

A month or so after she left, Suzanne came upon one of his business cards tucked into the back flap of her wallet. She recalled how he agonized for hours before deciding on the color, paper quality, font and size, middle name or middle initial. Then to his name, added the priceless "PhD" and underneath, in italics—*Psychotherapist.* With delicious delight, it took only seconds for Suzanne to black out the last few letters, leaving—*Psycho.*

Needless to say, Suzanne had very little respect for the field of psychology. But Dr. Markowitz seemed different and she was grateful Markowitz wanted to get to the bottom of this.

"My daughter ordered a birthday gift online. Lucy's an intern doing research on a boat. Calls…every now and then…I learn more about her from her photos on Facebook…." Suzanne rambled on, "…the gift was a medical alert tag."

Suzanne can't remember if she mentioned this before to Markowitz. Just to be sure, lifted the chain from around her neck pressed the button, but nothing happened.

"It's not set up yet." She explained. Then as if on cue, sweat ran down Suzanne's neck, the fabric of her blouse stuck to her. She was burning up. It's obvious this medical alert affected her. She needed help.

Suzanne accepted Markowitz's offer of the big, soft, leather chair—a recliner. She put her feet up.

Analysis was new to Suzanne. She had been under the impression the longer psychotherapy takes, the less effective it is. Some people just love to *get into it.* There were those Beverly Hills housewives who go nuts if they don't get their weekly, or even daily, dosage. For them, therapy was like a spa treatment, relaxing, looking good for twenty-four hours then the wrinkles would come back. Suzanne wanted the anxieties and nightmare to stop. If this was what it was going to take—she was into it.

"This thanatophobia scares the hell out of me."

"We all have fears," said Markowitz. "Heights. Flying, spiders, darkness, needles, mirrors, germs and even doctors and dentists! Some fears are reasonable while others not. I have a patient who's afraid to go into a swimming pool alone."

"She can't swim?"

"No. She's afraid of sharks."

Markowitz continued in her clinical manner, "That's a serious fear. Many women fear becoming a bag lady ending up homeless and wandering the streets. Even Oprah…if you can imagine it…had a fear she might one day be penniless. It's rumored she stashed fifty thousand dollars into a special account, just in case."

Suzanne didn't want therapy to make a big dent in her small savings. She was a do-it-yourself-kind of woman. She'd brainstorm with herself, go over the issue in her head a million times and then take responsibility for her decisions. Suzanne believed if you can step outside yourself and look at the situation, you could be objective. After all, didn't people always have answers for other people's problems?

"I'm an adult and should listen to my intuitive self." She'd tell herself taking great pride in not running off to seek professional help at every fork in the road of her life. If she could figure out how to caulk windows, she could figure out what's going on in her head…so she thought.

Markowitz got back to the issue.

"Thanatophobia is an irrational fear of death." Markowitz explained bringing her back into the reason for sitting across from her.

In a professional voice Markowitz explained in analytical detail, "It's an extreme case of necrophilia, which is a general fear of things associated with death, like coffins or corpses. Many people are afraid of dying. It's common. But in your case…."

Suzanne tensed up, folding her arms sensed bad news coming.

"…you have a fear not only of dying, but of dying *alone*. And even more intense is the fact…not only do you fear dying alone…"

Suzanne's shoulders caved in. She wanted to protect her head into her hands from what was about to be thrown at her. Then it came, the worst news ever.

"...you are afraid no one will know you are dead and won't be found for days.

"*Just like my mother!*" she screamed.

"Well, that's interesting!" said Markowitz, but didn't go there. Instead, made a note. "Any phobia can be controlled, even cured, but... you have to make a real effort. People afraid of flying don't go out and hop a plane. They work to control their fear, they take...."

"Baby steps!" Suzanne cut in. "Isn't fifty-nine...too *young* to be haunted about dying?" questioning Markowitz's analysis of the dream.

"There are five-year-olds horrified about death."

Markowitz put her note pad down.

The hour slipped by. Or did Suzanne like this therapy stuff? "I guess we need to talk more?" she felt stupid once those words left her mouth.

"Of course! Meanwhile you need something for this." Markowitz took out her prescription pad.

"I'd be happy with Xanax or Ativan or Valium, *anything.*"

After closing her notes, Dr. Markowitz scribbled on the prescription pad and handed the sheet to Suzanne.

Puzzled, Suzanne read it back.

Markowitz didn't smile.

"Plan your funeral?"

CHAPTER 7

Rosemary Married Jimmy

———

N olan's Funeral Home located at the edge of Mill Valley on Tennessee Valley Road to be exact, appealed to Suzanne. She found it in the local yellow pages, so she Googled it. The hook—it was small, basic. But what cinched the deal with Nolan's was its minuscule parking lot.

As Suzanne drove up, she mumbled to herself, "I don't expect many guests —Oops, mourners." The small lot would appear filled, and Suzanne thought she'd look more popular.

The chapel didn't have the nauseating smell of decaying carnations or mold, although dark sitting under the pines. The mortuary had been a family operation and Suzanne felt good supporting local, besides she didn't see herself in a vast Forest Lawn type of resting place. Actually, if possible and in the top 1%, she'd have a plot on a cliff with an unobstructed ocean view off the coast of Santa Barbara. In case climate warming caused a rising tide, she'd be dry.

At first Suzanne questioned if Markowitz was trying to discourage her so she wouldn't come back. This seemed fine, as she would find another doctor someone who would give her pills for immediate results. So went her inner self-dialogue, a form of self-therapy. — *If I could sleep through the nightmare, I'd have no panic attacks. If I have no panic attacks, I would not be so exhausted and depressed. It's all one circle of reactions. All I need is a pill.*

Then on a second thought, Suzanne didn't want to be taking pills to get into bed and then more pills to get out of bed. She guessed Markowitz was right. —*Get over it.*

Suzanne did call Nolan's in advance figuring it would be best to visit on a slow day, if there is such a thing at a mortuary. It was not like shopping, but then again it was. —*If I'm not dead yet, do I have to come up with the full payment?*

To be on the safe side, Suzanne decided to select the *el cheapo* casket and not get persuaded by the top-of-the-line silk quilting and brass trims. In most cases, the deceased didn't get stuck with the bill. In her case, Suzanne will.

She knew cleaning out her console was a delaying tactic, but being hot in the car led her to the dim, heavily draped interior to meet the director, James Nolan. Jimmy was not thin, as expected. Actually, he appeared well fed and his voice sounded normal. Why this took Suzanne by surprise surprised her.

Jimmy believed the more Suzanne knew the setup, the more comfortable she'd be. Most people in this business didn't get involved with someone who has the fear of death phobia. Jimmy was extremely sensitive and unbelievably understanding, almost to the point of being too nice. Then again, that was his job. Suzanne was not the first and he promised, "I can handle *everything*, except the date."

Suzanne walked into the back room marked PRIVATE.

Rosemary, the perfect plain Jane type, worked on her current client a petite woman in her nineties—someone's grandma. But sadly... Suzanne didn't mean to be mean...this woman reminded her of a costumed, stuffed, old-lady dummy.

Rosemary married Jimmy and has been doing styling and makeup since high school. She became Suzanne's new BFF—at least for today. Suzanne unfolded a dress she packed earlier and carried in a shopping bag. She showed it to Rosemary.

"It's sleeveless. Do you really want people to see your arms?" Rosemary commented, sounding like Suzanne's mother. "You're going to be in church. It's pink...*hot* pink."

"It's *magenta!*" Suzanne insisted pulling out the Neiman Marcus price tag still tucked inside.

Yes, Suzanne picked the dress up on one of her shopping sprees when you check out the sale rack and something screams, *Mexico!* She had a dozen of these sexy-little-dress purchases sitting in her closet—new, never worn. Perfect for when you go to Mexico with a guy. Still she was not fooling herself...Mexico was not going to happen. After all these years still single, this dress was going nowhere.

"It's kind of cut low." Rosemary continued, again in a motherly tone.

"Your...." Rosemary hesitated before lifting her breasts with her hands.

Suzanne ignored the innuendo and her gesture. She wanted to move on. —*How long with this take?*

"I should wear it at least once...can't you stuff the bra?"

While Rosemary continued to work on the elderly woman's face, Suzanne's eagle eye spotted something askew around the old ladies' lace collar. It wasn't centered. With Suzanne's eye for detail, she couldn't help but reach out to adjust the collar.

"YUCK!"

She backs off after accidentally touching the corpse, smudging Rosemary's makeup job. —*So much foundation! It's overkill.* But Suzanne said nothing, sweating and feeling nauseous. She felt really, really sick and couldn't wait for this to be over. —*I'll come back again. Can't do this in one visit. It's just too much.*

Rosemary noticed the smudge. She retouched it and smiled at Suzanne.

"It's OK.".

"Sorry."

"She's dead." Rosemary confirmed.

"I know, but...."

"Does anyone ever say they look like *shit?*"

Suzanne ignored her comment. Remembering the makeup bag and rummaged through her purse. She dumped the cosmetics onto the table. —*I have got to be nice to this person. She's going to be doing my face.*

"I just want to look like me."
Rosemary checked the stuff.
"Hot pink?" Rosemary asked quizzically rolling up the lipstick.
"It goes nicely with the magenta dress." Suzanne said with a shrug.
"Hey, whatever works? It's *your* funeral."

CHAPTER 8

Bridge and tunnel people heading into San Francisco....

———

Suzanne looked for something, anything to create some interest, some excitement. Then an opportunity came, in her radio voice, "... North Bay, highway #101, stop-and-go as you head south from San Rafael. It's not your usual in-the-fast-lane ladder, folks...it's a real treat this morning...looks like a port-a-potty fell off a truck and is in the second lane, southbound. I repeat, that's southbound highway #101 coming out of San Rafael...need to slow down! I cannot help but wonder if the truck was going to...or coming from...a construction site? If anyone hits it, you know what will hit the proverbial fan!"

Suzanne took one quick but deep breath, using it as a stress reduction exercise while on air.

"Stuck in traffic? Call and tell us the *hot* spot." She managed to add, "KABC radio, your traffic and weather, every ten minutes." Not only did she relay the traffic, she used the drag time to get the Call Letters in per FCC Rules.

———

There were the usual listeners who traveled daily over the Golden Gate Bridge. Italian sports car dealer, Luca Mastrocola was one of the advertisers. Luca acted as if he owned the radio station, which gave him the right to call and complain. A copy of his ad on file at the station showed a very attractive racecar driver in a red protective suit, late fifties to early sixties, dark glasses, a sexy day-old beard and holding his helmet revealing a perfectly shaved head. Can't get more Italian!

The fog can be thick, the temperature freezing, and even a heavy drizzle never stopped Luca from keeping his top down. Typically Euro, he wore his reflective aviator sunglasses even on dark, foggy days along with his shinny fabric racing gear smothered with logo labels. From his running commentary on the car phone, he maneuvered his sports car as if he'd been driving on a raceway.

He loved FasTrak. While a faithful listener...always checking the bridge traffic...*impatient* would be Luca's perfect middle name.

"What the *fuck* is going on!" he yelled at Suzanne from his mobile to the station after getting caught in traffic.

From his ads Suzanne knew Luca had a machine shop in Marin for the custom made parts he installed at his Italian Sports Car Restoration Shop in South San Francisco. Luca traveled daily via the Golden Gate Bridge. Working nine hours behind Italy, he reminded the traffic reporters, "Every minute I'm late, the cash register in my head rings red!"

Suzanne had never met Luca. But she suspected he was under the assumption every helicopter flying over the bay area was there to film the traffic and to feed the footage to the station. Always listening to traffic, Luca recognized Suzanne's voice.

"...looks like another Monday! Bridge people heading into San Francisco from Richmond, the wind is blowing debris from an open garbage truck. Keep your eyes peeled for a storm of flying plastic bags. These are not party balloons, folks, this is garbage." Suzanne reported, and then took a quick deep breath—stress release.

"Golden Gate Bridge...smooth as silk." Her radio voice announced.

Another early morning Golden Gate Bridge commuter and faithful listener was Suzanne's favorite hair stylist, Dianne. She didn't know how old Dianne was. She hid it well having worked her way up from shampoo girl to big-time stylist with her own shop. When Dianne got stuck behind a slow-moving delivery van...no problem...Dianne applied mascara while chewing gum with the tiniest, almost unnoticeable movements of her jaw, saving her smoking for some pot. Her downtown shop on Sutter with a high-price lease catered to high-price clients. She couldn't afford to be late, but Dianne knew there was nowhere to go, no way out when the bridge got jammed. When stuck in traffic, Dianne popped in *Adele,* sat back and accepted the slow flow, all the while checking her hair in the rearview mirror.

A few cars ahead of Dianne, Luca sat at a complete stop with his top down caught behind a city bus. Wearing Italian leather driving gloves he tapped his fingers on the steering wheel. Exhaust poured out of the bus' tail pipe. His fine Zegna leather jacket became covered with specks of soot. Worse, he couldn't breathe. Looking up, he read the ad on the back of the bus:

SUZANNE ROBINS AND PAIGE MILLER
KABC TRAFFIC AND WEATHER EVERY TEN MINUTES!

Suzanne, on the air had just reported: "Jammed? Stuck in traffic? Boy can I identify with that! Call and tell us the *hot* spot." She loved that word, a wake-up call that got drivers to pay attention.

And of course Luca was listening to KABC.

The station light blinked green, a warning to turning red.

The broadcast assistant opened the door and handed Suzanne a note from a caller. Done, Suzanne read the note, anyway. "Nothing I can do, it's too late." But then knowing the caller sponsored the station; she gave in. "OK, OK! I'll take the call, off the air." Suzanne grabbed the phone, smiled to sweeten her voice.

"Hello Luca, what's it like this morning?"

"The bridge is jammed! Where are you? You need to pay attention. Change your tune." Luca's voice sounded even more furious coming through his Bluetooth. His Italian accent was thicker when mad.

"I don't *sing* the traffic report, Mr. Luca." Annoyed, Suzanne kept cool. "I try to report the facts as I get them. Now…thanks to you, I know the bridge is jammed and will report it in my next broadcast. Thank you, Luca." Then she handed the phone back to the assistant.

"Do these people think I'm actually there, on the bridge?" Suzanne asked the room.

CHAPTER 9

Therapy

G etting paid to listen to people's problems, then telling them what they already knew seemed like a rip-off. Then again, Suzanne felt guilty judging all therapists by her ex and his inappropriate sexual behavior. But this was different. Jessica Markowitz was a real doctor. Paige was right. Suzanne's case was way beyond everyday issues.

Markowitz started with the basics believing Suzanne's phobia didn't happen overnight. The more she knew, the better she'd be able to help her.

Suzanne saw it as a direct shot to the cause and was not one to fool around.

"Married?" Markowitz asked.

"Been divorced, ever since Lucy was four. You know, the typical college romance. We thought we were in love...got married. Neither one of us would admit we weren't. We were way too young. Then...got pregnant. Yep, we're better off."

"Working?"

"Yep...I love it. And Lucy is taking a year abroad. I didn't push her rushing through college, especially after my disaster. So this is a good compromise...if you don't listen to the news...she's in Greece."

It hit Suzanne. Dr. Markowitz must think her an unfit parent to send her only child off to a politically unstable country. She needed to justify this right away. "Lucy's on an internship doing research for National Geographic searching the Aegean Sea's floor for sunken Greek and

Roman ships. It's non-profit-non-political. She had childhood dreams of being an archeologist...don't think there's any money in it.

Really don't want to convert the basement into a permanent apartment. Still...I do miss her. I miss her...a lot."

Suzanne sensed Markowitz judging her. —*What mother would let her one and only daughter go off so close to the Middle East to look for buried treasure?*

She wanted to give more backstory, but Markowitz moved along. Feminist or not, that alone would declare Suzanne crazy. However, moving on was a good thing since Suzanne saw the dollar signs adding up.

"An empty house, then?" Markowitz asked.

"Well, not exactly. There's Bob."

"Boyfriend? Lover?"

"Bob...is my dog."

"OK...medications?"

"None."

"Alcohol consumption?"

"Wine...Martini..."

Markowitz looked at her waiting for more information.

"...daily." Suzanne finally answered.

"Sex partners?"

"Sexually stale...sorry." —*Am I sorry? She's probably disappointed. Or, am I sorry for me? I think anything to do with sex has got to perk an analysis' radar.*

"Fantasies?" Markowitz moved without pausing a beat.

"Getting it on with a boy-toy!" —*Where did that come from?*

Not even thinking about the question, the answer came out. She laughed to hide her embarrassment. Uncomfortable in the club chair, she was sure Markowitz read some underlying, suppressed desire or other clinical description into her answer.

"I live a pretty normal life." Suzanne continued.

Markowitz did not want to go into past baggage choosing instead to stick with this particular anxiety.

"Changes in your life?"

"No…well…?" —*Oops! Here I go again. I have just opened a can of worms.* "…I just don't enjoy things as much as I used to. I can wander the supermarket for hours—in my pajamas. Polish off a half-gallon of ice cream watching dumb TV especially since I've been an empty nester." Suzanne slowed down letting the words flow without thought, "…I try to keep on top of the repairs on the house, but not as quick as I use to…the enthusiasm was gone." She paused again. "Vacuum? Hardly ever. I leave dishes in the sink. On Saturdays after I sleep in, I'll have a really nice latte with two strong scoops of espresso, and when I'm finished I go back to sleep. I don't know, but I feel exhausted…sometimes…I feel lost? Depressed?"

"Let me throw some things out there. Don't go into detail…just a yes or no."

Markowitz sensed tension in Suzanne's body language. She forced an element of a smile. And Suzanne felt it really helped…she never shared her inner self with anyone. It helped that she didn't know this person…nervous, but becoming less uncomfortable.

Markowitz continued to interrogate her.

"Do you wash your hands over and over again?"

"No."

"Do you check your e-mail too frequently?"

"No."

"Have you started collecting things?"

"Shoes!"

"By the *hundreds*?" Markowitz asked.

"Almost!" Suzanne laughed.

Markowitz got it and laughed, too. Suzanne was convinced she was human.

"Let's get to the bottom of this. Oh…one more question. Have you started shoplifting?"

"Shoplifting? Not intentionally. Sometimes…I forget to put all the items onto the counter…." Suzanne tried to explain, but Markowitz moved on.

"The panic attacks, have you ever had one before the nightmare started?

Dwelling on her past life seemed like a waste of time to Suzanne. — *Single, independent woman, I made many mistakes in my life...relationships, wrong choices in everything from food to clothes...especially clothes on sale, paint colors and for sure—men. Name it.*

And her mind went farther. —*Growing up, I could never talk to my sister or my mother. The only girlie conversation my mother ever had with me was to tell me to let her know when I found blood in my panties.*

Suzanne seemed miles away. —*Maybe it's just that my life was so nondescript.*

CHAPTER 10

Paige

———

Long, slim, bare, legs extended down to a pair of stilettos as Paige crossed her legs several times before she got it right. With each passing day, Paige became more comfortable in her new self, especially her hands. She spent a lot of time on her hands, as they were a dead give away. To become soft and delicate, every night she soaked them in paraffin and had the best manicurist in town.

Determined to erase every aspect of her past life as a man, Paige hid and buried any suggestion she was different. Her new name came after pondering for a long time. Most transgender men use the feminine of their male name. John becomes Joan or Joanne. A Peter would take some form of Piper or Petra. This became a challenge, as letters had to fit in the same print space on the bus ad for the radio station. Paige wanted a name she felt had substance—attitude.

Committed to appearing as feminine as possible, Paige was familiar with how much a plastic surgeon can do. And over the years she did it all—masculine facial structure softened, Adam's apple shaved, breasts implanted, tummy tuck to remove belly fat, liposuction to contour the back, knees, and legs and even a hair transplant to fill in and create a more feminine hairline. Larynx surgery for a voice change did concern her. She feared the radio listeners would notice and not like it. Because of her height, she felt she could get away with a deeper, but still feminine tenor.

Paige did the surgeries gradually. Even with all her precision planning, she did not consider herself a plastic surgery junkie. The final male genitalia removal was on hold until both Dr. Markowitz and Paige felt the time was right. With surgery, hormones and time, a perfect male can become a perfect female—except for the hands.

"It helps if you're lucky to have long, slender fingers and to have not been a carpenter." Paige often said while looking at her hands...fearful her hands would give away her birth identity. So Paige gave them a lot of attention, as well as her choice of scents—Chanel No. 5.

At five in the morning, who would care what they looked like? Paige cared. She cared because it had taken her ten years to get to this day. Her journey long and difficult, telling her wife and daughter was heartbreaking. Now, relishing every moment of her new life, today was no exception. Her cashmere sweater tucked into a pencil-thin skirt resting just above her knee allowed those long legs to enjoy the stilettos.

Suzanne, on the other hand, looked like a sad wet rat.

"What's going to happen when they move you to TV?" Paige teased.

"Not funny." Still, Suzanne laughed because she knew she was joking. Suzanne would never be on TV. "The nightmare and panic attacks are every night now. Paige...it's a sign," she said. "Death waits around the corner."

"You think you're the only one who dies?"

"It's not the dying. It's just...I don't want to die like my mother."

"Like your mother?"

"She died *alone.*"

"What does Markowitz say about that?"

"You know, the usual...I have to face my fear to deal with it. Make the funeral arrangements...write my obituary."

"Write your obituary?"

"It's what people remember about you." Suzanne took out her iPod and read what she had so far, "Suzanne Robins, divorced, was found after a week. She died alone. The police found no reason to assume foul play as she was discovered in bed with the light on holding a novel. She is survived by her daughter, Lucy, and Paige, her co-host at the radio station." Then added, "And Dianne, her hair stylist!"

"Forget the newspaper. It'll be trashed...recycled. It's the engraved tombstone that's tricky. Wonder if mine will be, Peter Miller, a wonderful father or Paige Miller, loving mother #2?" Paige questioned.

"Guess it depends on what you are when you die?"

"What if I'm still half-and-half?"

The broadcasting light blinked red, giving Paige her clue.

"Sunday I watched a movie, alone. Sasha isn't talking to me."

The solid red light turned green and Paige began, "Temperature currently at sixty-one degrees in the South Bay. Clear skies over SFO...."

Paige's voice faded out. Suzanne couldn't help, but notice her long, gorgeous, shiny black hair, Prada dress, Luis Vuitton shoes, classic pearls and immaculately applied makeup.

Paige looked at Suzanne in her baggy sweats, smiling at her while she reported.

Suzanne will never change.

CHAPTER 11

Dianne Reeked of Sex

Wearing black tank tops, tights or a miniskirt gave Dianne a solid backdrop for her own hair, while she stood all day in four-inch patent leather Jimmy Choo's. Her only wardrobe decision was to pick the color of her stilettos, going from yellow to bright blue to silver. Her never-failing, low cut, tank top exposed her best assets.

Dianne's Salon located on the second floor above a boutique dress shop on Sutter downtown San Francisco was upscale, very chic, and intimate. Like those expensive jewelry stores where you got buzzed in and eyes watched you on the video screen, it was Dianne's impression of security, except the front door was unlocked. Her clients were professional, career yuppies in Armani suits. If not a suit, an Armani jacket over a $500 pair of jeans.

Yet Dianne was at the opposite end of this spectrum. For openers, she had incredible long, wild-curly, strawberry hair. Unlike many hairdressers who let themselves go and look like shit, Dianne practiced what she preached. Talented, trendy and having a sharp eye for detail was what she sold.

Being attractive and sexy with a body to die for, she had no trouble attracting men. Playing with no strings attached...divorced three times...never dated her clients. "Never bite the hand that feeds you." She followed her own advice.

Dianne had a long affair with Match, her main source of introduction to new male friends. So addicted, she kept a notebook of whom she dated, along with their printed photo. In that way, she remembered who was who.

"The experience is what's important," she insisted.

Harrison, Dianne's manager in the salon, thought she was decorating her headboard with little notches—one for every fella she bed.

"Soon you're going to need a new headboard," he teased.

Young and good-looking, Harrison was one of the few straight male stylists in all of the Bay Area. He trained at Sassoon in Santa Monica, and then went on to work in Beverly Hills. Not being a Hollywood type moved north and has been a business partner with Dianne for more than five years. They got along well. Harrison was smart and passionate about social issues and while he didn't look straight, he didn't look gay either. Harrison attracted both sexes and those in the middle.

"Better this way, keeps them guessing. I get the gay guys and the women, too...both best tippers."

Not sharing much about himself with his clients, he and Dianne were tight watching each other's back, so to speak.

Major big named clients came into the shop, the core of their business. But the unknowns were Dianne's favorites...the artists, writers and single moms. Dianne called herself a hair therapist listening to their stories. Donating as much hair as she could to the Children's Cancer Center, Dianne had a huge heart.

Once a month a trio of former New York Broadway actresses ferried into the city and spent the day at the salon, the first stop for Margie, Patti and Joyce before their happy hour at Kuleto's around the corner. Afterwards they caught the 6:45 Sausalito ferry back. They met years ago while doing musicals on Broadway. Originally from San Francisco, it seemed only natural for them to return home when they retired from the stage life. Once a week the three would meet at a Sausalito studio for their doctor-prescribed exercise by dancing with a toddler's jazz group, and a tap dancing session with the teens.

"Yoga is for sissies!" Joyce ranted lifting her leg to the ceiling pointing her toe.

Although in their late seventies and living in senior housing, they treated themselves to a beauty day—manicure, pedicure, color, cut, set and anything else Dianne thought would perk them up.

"I hate those gray hairs that grow on your chin! Like old men!" Margie complained. Dianne took care of them. She also tinted and trimmed the wild, hairy brows.

"Can do pussy hair!" Dianne rallied. They were not at all embarrassed.

Dianne referred to the three as The Golden Gate Girls and anticipated their visits. Outspoken and opinionated on everything from world events to hot Hollywood gossip, she found them refreshing, especially after dealing with her high-profile career clients who only talked about divorce, sexual affairs, the market fluctuations, kids on drugs, kids living in basement, kids refusing to getting a driver's license and even more personal stuff, like herpes and urinary infections.

The Golden Gate Girls loved reading the rag papers for gossip. Dianne kept the walls filled with photos of celebrity clients from her earlier days in Hollywood along with the framed cover story from the *Enquirer*—her affair with a famous film star.

"Yep! That's me!" Dianne pointed at her photo.

Their bodies amazed Dianne, erect and incredibly limber. This caused Dianne to worry, "How long will I stand tall and straight after being on my feet all day? Wearing flats will kill my image!"

When Dianne and Suzanne were alone, they'd discuss the never-ending stream of younger, thirty-something women who came into the salon, and like many single women—fearful about the future.

"My toes will never look like Joyce's," Dianne told Suzanne. "And my body will *never* look that good at seventy."

Never been one to take time for herself, Suzanne didn't understand spending money on a facial when within twenty-four hours the winkles came back. Botox disappeared. Fillers shrunk. It was simply, money down the drain!

On the other hand, talking to Dianne was girl-therapy and the fabulous neck and shoulder massage she gave after the haircut renewed the spirit. Suzanne often thought how luxurious it would be to enjoy a massage on a beach in Hawaii with *a man*. That dream faded with every year. She didn't bother with manicures or pedicures…her garden came first. And if it weren't the garden, it would be painting the kitchen, or cleaning the grout in the bathroom. A beauty day for Suzanne was hanging wallpaper.

Dianne worked her hands through Suzanne's hair checking its texture, color, split ends and overall condition, a technique she used…a mental record of how a client's hair grew.

"You really need a cut!" she told Suzanne. "Good timing."

Harrison handed Suzanne a *People* magazine knowing full well this would be the last magazine she would pick. They both chuckled.

"I hear your broadcast every morning, Suzanne…always construction somewhere. Richmond Bridge…Bay Bridge. Those commuters are jerks! You'd think people would figure it out. Like—take public transportation…BART!" This was only one of his many pet peeves.

"I know…people don't change."

"Suzanne cannot talk now. I'm c-u-t-t-i-n-g," Dianne warned Harrison.

"Think maybe you need to tint your hair, Suzanne? I don't know, but it seems dry…there's…uh…no shine? Doesn't look healthy."

Dianne pointed to the blonde woman on the *People* cover.

"She's dead!" said Suzanne.

Suddenly Suzanne pounded her chest, she felt a panic attack coming on. She couldn't look at the photo. Slapping her chest, she grabbed her water and gulped down as much as she could without choking. Hot and sweaty, her palms were wet and the back of her neck drenched. Suzanne was nauseous.

"Oh my God, you OK, Suzanne?"

"She's *dead*." Suzanne barely got it out.

Dianne grabbed another bottle of water, unscrewed the top and handed it to her.

"You're thinking of Nicolette Sheridan. She got knocked off on *Desperate Housewives*, but she's really *not* dead!" Harrison corrected.

Dianne took a towel and waved it like a fan to move the air encircling Suzanne's body.

"I have *thanatophobia!*" Suzanne said softly under her breath.

"What?" Dianne's eyes opened so wide, you'd think they would pop out.

"I'm going to die...like my mother."

Patti picked up part of the dialogue, "Her mother's dying?"

"She got her plot picked out?" Margie asked from under the second dryer next to Patti.

"My mother's already buried." Suzanne explained.

"Her mother's dead already...buried, too." Patti clarified.

"So what's the problem?" Margie asked, confused.

Joyce being hard of hearing and unaware of the conversation, stared at Harrison until she nodded commenting, "I think he's gay."

"I have *THANATOPHOBIA!*" Suzanne announced to everyone.

"It's a disease?" asked Margie.

"I'm not sure?" Dianne answered.

"I'm going to get cremated and then sprinkled from a plane. It'll be the only way I'll ever see the world." Patti chuckled at her own humorous twist.

"She got her dress yet?" Margie asked. "I'm going wear...red."

Patti and Margie lifted the dryer hoods not to miss any of the conversation.

Joyce finally caught up, "OhmyGod, is it sexually transmitted?"

Not having any idea how fragile the Golden Gate Girls might be, Suzanne got out of the chair and stood up. She needed to clarify any misunderstanding.

"Look ladies, I have this extreme fear of dying *alone.*"

"You don't have to worry, it's a *phobia,*" Harrison explained to everyone.

"My therapist says I need to face my fear, plan my funeral and write my own obituary,"

Suzanne made it sound like it was no big deal and everybody did it.

"Don't you have to die first?" asked Margie.

Patti disagreed. "She's right. Who else knows what you've done? It better be interesting!"

"Oh, dear, I'm in trouble. I've had eighteen years at the radio station and a trip to Mexico for my divorce. There's nothing else. My life has been an embarrassment," Suzanne confessed to everyone in the salon.

Harrison wondered, "If you're dead, how can you be embarrassed?"

"I care what people think."

Dianne coaxed Suzanne to sit back down and took another shot at cutting her hair. Secretly chewing gum, asked, "Let me get this straight. Death is OK. It's just doing it all by yourself?"

"She's planning a suicide!" Patti shouted, confused.

Harrison concerned removed the dryer hoods from Patti and Margie, so they could move their heads and hear.

"No. She's not planning a suicide, and Joyce...I'm not gay."

"OK Suzanne," Dianne asked, "What you're saying is the cure for than-a-to-phobia, which is not a disease...it's a phobia...is to plan your funeral? *And* you have to write your own obituary. And at this moment... your *problem* is that you have nothing to write?"

"Exactly!"

"Honey, to have a good obit you need to have *lived*." Joyce was dead serious.

"That's it, Suzanne! You need a life!" Dianne got it.

Patti stood and demanded full attention, "You need one good orgasm!"

"Then you can write about it!" Dianne cracked up laughing.

Serious, Margie shook her finger at Suzanne. "You...are depressed. You...are lonely. You need to love and be loved."

"I have Bob. And Bob loves me."

Suzanne cringed at the sight of her nude upper torso reflection in the dressing room mirror. Fortunately the light was dim. Droopy breasts, folded lifelessly into Suzanne's beige, wide-strapped, crisscross bra. She cupped her breasts into her hands. They became rounded and full. She lifted them up. They were high and firm…breasts men are attracted to. Suzanne liked the look. But then let her breasts fall back.

"Why bother, who sees me nude?"

———————

Back in the salon, a tall blonde pranced in 4-inch platform stilettos. She was *hot*. Envy percolated in Suzanne's veins.

"Thanks, Dianne. I'm going home to write my obit."

"I thought you had nothing to write?" Harrison had this quizzical look.

"I'm copying the obituaries in the newspaper." "You're getting weird, Suzanne." He said lifting his eyebrows.

Dianne eyed the tall, blonde who sat in the salon chair reading. "That's Sydney."

"Can't add six inches to my neck!" Suzanne whispered shaking her head.

"Look at the color of her hair." Dianne whispered back. "Look at her hair."

"Me, go blonde? Never going to happen. Nope. It's just not me."

Dianne gave up and changed the subject. "You know Suzanne, Margie's got something. You need to get out more and get yourself a *man*."

With mousy brown wet hair and gesturing with her arms, Suzanne stood in front of the mirror.

"Take a good look at what you see…baggy pajama bottoms tucked into my Uggs, over-sized coffee stained t-shirt, Birkenstocks with unmatched socks." She steps out of her pajamas and rips off her t-shirt getting everyone's attention so there would be no misunderstandings.

"And what your eyes didn't see hidden underneath…old bra and, yep! Baggy panties with the elastic all stretched out."

Suzanne pointed at herself in the mirror.

"A *man*? Just look at me!"

The Parking Garage

Retreating to the parking garage across from the beauty salon, Suzanne scrunched her wet hair in the rearview mirror. The mousy strands didn't help. Not in favor of blow dryers she let her hair dry—naturally.

"It'll be better after it dries," she struggled to convince herself.

Still scrunching her hair Suzanne inhaled, started the Volvo, and with pursed lips exhaled releasing a sigh of relief as the engine turned over...a technique she performed in childbirth. Shifting into reverse it rolled backwards, instantaneously she hit the brake. The dented, pre-historic Jeep splashed with gray paint primer stopped. A man wearing a faded baseball cap sat behind the wheel, one hand on the *h-o-r-n.* Leaning out his window he flipped her *the finger!*

Pissed, Suzanne rolled down her window, "Are you wishing me a pleasurable experience?"

"You wish, bitch...never goin' to happen!"

This obscene gesture and his derogatory tone provoked Suzanne. Pulling back into the parking space she killed the engine and recoiled across Sutter Street.

"OK! OK! I'm back! Where do I start!" pulling on her hair, Suzanne demanded attention. Amazed and delighted, Dianne pointed to the empty chair.

51

"Men love blondes," Harrison said in a *I told you so* tone.

"Blonde? I'm thinking more like highlights…or something? Dianne, what do you think?"

"Trust me, Suzanne. Change is good!"

"Change? My life's set up with no complications. Don't have to pick up his dirty laundry, wash his dirty dishes…or find his secret porno site on the computer or check his texting. Why go backwards? And then…no matter how young you are, there's always a *younger* woman."

Fearing another panic attack, Dianne reassured her, "Suzanne, it's OK, I'll just do highlights." But tiptoed around her reasoning, "Maybe just a gay-guy roommate?"

"My life is so tightly choreographed, it would never work with any man." Suzanne admitted.

"Nice to have a playmate…." Harrison popped, "Maybe hang out with Paige?" Then Harrison quietly probed, "I'll bet she has some *hot* friends." Harrison had a thing for Paige.

Not letting it go Dianne defended her point, "It's true, Suzanne. You've been out of the dating scene…Lucy's not home any more…motherhood's long time over—been there, done that—maybe a nice guy would be just the thing you need?"

"Yeah! Get out a little. Live!" Harrison backed her up.

"You know, I have a few divorced clients." Dianne fostered, "Can't hurt to just meet…a drink? Not suggesting marriage here!"

"A blind date? Don't think it's worth my time."

"A drink?" insisted Dianne.

"How long has it been since you've been on a date?" Harrison froze, waiting for Suzanne's answer.

"You mean like…he calls…picks me up…we dine? Go back to my place…or his?"

"*LAID?*"

"*Ten years!*"

"*OhMyGod!* My grandmother's doing better than that!" Harrison quipped.

"*WE'RE GOIN' STRAIGHT TO BLONDE!*" Dianne howled.

CHAPTER 13

Do blondes have more fun?

———

U nable to stop herself, Suzanne picked up a dishtowel and wrapped it around a wooden spoon as a pretend microphone. Throwing her head back—Hollywood drama style—stepped up to the hall mirror jokingly asking her image, " Good morning bridge and tunnel people...Do blondes have more fun?"

Bob stared at Suzanne, attentive wagged his tail...her best audience.

Playing the diva role, Suzanne's eye caught the obituary clippings taped to the edge of the hall mirror. Pulling one notice off read it to Bob, "Ellie Murray died of a heart attack at eighty-nine. She was a life long member of the Polar Bear Club." Suzanne shook her head. "Don't they jump into freezing rivers on New Year's Day? No wonder she had a heart attack."

The phone rang interrupting her conversation with Bob.

"Lucy, everything OK?" Suzanne never knew when she would hear from her and not sure when she'd hear from her again. So she dropped the wooden spoon.

"Oh, checking in on me? Yes. I got the package....No. I've not tried it, but hold on...." Suzanne pressed the medical alert button hanging around her neck. The beeper *beeped.*

"It works! But I don't have anyone to call…. Oh, it's already set up?" Suzanne listened carefully as the connection was poor, and kept breaking up. She repeated word for word what Lucy said even though she knew it took up international cell minutes.

"…dredging the sea bottom is at a standstill until the lab identifies the pottery pieces you found?"

Multitasking, she put the groceries away as they talked.

"Oh dear God! Do you think it's really from a pirate ship? Any coins? …. Too, bad…. You think I should take a vacation and visit you now that you're on land? Lucy, there's nothing there but dust and dirt…. Oh, there's goat wrestling? That's not enough to temp me, and you know I'm not into camping, not my thing. Besides I have *hot* water, I'm more into Italy…. What! Your dad's getting a divorce from (she was thinking "babysitter" but didn't say it!)…um…what's her name, Mary Jane? Nice that he still makes that annual phone call…."

If anyone has had a secret, Suzanne did. It seemed to never fail every time her ex came up she'd be the one who felt guilty. He was wrong, no question there. It was the reason she quietly slipped away getting as far away as possible and never allowed contact with Lucy until Lucy was old enough to put the pieces together. Suzanne never trusted him. And he never challenged her. Isn't it the mother's job to protect her children? Suzanne wished he would at least call Lucy on her birthday, or send a card. Better yet—money.

Of course, she was not going there now actually glad he married the babysitter…it became her problem. Suzanne wasn't kidding when she said he was the luckiest man alive.

"…oh! Your father still believes the right woman is out there waiting for him! Ha! What a dreamer! OK, sorry…I know the best thing is your half brother. We'll give him that…. What? You've got to be kidding. I should start dating, too? It's not good to be alone for the rest of my life? Lucy…I think you have been in the desert too long. I'll wait to see you at Christmas…. So, what am I doing? You mean today or the rest of my life?" Here's where Suzanne kept the laughter to herself.

"I've been thinking of redecorating your room. Do you know I still have all your stuffed animals? Some of them are twenty-two-years-old… OK, you have to go…I love you, too."

Lucy took advantage when she found an Internet Café to post photos. The photos showed a rocky, desolate coastline with sparsely dotted goats, but her life was a ball. Suzanne didn't get it, but praised her for being adventurous…millennium kids never grow up and in Lucy's case, still like digging in the sandbox. Jokingly she reminded her, "I'm proud of you. You could be living in the basement, without a driver's license, snacking on cold pizza, claiming Facebook, Twitter, Snapchat, and Instagram to be your employers." But it was Suzanne who felt lucky. She could have waited to have a kid and be fifty-nine with a fifteen year old, praying that her daughter didn't get pregnant or drugged. And not uncommon in today's world of career women having babies in their late forties.

In reality, Suzanne cried for a week because she missed Lucy. Being a single mom, Suzanne spoiled her! Was that how millennium kids got that way? Suzanne kept Lucy's stuffed animals individually named, piled on her bed—once a mom, always a mom.

Just as Suzanne hung up, the phone rang again.

"Who?"

The medical alert response person called checking on her.

"I'm fine. It was only a test."

Suzanne felt flushed…wet hair stuck to the back of her sweaty neck.

CHAPTER 14

The Bar At Bix

———

Suzanne's obituary was due at her next session with Markowitz, and she needed to get home to feed Bob and do laundry. But when Paige suggested going to Bix a classic after-work bar, she hesitated. After months of going home to an empty house, she had second thoughts.

"Sure! I need to get out!"

You'd find Bix deep in the financial district where a well established bar crowd gathered when the stock market closed...on the West Coast it was early. But it meant Suzanne would have to kill some time after reporting at the radio station.

"I can check out shoes at Neiman's," she suggested to Paige. "How about...catch up with you there?"

Bix was true to its reputation located on an enchanting back alley named Gold Street. The old world charm of this marvelous, architecturally renown building detailed with turn-of-the-century craftsmanship, first class service, and flawless food—like their famous steak tartar prepared at the bar and generous drinks—has been a man's place for ages. Even the valet remembered your name.

Would Suzanne go there alone? *Never.* If it weren't for Paige, she would never have stepped inside, even though she was curious about the building. And yes, it was something to put into her obituary—architecturally sensitive.

Josh welcomed them. The packed bar was dominated by suited males and crowded with twenty-something females networking...i.e., taking selfies.

"Paige, I'm the oldest woman here!" Suzanne nodded toward a sixties guy with a younger girl/woman in a mini-skirted-bare-midriff outfit accentuating every detail of her body.

"No, you're not." Paige pushed a drink into her hand. "I am."

"I need this!" Suzanne said accepting the martini.

"Work the crowd, start a conversation." Ignoring the couple, Paige forced a smile and took the lead…such a natural.

"Haven't seen you here before." Said a voice from behind.

Wiggling off balance in her new stilettos Suzanne turned, finding herself eye to eye to this guy.

"T. Rowe Price and you?" chanted this overly friendly boy-man who appeared to work out…or his suit was padded.

The blonde is working. Thank God, I'm not standing alone.

"Will Douglas."

"Suzanne Robins."

Suzanne waved off the selfie handing him her business card.

With a squeamish expression he quizzed, "Does anyone do radio anymore? Thought radio died with black and white TV?"

Suzanne stood there, dumbfounded. Finally words came to her lips, "Never heard of Sirius? Howard Stern?"

No way can I make small talk with this kid. He probably doesn't have any big words in his vocabulary! Bet he doesn't drive either and lives at home—in the basement. Besides, you can't trust a man with two first names…I read that somewhere.

Uncomfortable, feeling out of place even in her upscale youthful platform four-inch heels, Suzanne made her way back to the safety of the bar. Easing onto a stool faked a conversation on her iPhone. Looking over her shoulder, she watched Paige in the middle of a male-dominated group soaking up every move she said.

Sliding off her new heels, Suzanne leaned in to the man next to her as he studied the financial market on his iPhone.

"Hi, I'm Suzanne." Displaying a Cheshire grin, "…I'm writing my obituary."

CHAPTER 15

The Back Room

———

"Anything else I can do for you, Ms. Robins?" queried Rosemary.

Suzanne wandered into Rosemary's back room. A couple of days have passed since she stopped by the mortuary. After her last visit, she feared sliding into perfection…selecting fabrics for the interior upholstery took an hour. Like restoring the Victorian, she wanted all the shades and hues to softly fold into each other, even inside the casket. — *After all, it will be a reflection of me.*

Earlier she tried, but couldn't deal with the music. On the table in the main office sat a three-ring binder with selections. You picked the number. The organ was set up electronically like a player piano, making this of all the arrangements the least personal. Being so computerized at such a personal time upset Suzanne. So as not to be asked to leave… people don't usually get to see the private, inner workings of a mortuary…Suzanne kept her cool. Instead, she visited Rosemary.

Suzanne's eyes gravitated to the photos in an open binder on Rosemary's desk. Inside a plastic surgeon's office, there were photo books filled with before and after pictures of patients who have had work done. Only Rosemary's people were dead. Suzanne had no clue why she would display them. But then after leafing through, she realized the results were quite good. —*How else can you show off your work?*

Suzanne felt compassion for this woman. —*How could she go out to a party and talk about her job? Does she have many friends? Does she have any? It's like she's a mole living and working just a few feet from underground. Rosemary is not old, so what kind of social life do Jimmy and Rosie have?*

Rosemary waited for an answer.

As Suzanne searched the shopping bag, she saw Rosemary out of the corner of her eye. She had the patience of a saint, Suzanne thought. In fact, Rosemary was a saint. *—If this were my job, I'd be at a bar every night with a half-dozen martinis lined up. Think about it, how could anyone do this job? Was formaldehyde her perfume of default? What must her home life be like? How did she answer the kids when they asked, how was your day today, mom? And smiling back—she's got to smile—"Oh, great. Really great, dressed six corpses, styled four more, burned one and buried two. Not a bad day." Who can you share that information with? Not your kids.*

"Oh, yes...."

Suzanne retrieved an old photo from the shopping bag...a headshot from the book jacket of her one and only published book. The editor remarked how casual it looked and rejected it. Yep, the editor was right of course. Still, Suzanne thought—baseball cap and blue jeans. She knew she would never look as good as she did in that photo.

"Can you make me look like this?" she asked, handing the headshot to Rosemary.

"It's black and white."

Maxed out with the sensation of nausea rising to the edge of the back of her throat, Suzanne decided to deal with the makeup and music another time.

Surprisingly she made it back to the parking lot without puking. Once in the Volvo, accidently slamming the door she heard a piece of rusted chrome fall off the car. It was an old piece, fragile and loose...just waiting for the right moment to drop. It could not have picked a worse moment.

Burning up Suzanne threw on the AC and took off her cardigan. Unfortunately, it took more than a few seconds to feel the blast of cold air.

"When someone is dead, you do what you think they would like. If you get it wrong, who really cares? It's always *so lovely*! But when you plan your own funeral, it's a whole different ball game. You have to do it right." Suzanne dialogued with her reflection in the rear view mirror as if rehearsing a part for a theater production. But the other character didn't answer her cue.

Finally the cool air began to surround her body.

Remembering the last parking lot incident, she took a good look before she backed up.

Suzanne's other brain kicked in as she pulled out of the parking spot. —*Saint Rosemary was right—no one ever said they looked terrible. Yet, they always look awful. And if they don't look terrible, they look weird.*

Suzanne brushed the damp hair off her neck. She leaned into the air duct and felt better the more distance there was from the funeral home.

Mentally she ran through the list. —*What about food? How do I know how many are coming? Will there be enough toilet paper in the lady's room? Just how far do I need to go with this? Searching for just the right dress took me all day searching my closet. Then, wouldn't you know Rosemary didn't like it?*

Frustrated Suzanne shouted, "How long do I have to do this, Dr. Markowitz?"

CHAPTER 16

The Comfy Leather Chair

"It's the obituary that's giving me trouble."

The comfy club chair had become familiar. As anxious as Suzanne has been to get this thanatophobia out of her system, she wasn't ready to charge ahead on her own. She sensed progress...aware of what set off the attacks. Or so she thought so.

Markowitz pushed, "Part of therapy is to get your obituary into *The New York Times.*"

"What if I'm not dead?"

"That's no problem. You email and cancel. But to be accepted is the ultimate." Markowitz assured her.

"So I need a really good obit?"

"Absolutely."

"Have they ever published someone's obit who is still alive? Now, that would really cure me!"

Markowitz didn't laugh.

"Does it have to be about me? Why can't I just write an obituary that's interesting, something people will enjoy reading?"

"That's not the purpose, Suzanne. When you get into it you'll see how much you have accomplished in your lifetime."

"...I'm not so sure."

Suzanne had not lead one of those quintessentially worthy lives. Not a leader in business or in the community. Not even a PTA president, vice president or on any charity board. She didn't even go to meetings. Not a philanthropist like Chelsea Clinton or Bono, accept for the five dollars in the church basket—occasionally, and not even conventionally virtuous like a candy striper volunteering at the hospital.

"There's no way I can do this. My life is not entertaining, accomplished, or unique," she complained to Markowitz. "I'm fifty-nine and have nothing to show for it. Maybe in the next twenty years!"

"Age has nothing to do with it. Many young people who have died have been quite accomplished. Olympic medal winners, start-up geniuses, rock stars, many actors don't fine success until their fifties…."

"My life is far from Hollywood. I'm a single mom. Do people want to read about the struggles of a single parent and teenage daughter-mom fights? A constant fear of not having enough money to pay bills? What about the horror and embarrassment of your ex-husband running off with the babysitter? I have only dirty laundry…No, don't think so." Suzanne took a deep breath. "Outside of that, my life has been and still is outrageously boring. I'm a traffic reporter on the radio. I work in a sound booth…Dr. Markowitz, no one sees me—*I'm invisible*."

"Then let's forget big bang events, look for something intimate. Trace every facet of your past and find something hidden, personal, and secret. Dreams. Something lost? Something no one knows about you."

"Can't people express their sympathy and be done with it?" Frustrated, Suzanne was desperate to move on.

"Suzanne, the purpose of this assignment is to take this opportunity to look back on your past…then you can look ahead and *savor* life as you are living it. Your next forty-some years will taste so much better. When you come close to death, you want to live." She paused, "I'm sure you can find something to write."

"…not so sure."

"For fifty-nine years, you've done nothing?"

"Yep! Nothing."

"Then it's time to become *visible*."

———

As Suzanne brushed her teeth, she faced obituary clippings haphazardly taped to the side of the bathroom mirror. Framed in rustic pinewood with a whitewashed finish, the clipping had to be removed carefully.

When Suzanne decided to make the attic into a master bedroom, she liked the idea of using rustic pine on the ceiling with a whitewash rather than the all white look which she did downstairs. She even added a bath under the eaves knowing full well the steam might cause the whitewashed finish to peel. Then at the last minute added a small window at the tub level, opening a view of the bay while soaking. Although Suzanne did the walls in white, the whitewashed pine ceiling created a mellow feeling. The brass bed and pillows, trimmed in white lace… added a soft touch.

"I dragged that bed around for years and finally it's got a perfect home," she patted herself on the back.

When Suzanne put in the dormers, the view became even more dramatic. Every morning she woke up to the sunrise across the bay and fell asleep watching the San Francisco city lights—"It's eye candy." She gave herself another pat on the back.

As she removed one of the clippings the words blurred.

"Bob, I'm so sick of these obits! I've done nothing to fulfill my dreams." She felt the breath of Markowitz. Bob responded to her call. She was sure he was asking, "What dreams?"

Suzanne brushed her teeth. Still unhappy with not finding the right obit to copy, she gave one more try. "Cherie was elected president of her senior class and active in the Head Start Program. She dedicated her life to helping young musicians…tireless in her generosity and efforts in this cause…Cherie's marriage…."

Suzanne pulled the obit off the mirror and ripped it up, immediately looking back to check if she left a mark.

"Bob, that's it! I give up…it's never going to happen!"

Suzanne threw the clippings into the trash. —*Who cares anyway? In a few weeks after you're dead, no one remembers what you did or didn't do. Maybe they'd remember you if you left them a nice jewel or two, a family heirloom. In that way when you wore it, you'd remember them.*

Yes, that would work, but it hadn't for Suzanne. No one had left her anything. Actually that was not true. It was her mom's savings that she used for the down payment of the cottage. She should not be so hard on herself. She loved mom. But mom was not on her mind and only came up every now and then. Maybe if she left Suzanne a diamond, it would be different. Suzanne would admire it and think of her every day.

Brushing her teeth she asked her reflection, "Why did I stop dating?"

Suzanne spit. After taking the used piece of dental floss from the towel rack, flossed, rinsing the floss under hot water shook it, and hung it back on the towel rack…having done this million times.

About dating? Being a good mom was important to her. And of course, she was involved in her career. But Suzanne knew that was not all there was…something lingered and it would come to her…she could feel it.

Yes, there it was popping up again, a fear she had after the divorce, secretly corroding inside. With her worst feelings and like most unpleasant things, she buried it. Probably not the only reason, but a big reason she avoided a second relationship. The thought came back piece-by-piece. —*I didn't want to get hurt again.*

And yet, starting over again took energy and time. Dating was a night job. Being a single parent was tough enough—no glamour there. Then there always was the chance of divorce…a whopping 67% for second marriages. Suzanne knew the stats by heart. After going through one failure, she put it off—been there, done that. —*Just how much failure can you take?*

Suzanne felt like Rosemary. You got into a groove and stayed there. You tried at first, but the odds were against you. So you slid back into that nice comfy zone, gliding along while dealing with the little ups that balance the downs. You told yourself, "You're happy." Even if you did smell of formaldehyde, you learned to live with it.

Searching for the truth, Suzanne realized she was terribly disappointed she never got remarried and never had a second child. In her deepest thoughts, she had always wanted another baby, an aching loss long past. And with that ability of motherhood gone, so went her desire to find love. She accepted her failure, her mistake—she married the wrong man.

Oops! That's it! I'm punishing myself for my ex's mistakes. If I had married the right man, my life would be different.

The session with Markowitz dug up old wounds. The doctor's drill that there must be something *hidden*, something *lost* was absolutely true. It was not what Suzanne had done in her life; it was what she hadn't. Markowitz encouraged her to move on, to live and *savor* life. Yes, those were her words. She made Suzanne poke deep finding the loss she had buried.

CHAPTER 17

Le Garage

Le Garage—small, expensive, and impossible to find, never had to advertise...a word-of-mouth place. Suzanne doubted they had a sign. Typically French they preferred to select their patrons...a steady stream of local followers who knew how to find it.

Le Garage used to be a car garage ages ago. Not sure it isn't a rumor. Somehow, it went from a simple café to upscale bistro over night. Located on the dock between the warehouses serving the San Francisco Bay boating and shipbuilding industry, it opened for a great breakfast, a delicious lunch and offered take out. Closed in the afternoon, come evening it was one of the most incredible foodie hangouts.

Paige ran into the chef at the Pebble Beach Food and Wine event and has been hooked on his cooking ever since. She'd drive from her townhouse in Pacific Heights over the Golden Gate Bridge without giving it a second thought.

Paige moved to Pacific Heights when she started her new life. She enjoyed the yard and garden of suburban life, yet longed for a home in the Pacific Heights area with a view of the Golden Gate Bridge. Then she found just the place...small, but perfect.

"Location is everything." Paige sounded like a proud homeowner.

Occasionally the old Peter-persona came out, "Every morning I can predict the weather by looking out my window. As a kid we lived with a similar view of the Golden Gate Bridge...never realized how special that place was until we moved away. In the sixth grade for a year, I'd get up at the same time and take just one photo with my camera on a fixed tripod. Discovering there were no two photos alike, and a fascination with the fog, sun and wind led me to be a meteorologist."

Paige loved the menu at Le Garage. Amazing choices were distinct and beautifully executed. "Honestly, I can't figure out how they do it in the tiny kitchen...might be the reason the chef serves only what's fresh," Paige raved. With little to no storage, every nook and cranny was designed into coolers...mostly for French wines. French Mediterranean cooking suited the Marin health nuts just fine. The tiny bar...the pulse of the restaurant...sat six. The bar—Paige's preferred place to be.

"If you want to meet someone and keep it quiet, Le Garage is the place," Paige had told Suzanne...another reason Paige frequented often. And tonight Paige had a date with Thomas De Santos, stunning with his clothes on or off.

Paige sat close. She liked his outdoorsy smell. Thomas found Paige exotic...her facial bone structure and those long endless legs were mesmerizing. His hands worked their way up her firm thigh, while eyes on her he carried on an intelligent conversation, chuckling occasionally at his own jokes.

Paige agreed to meet him when he suggested Le Garage. "If you know how to find it, he's my kind of guy," she told Suzanne on a number of occasions.

"Squash blossoms stuffed with Dungeness crab, and the pepper coulis." Paige requested without even peeking at the menu. Akira, the young Japanese bartender, took the order knowing exactly what Paige liked.

"*Foie gras au torchon*," Thomas added copying her manner, as he knew the menu as well.

Akira served a small ramekin of truffle butter with toasted brioche.

"And...the *mussels mariniere*," Thomas suggested smiling.

"One more plate? The *duck confit*? It's unforgettable, comes with a huckleberry *gastrique*," Paige whispered to Thomas, who gave the OK to Akira.

"Bringing it all at the same time." He added, then surprised Akira by saying "thank you", in Japanese. A smiling Akira added more champagne to their glasses from the bottle of Perrier-Jouet sitting on the bar in a very cold ice bucket.

Paige told Suzanne, Thomas' best friend ran into Paige at an ecological seminar at Berkley and again, earlier that year at a brainstorming session for the Weather Channel. Paige not only reported for the Weather Channel, but did major research for the program. The friend was impressed by her knowledge, and at the same time liked her company. But happily married suggested she meet his college buddy, a partner in his advertising firm and best friend. Understanding his friend was the hard to please type, it occurred to him maybe the bright and gorgeous Paige Miller would be perfect.

Paige wore her pewter mini Herve Leger that fit like a glove... only someone with a Paige body could carry it off. So distinctive, the garment needed no accessories except black stilettos. Paige's taste in clothing changed from Polo classics worn by Peter, to more of a Chloe female—sexy with class—as Paige changed. "Can't take that innate talent for style away from you." Suzanne stretched it further, "One day that TV job will happen. You're perfect."

"I'd love to do TV." Paige never denied it. No one appreciated clothes more than Paige. "Most women have no clue how much a man enjoys a woman in a dress." She'd preach.

Paige impressing Thomas was no surprise.

"Girl, you are...hot," Thomas whispered, reaching for the warmed bread in one hand and rubbing her leg with the other.

Paige gently took his hand away. She couldn't let his hand get to close to the cookie jar. But no question strong chemistry stirred.

"I do like him," Paige teasingly whispered to the bartender.

Thomas was successful. He got his first Cleo Award at twenty-five. He never married, but didn't want to be single either. He had a liking for smart, creative, attractive, contemporary women, but hadn't found her...yet. However, Paige interested him. Not seeing fatherhood in his resume, he liked the idea Paige already had a kid—just not his.

The night happened fast...nothing they couldn't talk about. Paige had dreams rerunning in her head of such an evening of conversation, many times. But she didn't want to get her hopes up.

"Great desserts!" Thomas playfully suggested. "Crème Brulée...and there's a molten chocolate cake stuffed with a berry ganache..." he read the list from the dessert menu. He caught Paige's silent smile watching him. He quietly smiled back continuing to read on, "...then there's the Lemon Zest Panna Cotta with a delicate passion fruit gelée...or maybe just a nice glass of Muscat de Beaumes de Venise La Pastourelle 2012..." Thomas struggled with the French.

Paige chuckled, "Very good." Paige knew how much she would love to indulge. It's only been once or twice before that Paige felt the demands of her job.

"Thanks...but I can't, Thomas. Must be at the station by five... another time?"

Paige gathered up her Hermes bag. Thomas helped with her cropped Jil Sander buttery leather jacket. While Paige knew anyone else would have added a scarf, she preferred her own long neck to be bare considering it one of her better assets.

————

Thomas silently walked Paige to her car. When Paige leaned to get inside, he gently pulled her into his arms and held her face in his hands kissing her while holding her tight. She felt his heart beating against her implants, sensing his heat. Passion drew them in. But Paige was afraid. —*What if he reaches between my legs?*

CHAPTER 18

Roger

———

Waiting on the sidewalk in front of the Sausalito Movie Theater on Caledonia Street, Suzanne looked both ways for some sign of her blind date. The bay wind blew. Wrapping her coat around her body checked her watch. Then, checked it again, and again.

Dianne's clients were San Francisco professional people, so he'd show. Suzanne had a brief phone conversation: day, time, and place. It was hard to understand his accent—cell reception didn't help. She got the important info and liked the idea of practicing her French, which should at least impress him...so she thought. His voice sounded upbeat and energized...another good thought.

This was a real date. How long had it been? Suzanne couldn't remember. She figured it must not have been so terrible because she would have remembered. And probably was not so great either. If there had been a second date, she would have remembered that. Standing in the wind, she tried to picture his face, the name, the place... anything that would bring back the memory.

The blind dates Dianne set up were going to be remembered. She had no great expectations...a night out with a friend...at worst a learning experience.

My hair looks good.

Suzanne felt good, Jeans of course. She hadn't let anyone see her legs for years.

"It's me he should be interested in, not what I'm wearing." Suzanne mumbled to herself, reinforcing herself. Then again she did put on a white, man's shirt. Somewhere...maybe *Vogue*, she read men love a sexy shirt look. And with it a wonderful un-glitzy tumbled green stone necklace that Lucy picked up from Turkey. The coat was a long-ago purchase, it felt good wrapped around her body, "Coats never go out of style, they actually serve a real purpose."

An aqua VW bus, straight out of the sixties, pulled up to the curb.

Now, Suzanne liked classic, but she wasn't so sure of this one. In her college years, they said you could judge a man by his car. Classic was good...not splashy or ego driven, but Suzanne felt this was over kill.

Roger, sixty-ish, was tall and slender, a classic himself. Suzanne wasn't sure if these were his best clothes or his only clothes. But he needed new clothes. Dianne's haircuts were pricey, Suzanne figured his financial priorities must be elsewhere, this peeked her curiosity. There were lots she could learn when you knew how he made and spent his money.

Jumping out opened the passenger door. "Hi, I'm Roo-ger," he said rolling his "r".

"Nice to meet you, Roger."

"ROO—ger." Like a French teacher, corrected her pronunciation. Suzanne didn't have time to feel like a dummy as the traffic was backing up. She quickly climbed into the VW bus. The old, worn interior had silver duck tape patches holding the seat together. Although a collector's dream, this vehicle had a long way to go.

"Suz—anne," she said stressing the "Suz". "Haven't seen one of these since I hitchhiked in Europe...years ago. Nice paint job!" she tried to break the ice.

"Buckle up!" he ordered.

Roger erratically drove onto #101 beeping at cars maneuvered into the fast lane. "I like jazz," he said. "Reserved a table at the Panama Hotel. They have this cool Brazilian jazz band and my favorite food."

"Oh. Dianne only mentioned drinks?" Surprised, but not wanting to discourage creativity, especially since she liked a man who came up with dining suggestions and had a passion for something, "Dinner sounds nice, but I have an early morning."

Roger heard her, but wasn't listening. Turning up the radio, blasted Latin jazz. As they rambled along, Suzanne decided she was not crazy about the vehicle. —*My old Volvo feels safer, and these belts are a joke. If we crash there'd be nothing to hold us...like riding in an oversized tin can. I should have been more specific and stuck to the plan—a drink. I should have taken my own car. How do I know I can trust this guy? Well, I can always taxi home.* Then she had another thought that pissed her off. —*Shouldn't he have cleared his plans with me?*

The Panama Hotel was an old jazz club hidden on a backstreet in San Rafael...colorful but worn. Actually quite seedy, but that was its charm. From the street they heard the music. The restaurant, jammed with a unique following, didn't lack in atmosphere.

The linens were original...the stains certifiably untouched by Clorox.

As seedy as it appeared, Suzanne was impressed that Roger went out of his way to pick such a unique place. Although she would have been happy to meet him there, she understood it was difficult to find hidden on a residential street. Suzanne sensed a take-care tone. It quieted her suspicious brain...he's OK. —*A glass of wine would help. Prosecco would be perfect.*

Roger took one menu from the Latino waitress and waved off the second. Sensing her concern, gave her a smile.

"I know what's good."

"But I don't eat hot, spicy foods."

Roger leaned into the waitress pointing to several items, ordered, ignoring Suzanne.

"Beer." Holding up two fingers.

She shook her head, but Roger was into the music.

The waitress brought the beer. Roger sipped exaggerating his response savoring it. Suzanne realized she needed to get into the moment and stop judging. —*I just need to go with the flow.*

Looking around, she took in the smells from the kitchen and wondered what spices lingered in the air, mentioning her find to Roger,

"Cinnamon hits me along with the aroma of citrus and the smell of hot red peppers."

Then she zeroed in on the wait staff's uniforms…totally black. The waitresses had black veils and the waiters had black shirts and ties. Even the Latino band members wore black with black felt hats. They played their music and marched in a funeral-style procession between the tables, stopping for an effective blast of New Orleans blues topped with an Afro-Cuban flair. A fantastic experience for any jazz lover, but the scene didn't sit well with Suzanne.

The food was piled high on oversized plates dripping with sauces, but Suzanne couldn't get her eyes off the black-veiled waitresses and the funeral-like jazz procession. Her palms got clammy. She found it hard to breathe. Her forehead dripped with perspiration, as did the pores in her scalp. Her hair was soaked. Her neck was burning. Suzanne felt a panic attack coming.

"I can't b-r-e-a-t-h-e," leaning into Roger, "I think I'm going to choke."

Roger's head swayed back and forth into the music. His hands drummed the table as his feet tapped the floor. Suzanne realized they are on a date, but she was totally alone.

"We're going to Costa Rica next month. It's perfect weather this time of year. Fishing is great…"

The jazz band blasted, Suzanne barely heard him. She dipped the linen napkin into the water glass. Splashing water everywhere, drenched her face with age-softened cloth. It felt really good.

"…I make this great grilled fish wrapped in seaweed. You do like fish?" He paused, "Oh, it doesn't matter…I do."

CHAPTER 19

Am I going backwards?

———

Dianne arranged the blind date, but Suzanne felt the need to be discriminating. She picked the eatery and took her car, making her feel in control. Was it the blonde?

Poggio, a quaint Italian restaurant with a great bar, had been known as the backbone of the eateries in the heart of downtown Sausalito…successful because of the foresight of a local entrepreneur. Being a social person introduced himself impressed Suzanne was a local celeb until she told him she did traffic on the *radio*. His interest waned.

Not to be disappointed with the date, Suzanne got the man's backstory from Dianne. The way she figured it…the more you knew, the closer you were to the second date. Tackling this as if a job interview, knowing the backstory got her in at a higher level.

David Holmes was a well-established financial advisor. Although the ferry could have dropped him in the heart of the San Francisco financial district, he drove his new Mercedes every morning over the Golden Gate Bridge. Dianne said the morning drive *inspired* him.

David lived in Sausalito for some twenty years. Ex-wife #1, his college sweetheart still lived in Sausalito in their beautiful home on Harrison with a magnificent view of both Belvedere and the San Francisco skyline. His kids grew up there. Ex-wife #2 lived in an oldie David remodeled for the two of them and her older kids. Her house on San Carlos located one street above ex-wife #1 also had a magnificent view of Belvedere and the San Francisco skyline. That worked for some eleven years.

If that wasn't enough information, ex-wife #3 now had their beautiful home on Sausalito Road, one block above ex-wife #2, and two blocks above ex-wife #1. Yes, she got lucky with the magnificent view of Belvedere, the San Francisco skyline, Berkeley, Bay Bridge...if you listened to David telling it, "She can see the very tips of the towers of the Golden Gate Bridge." Yeah, right! That was impossible.

When Suzanne arrived, David seemed older than his sixty years. And knowing his backstory...not surprised. David seemed to be in a hurry to get through life wanting to be the first to the gate and win the golden ring. Yes, he'd been competitive by nature...material possessions were important, so were young pretty wives.

Spotting him—belly fat hanging over ostrich belt, shirt buttons barely hanging on without popping—was reminiscent of the doctor Suzanne dated years ago.

Am I going backwards?

Suzanne checked out his pants and jacket, finding that they were from the same suit even though he had out grown it...only kids did that, she thought. Recognizing the custom tailored look, she figured his wives had good taste.

Interesting to note, David lived in Marin County a sport heaven. Men were lean, mean and good looking. David was overweight, a softy and not attractive. With all his money, he could have afforded a trainer. This turned Suzanne off. —*This was going to go nowhere.*

With respect to Dianne, Suzanne fathomed, "A drink won't hurt." After all, down the road he might have a buddy who would be perfect for her. Rather than being a waste of time, Suzanne considered it networking.

David waved for her to join him, and pulled out the other barstool.

"Two Belvederes with a twist...make'm doubles, *shaken, not stirred!*" David reminded Tony, even though Tony has made this exact drink for David all these years.

Suzanne rolled her eyes. Tony got it.

She introduced herself, "Suzanne R—...."

"David Holmes! I recognize your haircut." David cut her off.

"Oh, cute!" Suzanne responded. —*Was that supposed to be funny?*

Proudly he handed her his business card. She noticed his fingers were perfectly manicured and polished with Revlon's clear. She doubted he had ever touched a garden hose or swept a patio since childhood… maybe never then. She guessed lifting his martini was the maximum physical effort he applied on a regular basis.

She checked the business card: CEO of some major financial corporation. And he was the III—as in third generation. Although curious, she thought names told a lot about a person, but she didn't want to show she was impressed. Then again if you broke down what he actually did, he was a salesman.

Suzanne gave him her card.

Without looking at it, put it on the bar as he tapped his glass against hers, "To Dianne…with two Ns."

"To Dianne," Suzanne mimicked. His dumb humor made her smile.

Leaning away from David, she took his hand from her knee and tugged her skirt down.

I give this date fifteen minutes.

Although Suzanne felt strongly about meeting someone who appreciated intellectual conversation, good taste, love of the arts, classic films, adventurous spirit and a healthy lifestyle, she liked to believe all of that outweighed sex appeal. She has ranted to her single girlfriends, "Isn't personality what it's all about? And if you do meet someone, isn't that what it becomes anyway? How many couples do you see at a dining table actually talking to each other? So forget the ability to converse on any subject and go directly to the food." Yes, a woman can actually go to a museum with a guy and not say one word the whole afternoon. Suzanne had seen it. —*Love at first sight? It's a myth and if it does happen, it's short lived. Don't we know better? Or, do we?* Suzanne's mind didn't quit when it came to relationship theories.

How many drinks has David had?

"Yep, she left me. I'm sure Dianne told you!" anxiously waiting to tell his tale of woe.

Poor guy needed attention, probably found it hard to live with himself and scared of being alone! Maybe he has thanotophobia? Suzanne didn't go there, but David did.

"Mia, my third…was perfect. Yep, ten years and *one* day! I adored her and watched her play every Saturday at the Harbor Tennis." His hand slid perfectly straight across his eyes, as he described the scene, "You play right at the water's edge, like swimming in an infinity pool." Then he paused, "She had the most gorgeous, blonde ponytail…yeah, she was young…probably too young." His eyes suddenly bored into Suzanne as if she accused him of pedophilia.

"Why the hell not? I'm successful?"

"Young like…maybe your daughter's age?" Suzanne dug in. Actually it came out unconsciously…maybe. Sometimes she couldn't resist not having the self-discipline to control her mouth.

"She was twenty-three. I was fifty. It's not the age difference that created the scandal…really! I've been watching her tennis games for years and then finally, I got up enough nerve to ask her to play with me. That did it! We skied Aspen, Sun Valley. Napa. I was in love." Gentle tears rolled down David's cheeks as he lowered his eyes with a blank stared at his martini.

Compassionately, Suzanne gave him time to gather his thoughts. "… and then, the dreaded papers!"

"Divorce papers?"

More tears, eyes swollen. "Well, I got tennis elbow. A new knee, so I couldn't ski…had trouble driving at night…kept forgetting my keys…." David polished off his martini and shook his head, "She knew I was older. For God's sake, she's my stepdaughter! Then she falls in love with the tennis coach…got pregnant. What's her problem?"

"Let me get this right, your ex…who's your stepdaughter…is now pregnant by the tennis coach? Doesn't that make your ex's baby-to-be your step-grandchild?"

"Yep." David's head slowly nodded. He didn't look at Suzanne.

No wonder they all got houses. He had to pay them off to keep peace in the family.

But Suzanne swallowed her thought when she felt David's hand take hers and hold it to his crotch, pressing it against his penis inside his unzipped pants.

"I take Viagra!" He said puffed up.

Surprised, Suzanne jerked her hand away the second she felt the wiggle of his penis.

"There are tons more young gorgeous things out there." Suzanne meant it…happy she wasn't a young thing. She pushed his roaming hand as she glided her chair away from his.

"Three down, more to go. Serial monogamy. It's a socially acceptable version of harem building." She tried to justify his marriage pattern.

"Said she loved me." David's voice cracked.

Is this guy stupid?

"It's the latest female career. Didn't you see it coming?" She *had* to ask.

David glared at Suzanne, eyes pierced. "She's not a hooker for God's sake."

Suzanne shook her head. "Wife player."

"Wife player?"

"There are baseball players, and football players. They don't have careers lasting a lifetime, but they try to milk it beyond ten years. Then live off the spoils. Right?"

"Yeah…so?"

"Wife players have a similar game. Unlike a male player who is in it for quick fun or an affair, a wife player with a ten-year marriage…even if she signed your prenup…gets more. That's why the ten year and *one day* timing from your ex." Suzanne was onto something now. She had no idea where it came from…perhaps the modern magazines gossiping about celebrity breakups.

David waved to Tony for a refill.

"Look, David, think about it. You don't even have to be naturally beautiful to be a wife player. All you need is a good plastic surgeon and dentist."

David was either totally mesmerized, or drunk. But he was listening…at least Suzanne thought so.

"Now, if I were going to be a wife player, I'd take those classes they have at college extension programs teaching how to flirt, dress your best and even how to break into an ongoing conversation with a great one liner…think you can get some sort of a college degree. In fact, I'm sure of it."

David stared blankly, no doubt wondering—*What the fuck was she saying?*

Now somewhat embarrassed, Suzanne paused to sip the martini.

"You'll be fine," she smoothed over her opinion. She felt sorry for the man.

But Suzanne was on a roll and found herself talking again, loving it! "I can't get my mind off these wife players…not to be confused with housewives…who just move on to the next guy, maybe two in a lifetime, possibly three if they start young enough. And with each time, they acquire vast sums of money. They never have to scrub a toilet or boil water. They get to play house in multiple houses filled with expensive possessions, have tons of help, foreign travel, and the A-list social scene. If you get fired or divorced, you end up with a really nice stash of stuff…"

"Are you nuts?" David asked.

David had more to say, but Suzanne didn't let him.

"…then, again," rebutting herself, "What about *love*? Of course wife players are in love. Like so many men, they love their work and the rewards it brings them!"

"I'm…very successful," David seemed to be repeating himself.

"Yes, David you are a very smart man." Suzanne bit her tongue, so desperately wanted to say but didn't —*I think ex-wife #3—the stepdaughter—might be smarter.*

"So how long has it been since you were divorced?" He tried to take the heat off himself.

"Twenty-seven years."

"I can see why." David, now pretty drunk, relished in his smartass answer.

Instead of digging herself into a deeper hole, Suzanne ignored the slam.

"What are you doing to move on?"

"Phone sex...medical marijuana...blowjobs." Looking at Suzanne with a big smile, under the bar David's hand grabbed hers. And with Suzanne's hand, he massaged his penis.

She pulled her hand back, again. —*He doesn't get it. This man is pathetic! I'd rather be alone.*

"How about another drink?"

Suzanne was antsy to get away from him. Nor would Suzanne ever want to meet or have any sperm belonging to him or his male friends. She politely refused, anxious to make an exit. Inconspicuously, she took back her business card still on the bar, and slid it into her pocket.

"It was nice meeting you, David."

"Nice meeting you, too...Sybil."

CHAPTER 20

The Clock Read 4:58 AM.

———

Suzanne's blonde tresses made even a seasoned sweatshirt look good. Paige had finished texting the fourteenth message to Sasha. As Suzanne hustled into the broadcast booth, she removed the half bagel from Suzanne's mouth as Suzanne unloaded her paraphernalia from her canvass bag.

The broadcast red blinking light changed to green.

Grabbing the headset and microphone, Suzanne slid in front of the monitor.

"Looking *good*, Bay Area commuters! Moving along on #680. Let's keep good thoughts. Don't be jealous of those ski bunnies heading up the Donner Pass on #80. CHP stopping all vehicles without chains in their back pockets. Snowflakes, black ice...not even Halloween, looks more like Christmas!" And then Suzanne turned her attention to the traffic on the bridge—"Golden Gate Bridge, you lucky bridge people... purring like a kitten."

Within seconds, the radio station assistant leaned up against the glass panel displaying a handwritten note. She had a caller on the line. Suzanne recognized the name.

"Oh God, here we go again!" She mumbled under her breath. Fortunately she remembered to cover the mic. With two fingers to her mouth, she forced a smile

"A caller from the Golden Gate Bridge! How's your Monday so far, Luca?"

"Can't you see? We're totally socked in. I never heard you say *fog!* It's wet. We're creeping…it might as well be snowing. I'm going to have to put my top up," Luca complained from his hands-free mobile. "I can't do it while driving. My leather seats are getting soaked!"

"Oh, Luca, so sorry to hear that. You need the weather! Stay tuned, folks."

The broadcast blinking light green turned red.

"Thank God!" Suzanne said after coming off the mic.

"What are you on?" Paige asked, concerned.

"This thanatophobia is making me nuts. Sorry."

"What happened to Valium?"

Returning to her bagel, Suzanne handed Paige the mic.

"We've got to talk. Lunch?"

Clock read 5:11. Broadcast blinking red light changed to green and Paige picked up the microphone.

"Big news this early morning, it's the first snowfall of the season in the Tahoe area. The storm front will hit us about three this afternoon. The Bay Area has an eight-five percent chance of rain as far south as the Monterey Peninsula…."

Paige reported the weather over the radio, but she could have been doing TV. Paige never failed to looked gorgeous, shapely—s-e-x-y.

CHAPTER 21

Lunch

S uzanne had been standing in line with Paige at a favorite lunch spot, The Slanted Door, only steps from the station. Located at the Ferry Building, Charles Phan the owner was one of those great American success stories.

Paige—a popular patron—often dropped in after work for a Singapore Sling and some wild California sea urchin. The bar made a long and beautiful statement attracting the after-work tech crowd just before taking the ferry to Marin…suited, successful Paige's type. Paige was good at separating the married from the single and could detected a *player* a mile away, even has been known to tease them…just a little.

Sophisticated and sexy in her Michael Kors sweater, eyes followed Paige. Male patrons stopped mid-chew staring. Her posture, edginess caught their attention. And then following Suzanne—the train wreck. She shuffled. The little café down the street from the radio station was her usual hangout. —*Thank God I left my slippers at home.*

Paige knew everyone's name, acknowledging the waiters and even the busboys as she proceeded to follow the host to a table.

A guy accidentally rubbed against Paige's backside.

"If you do that again, I'll kill you." Paige said under her breath yet loud enough for him to hear. She lifted her head expressing a slight mischievous grin.

Suzanne wasn't surprised when the host led them to a table leaving the standing patrons to wonder *who's that?* Paige's iPhone rang. She answered in a soft, almost whisper tone, while strutting tall in her stilettos to a bay view table.

"Thanks Brandon, nice words! Love to...just starting lunch, text. Ciao!"

The Slanted Door has been world famous. Phan, a Vietnamese immigrant, began with a vendor's cart. Young and very bright, learned exactly how Americans like their Asian food. He took the best of Thai, Chinese, and Vietnamese and tossed them together.

The results were incredible tastes, incredibly served. Phan also had an eye for exceptional, sleek design. With exotic, pale green tinted glass and a sophisticated ambience along with incredible food, The Slanted Door became an instant success in a competitive city—proof of the American dream.

At the table and anxious to talk, Suzanne reached into her shopping bag and pulled out a bunch of books: *Men, Love, and Sex*, and two more *Love Smart, Love at Second Sight*.

"I have more."

Tipping the bag Paige peeked into a shopping bag.

Paige's iPhone beeped, this time a text: THOMAS. She smiled as her eyes read his name. But she didn't answer it.

Picking up a book, Suzanne looked around checking to see if anyone was listening, as if people knew who she was. Opening the conversation she kept her voice low, "Dr. Phil always makes good sense...so practical. *Second Chance* deals with the divorced woman...."

"Really Suzanne, when do you see Jessica again?"

"Jessica?"

"Dr. Markowitz."

Suzanne forgot Paige was on a first name basis.

The waiter interrupted. Having eaten at The Slanted Door so often, Paige politely refused the menu.

"Two green papaya salads. We'll split the oven-roasted red snapper and cellophane noodles...a couple of raspberry-mint coolers." Paige concluded the order with a huge thank-you smile.

Suzanne looked at him and smiled, too. Banking her delightfulness if ever she came back without Paige. He'd remember her. Suzanne had eaten almost everything on the menu and there wasn't anything she didn't like, even had no problems with the cellophane noodles that reminded her of unborn worms.

With so much on her mind, she leaned into Paige speaking softly, "Paige, eighteen years ago I met you as Peter. We became friends. Close friends. You told me how you always felt different even as a child. You made up your mind to be true to yourself...to be honest with your wife. Then, you made this incredible, drastic life change...."

"OK, OK, tell me what's on your mind." Paige didn't want Suzanne to lecture her or rehash her backstory.

"These panic attacks are a wake-up call."

"To go *blonde!*"

"To make a lifestyle change before it's too late. Two-thirds of my life is over. Every day I talk to all those bridge and tunnel people *stuck* in traffic. But at the end of the day...they've gotten to work and home again. Paige, I'm *stuck* in my life." Suzanne took a beat. "I'm going nowhere."

The food arrived. The flawless presentation, smell of delicious spices, the hum of background voices, Suzanne tried not to breathe as it might upset the balance.

Paige careened closer and duplicated her serious tone, "I love being a woman, but it cost me a lot—my family, my body, not to mention hours of therapy." Then her tone changed, "Suzanne, I thought you were happy. You're independent, have a great cottage with a million dollar view...an adult daughter. A career most people would die for...besides being really good at it. And you have a perfectly choreographed life, you have said so yourself...Suzanne, you've lost me!"

"I know, but this nightmare has changed everything...look, it's like I've been on a self-imposed diet for twenty-seven years. And now...I'm starving. I think the panic attacks are a warning."

"OK, now you're starving and you want to eat everything on the pastry cart?" Paige's face crinkled up. "What's your desert of choice?"

"I want to open my single existence to include a *man*."

"A *man*? Why? Just have s-e-x!"

"Think about it, Paige. If I have a man in my life, I won't die alone."

"A guarantee comes with that?"

"I have to stop being *invisible*. A second pop at life…a second chance at love—*a relationship*."

There was silence.

Paige chewed slowly. "So you want to love again…what's your plan?"

"Paige, this time…I don't want another mistake." Suzanne anxious to get her point across tried to keep her voice down.

"So this is your wake-up call?" Paige teased.

Paige saw Suzanne was dead serious. She understood what it was to feel like you are loosing out if you don't get your life together. Paige understood the pressure of time. "Well you can't just love any man. He's got to be a really great guy."

Then Suzanne asked, "Paige, will you be my *dating* coach?"

"Oh, the blind leading the blind?" Paige wailed and raised her eyes to the ceiling.

"You know it from both sides devoting your life to becoming a woman, and you know what men want. There's no one better than you. I need your help. P-l-e-a-s-e?"

Paige sat motionless while a very long minute passed. Paige never thought of herself as anyone's mentor. But did she really know both sides? In many circles, she would be considered totally unacceptable for the job—a failure as a man and inexperienced as a woman.

"Paige, I can't write my obituary. Ask Markowitz, she'll tell you…I'm failing therapy!"

"That's not going to happen!" Paige burst with renewed energy. Pushing the books on the table back to Suzanne.

"You got a deadline?"

"Any time before I die.

"I guess if you don't want to die alone…a man could work."

Paige caught the eye of their waiter, "Check, please!" Suzanne smiled again ingraining her face into the young man's memory.

Paige turned to Suzanne doubled checking, "Do you really want this? I mean really?"

"Paige, I'm stuck. All I want to do is strip naked and start all over."

Then Paige leaned in, a mischievous grin spread across her face. "Why can't we blame this on your ex and be done with it?"

Paige stood up, grabbed her bag, looking at Suzanne tried to keep a straight face.

"Wear stilettos to the supermarket...the best place to meet men."

CHAPTER 22

Faking It

———

"These might be worth something, look at that heel! They're vintage." Suzanne pleaded.

"You've got to be kidding." Laughed Paige.

"What if it comes B-A-C-K?"

"OhmyGod! You can't be caught dead in these!"

Suzanne had a walk-in closet, a woman's dream especially in a small house. Cleverly she managed to use every nook and cranny even though the organization seemed awkward from a designer's view. She found unused space for mini shelves, higher areas for hooks and a great shelf just for hats. Shoes had their special spot. Hanging clothes got a wood pole...she wouldn't dare use metal. Coats shared a special corner with the one and only full-length dress.

Actually, this dress was not just any dress. It had been waiting for an event to happen—with a man of course, like the magenta dress Suzanne purchased for Mexico. Only this dress was a fancy gown—Ralph Lauren Black Label, gorgeous celery green silk satin. Turning Suzanne's blue eyes green, fit like a glove...low-haltered neckline and a low back. *Gorgeous?* Yes.

Suzanne found it at the Ralph Lauren outlet store in Gilroy tagged $3,999, now on sale down 70%. Studying it she noticed a tiny pulled thread way down near the hem.

"You get an additional discount for the damage," the young salesgirl offered.

Trying it on, Suzanne waltzed around the store. It needed hemming, but she felt princess-elegant lifting the skirt as she walked as if attending the Oscars. But actually she was buying time trying to figure out what the final sales price would be. At 70% off...not dealing with the penny came to $1200. No question a good deal. But to justify the expenditure when the chance of needing something this gorgeous, was nil. That was until the just-past-teenage salesgirl pointed to the sale sign, "Today only, additional 50% off any sale-priced item."

"OK, it's way more interesting, now." Suzanne admitted.

"*AND...*" the sales girl continued, "...you get the damage discount as well as an alteration discount. But...you do have sales tax."

"What would the adjusted price be?"

"Do you plan to return it?"

"Didn't think I could?" Suzanne was surprised at the question.

"Well then, you get a no-return discount as well."

While waiting for the computer to figure the multiple discounts, the salesgirl questioned one more time, "Are you sure you will not be returning this?"

Suzanne shook her head.

"That comes to, with tax...$121.32," she announced with a huge smile of amazement.

"*SOLD!*"

And into the closet it has hung never worn, down the pole from where the magenta dress resided, also never worn but now into good use. Best of all, the closet was cedar lined. Yes, when you opened the door it smelled wonderful. It also had a window. Although it was on the north side Suzanne hung a pair of wide slatted blinds to be extra protective. Keeping a closet neat was the beauty of Suzanne's personality, except for today when even her celery silk gown could be stuffed into a trash bag to go to a homeless shelter.

Paige threw dresses, blouses, sweaters, skirts, jackets, and almost everything else from inside the closet to Suzanne who stood at its doorway. More things came flying out the closet door and piled up on the floor. It was painful...like watching old friends being thrown out of the house. Suzanne was attached. Even Paige, a superstar at putting together an outfit from nothing, and making it look like it just came from latest *Harper's Bazaar* was frustrated by this collection.

Paige had this philosophy—if you dress the part, you play the role. Not an original theory. Psychologists encouraged people with low self-esteem to feel better about themselves by first pretending—*fake it till you make it*. Paige has had years of practice and it paid off. Peter developed into Paige with the encouragement from Markowitz with this *fake it until it becomes you* attitude theory. Paige was happy inside the half empty closet…the good half.

"You want people to treat you differently, don't you?" Paige kept the conversation going from inside the closet. "The trick is…they need to *see* you differently to treat you differently."

"I'm not very good at acting." Suzanne shouted back as she scooped up the cyclone of stuff flying off the hangers.

"You are not acting! You're showing your real-self, who you really are!"

"If that's not acting, then what is it?"

"It's your *fucking real-self-faking it!*" Paige laughed, climbing over the hill of clothes she created. "I'm *not* talking sex here. It's all about playing the *real-self*…the person you want to be until it becomes a deeply engrained attitude you express every moment you breathe. A child didn't think about how to play. He's just being himself as he plays at being a cowboy or race car driver."

You can tell Paige has been in therapy.

Suzanne turned to see if there was anything left in the closet, relieved seeing the celery green silk satin still hanging there.

"Halloween is such fun because we get to dress up. Guess whom most people choose to be? Whoever they most want to be. That's why you're always Marilyn Monroe!"

Suzanne got it. She couldn't help but agree.

Paige folded the rejected clothes putting them in a trash bag, helping to get a handle on the overload. Together they piled clothes into bags.

"Over the years life takes twists and turns." Folding the clothes didn't stop Paige from lecturing Suzanne. "We no longer get to choose who we really want to be. We follow a plan that's somehow been carved out for us. Much of it was our own doing. When we realize we've drifted off the main road, it's too late…we have six kids and a scumbag husband. We're stuck. We do what we have to do…we hang on to things. We're afraid to let go. We are afraid we'll have nothing to show for our lives. And then, there's the bigger picture—the social expectations. What will our friends think?" Paige stopped to take a deep breath.

Suzanne thought she was finished—Oops! She was not.

"That's why you have these panic attacks. Who cares if you're afraid to die?" Paige was now spread eagle on Suzanne's bed…still going strong, "What difference does it make if you die at thirty, forty, sixty or eighty? Once you're dead, you're dead!"

"So what do you do?" Suzanne's face scrunched into painful antics.

"You get your act together and become visible…Markowitz is right."

"I don't know how to start."

"That's why you-*fake it*! Don't give them any opportunity to see you are scared shitless!"

Suzanne thought Paige would go slowly. Having her try on an outfit, wearing it around the room breaking it in like a new pair of shoes. But maybe Paige knew nothing Suzanne had in her closet could you get excited about…except the celery green silk gown. The closet was filled with clothes that looked great in the window, but once home, were not.

Paige approached with action believing that if you want real change, you need to take drastic measures.

"Time is not on your side!" Paige said, leaping back on her feet.

"I don't think Dr. Phil's book has anything on throwing out your life-long collection of precious garments." Suzanne defended her position.

"Single? Sixty? Sexually stale? Looking for a man?" Paige shouted once again from inside the closet.

The last few pieces of clothing flew out landing on top of Suzanne's neatly arranged eight trash bags. Once again she picked up each item, folded it neatly before placing it inside the plastic bag, giving it a last pat goodbye.

"I'm not geriatric…yet. Why are you picking on me?"

"You asked me to be your dating coach, remember?"

Suzanne folded faster.

"There are more single females than single males with the percentage going up the older you get," Paige stated facts.

"So why in the hell *do you want* to be a single female if finding a man is so hard?"

"My wife hated me!"

Suzanne picked up one dress carefully, putting it back on its hanger. "She did not!"

"You remember when I told Rebecca how I wanted to live as a woman and wanted a sex change? She looked at me funny and asked why I couldn't just be gay?"

Paige stepped out of the closet again. "I told her, gays don't feel… inside, the way I feel… the incredible sensitivity, the reaction to the smell of a man's cologne. The attraction to designer clothes, Jimmy Choo shoes. And gossip! I always thought I was a woman. At thirteen I would have appreciated big boobs, not a big *dick*."

Paige looked at the dress Suzanne put back on the hangar. "Oh, that one…the museum piece, wore it with your ex? Get over it!"

Taking an empty shoebox thrown to the floor she said, "Write down all those Richard-the-Ex haunting memories and stuff that old baggage in here. Then we'll bury it. Ha! Markowitz didn't tell you that one, did she? Therapy in a box!"

In fact, Suzanne felt as if she just had ten years of Markowitz therapy. Every word she said made sense. The problem—knowing and doing were not the same.

Slowing down, Paige pointed to the faded pajamas Suzanne wore, "*OK*, give it to me! *And* the panties and bra! Say goodbye…some homeless lady is going to be ecstatic."

Suzanne stripped.

And before Suzanne could grab her robe, Paige threw several hard-cover books at Suzanne and had her walk across the room—nude—with the books on her head.

"Posture! Don't walk like an old lady." Directing her to turn and to go back she added, "You have only seven seconds when you walk into a room for that man to notice you. And he's not going to see your eyes if you are looking at your feet."

———

Paige was on a roll. Going into Suzanne's bathroom she threw out old makeup jars, tubes, lotions, hundreds of saved samples, many dried up. Paige stared into the bathroom mirror touching her smooth face, "L-o-v-e those hormones!"

Seeing Suzanne's reflection, "You, my friend…need Botox."

Finally Suzanne heard the words, "We need to shop."

Completely exhausted and totally overwhelmed, Suzanne jumped onto bed, burying her head under the pillows screamed, "Where did I go wrong?" Having second thoughts she whined, "I can't believe I'm doing this. Dating is hard work."

"It is work. It's a second job," Paige agreed.

"My thoughts exactly. Can I collect retirement?" Suzanne poked out from the pillows.

"If you play your cards right, there'll be a return on your investment."

———

In the kitchen and off to one side of the counter dangled an IV pole with a bag of IV fluid. Paige stared not quite sure what to make of this piece of medical equipment.

"The wine?"

"In the fridge."

Opening the refrigerator Paige discovered six pints of blood.

"Expecting a vampire?"

"Oh, it's my emergency supply. You know, just in case I'm...you know...dying."

"OK, I guess lots of people have blood cooling in their fridge,"

"What?"

"Nothing."

———————

In the living room sat a new club chair. The soft, dark, leather reminded Suzanne of the chair in Markowitz's office. "Not sure it goes with shabby-chic," she mentioned, not wanting to sound ungrateful for Paige's gift. But it didn't belong in the house.

"It's not for you. It's for *him.* You have to visualize him sitting in it."

"Of course, it's positive thinking...the live one!" Suzanne got it. She moved the chair over to the fireplace.

Completely exhausted from closet de-cluttering, the head cleaning took its toll as well. It was not the trashing of a closet full of old clothes, it was throwing out years of life. One new outfit could make Suzanne look good. But it was the *fucking-real-self-faking it,* that was going to make Suzanne a new person.

One thing for sure—it was Suzanne's new favorite expression.

Paige brought the wine from the kitchen and they crashed onto the sofa. Bob liked to snuggle between them. Sipping the Italian red, Paige tried to reach her daughter adding another text.

Paige casually moved a square glass bowl of fresh cut flowers sitting in the middle of the coffee table. Unconsciously, Suzanne slid the same bowl back. She caught herself in the subtle move. Suzanne had difficulty picturing a man in Paige's spot on her sofa. *—Even if the IV pole wouldn't make him uncomfortable and the pints of blood wouldn't scare the hell out of him, how could he put his feet up on to the coffee table without moving the flowers"*

"Paige, what if I never find this *man?*"

"Guess you can always tell yourself…when you're dying alone…that you tried."

Paige put in the DVD, pressed the PLAY button.

Sex and the City began.

CHAPTER 23

Bury Old Baggage

Sunday mornings were quiet in Sausalito. If you wanted to know the local gossip, hang out at Poggio's breakfast bar.

Mr. and Mrs. O'Brian didn't go there. They went to church.

The O'Brians lived across the street from Suzanne. Now in their eighties, they had always lived there as far as she knew. The front garden bloomed every season. The house trim painted in perfect condition. Suzanne never heard voices, except maybe on Saturday afternoons when the NPR station was tuned to the Symphony. Then you listened remembering what it was like before the iPod. Thanks to the internet, and face chat they had a close relationship with their grandchildren three thousand miles away on the East Coast. Mrs. O'Brian taught her granddaughter how to knit via Skype and on one Fourth of July, showed her how to bake an apple pie. They would also text.

Suzanne usually saw the O'Brians working in the yard, but this morning they walked home from the Farmer's Market…canvass bag full and the Sunday edition of *The New York Times*. Passing her house, they crossed the street. Having married in their early twenties, adore each other like teenagers. Isn't this the relationship in your later years suppose to be?

Suzanne reflected on current couples who endured years of marriage, they separate and go separate ways. It seemed lately women were waking up not wanting to go down in history as being a Mrs. Nobody, instead looking to be a Ms. Somebody. Neither partner did anything wrong, she only wanted an identity. Suzanne got it. And unlike David's younger wife who had earlier plans, traditional expectations where changing.

Suzanne reflected on her marriage that didn't work and worse yet, she gave up. She needed to move on from old memories. Paige was right. — *Stop wearing pajamas to the supermarket and leave the Uggs at home!*

Seeing Mr. and Mrs. O'Brian walking together was another wake-up call. Their body frames compressed with age were far from shuffling along. Every step—short, but perfectly coordinated. Energy flowed. Did Mr. O'Brian walk to accommodate Mrs. O'Brian, or was it the other way around? Did it matter? He had the newspaper tucked tightly under his arm. But Suzanne's eyes were fixed on Mr. O'Brian's other hand—holding the hand of his wife.

"I wonder if they care about their obit?" Suzanne asked, once again dialoging with herself.

Not into social media, seldom did Facebook and not crazy about Tweeter, Suzanne felt she had nothing to say...instead got hooked on daytime talk shows. *Oprah* was her afternoon staple for the longest time. Then came *Dr. Phil.* The reality show producers made fortunes exposing viewers to lives of the worst of the rest of the world. The topics were unbelievably amazing—Botox for five-year-olds to sleeping with your sixteen-year-old daughter's boyfriend. How about the woman who gave birth to twins from two different fathers? Yes, this was possible. They dredged up stories about family secrets like the one about the young woman from Rhode Island who hid her dead baby in a shoebox under her bed for fourteen years. How in the world did she get away with that? She must have been a teenager who never cleaned her room. Possibly a stillbirth and the young girl...so scared...didn't know what to do? Then the reality button—she must have been fat. How else could she have hidden a pregnancy?

Suzanne dragged herself back to reading the newspaper obituary section...she needed one obit to bring on inspiration.

"Bob, listen to this, 'her extensive, dramatic, and comic dexterity in television....' Hey this is easy, change the word television to radio. *Bingo!*"

Bob's tail wagged like crazy. The *bingo* caught his attention.

"It's not a lie Bob, what great words—dramatic, dexterity."

Bod panted as if laughing.

"Look Bobby Boy, I need something. Got to start somewhere. I think this fits *me* pretty well." Suzanne knew Bob wasn't going to give her any grief. Markowitz would do that.

Skimming more obits from *The New York Times* determined to get something down on paper, Suzanne needed only one line that had some truth in it. Something merit worthy.

"OK, how's this, Bob? Suzanne Robins loved animals. She found Bob at the shelter." She crossed out *found* and substituted *rescued.* Now Bob really perked up.

"Think about it, the word—*rescued,* is far more classy than the word—*found.* People don't tell their friends how they got a dog from the shelter. It's all about having *rescued* a dog." Then Suzanne realized she hit on an important issue…lots of money got donated to these rescue shelters by rich people, older women in particular. The word—rescue, rang with status and soothed the conscience. "There's nothing wrong with that, Bob. *Rescued* is the word of choice." Suzanne imagined Bob smiling.

Didn't take long for Suzanne to become incredibly bored, "With the price of therapy, I got to stick with this," she admitted to Bob. Having him a good listener, she read one more obit, 'Violet in her lifetime did thousands of hours of volunteer work for the American Cancer Society, Salvation Army, United Way, WHIP, Boys and Girls Club, ASPCA, Sausalito Women's Club, Meals On Wheels, CASA and Dorothy's Soup Kitchen'. OhmyGod, Bob, you name it Violet did it."

Needing to remedy the guilt of having a selfish life, Suzanne called Paige. "Were you ever a Girl Scout? Just kidding! What are you doing for Thanksgiving?"

They made a plan.

Suzanne took an aspirin with her coffee.

Discouraged, Bob followed her as she wandered into the bedroom where she picked up the small notepad laying bedside and compiled a list: False expectations. Bad marriage. Richard-the-Ex.

"So much baggage!" She took the handwritten scribbles and opened the shoebox Paige set aside in the closet. She chuckled when she noticed the shoebox was Prada, and relieved to find her Prada shoes still on the shelf. Suzanne felt they gave her closet a touch of class.

Throwing the note into the shoebox closed it giving the cover a pat...as if there were a physical connection. Tippy-toed, slid it back on the upper shelf.

"Bob, Paige is right. I need to bury my old baggage so I can move on with some *new* baggage." She caught herself conversing with Bob, confirming her opinion about lonely people.

Bob wagged in agreement.

"At least if I have new baggage, I'll have something to write about."

CHAPTER 24

Today is the first day of your new life.

———

"I'll pick you up in ten minutes. Wear something baggy, which I'm sure you have hidden from me." Paige snickered.

The Pilates studio in Sausalito had a faithful following. Paige never thought yoga gave her enough of a workout. The stretching was good, but left her unsatisfied...too soft, cushy. Her masculine frame wanted something more demanding. She also knew it was this structure that gave her a long, lean, model figure woman died for.

No matter what excuse Suzanne made for being overweight and how much she complained, Paige retorted with her usual response—"Underneath the fat there is the ultimate female body, long, lean and fit with high-flying boobs."

Paige discovered Pilates. Got hooked.

Marcy, this tight-bodied young woman stood sergeant-like, in the background several reformers reflected in the mirror of the gym walls. Pilates was work to Suzanne and like a lot of other things in her life, never followed through with the training sessions. In fact, over the past ten years, she had zero activity in anything athletic.

Suzanne stopped playing tennis a long time ago. Skiing was now definitely out of the question...cold then and colder now. When she did ski, Suzanne skied the best places—Tahoe, Vail, Sun Valley, mainly to meet men. Besides the cold, she was never crazy about the sport, *but* she l-o-v-e-d the clothes. She looked thin and very chic in the tight stretch pants and got hooked on large-framed, reflective, aviator sunglasses.

Ski outfits had an aura of the European jet set lifestyle. At the resorts men were abundant and martinis the rage. Suzanne loved a good martini.

Suzanne and her Sun Valley condo-mate discovered…after a heavy après ski drinking night…they slept with the same guy that same week, but only after they recalled the same white bear rug.

But for Suzanne turned on by his 6' 4" body, fitted midnight blue ski pants, baby blue eyes, silver curls, day old beard and programed charm, it was her first sexual experience after the divorce. The weight of his nude body on top, pinning her down on this white bear rug was incredibly exciting. Recalling zero foreplay—strip, immediate sex—she thought she had multiple orgasms like never before…not sure if it was alcohol or actual fact.

Just when she thought that was the end of her evening, a knock on the door brings a young woman nude under a full-length fur coat and fur boots. "You're not leaving?" Suzanne was not into a three some, yet the other woman wouldn't accept the rejection and grabbed Suzanne's face and kissed her as she massaged her breasts. The silver curled guy watched, smiling.

Walking back to the condo…nude under her down coat…Suzanne needed cooling off.

Tennis on the other hand Suzanne had no trouble giving it up as the skin around her knees began wrinkling and her thighs developed unattractive dimples. Other women in the club wore stockings and didn't care how they looked. This appalled Suzanne. She cared. She quit.

Paige set up the training session with Marcy knowing if they did it together, she wouldn't back out. Paige enjoyed the graceful stretching and rhythmically moving to the music.

Suzanne struggled to keep up. Marcy kept on her case.

"Tomorrow, kick boxing." amused Paige, making every move count mesmerized by the rhythm. "That's it for carbs (deep breath, exhale)…sugar and salt from this moment on."

Suzanne's body slowly collapsed. "I hate this. I'll starve!"

"Today is the first day of your new life." Paige patted her on the head whispering into her sweaty ear.

CHAPTER 25

BOTOX

"BOTOX...the face has a mind of its own," Paige insisted. She knew Suzanne wasn't into pain and feared the sight of a needle might set off a panic attack, but Paige convinced her no matter how much Pilates she did or how good she got at Zumba, none of those helped to remove frown lines.

Taking a break from the obituaries Suzanne clipped an ad offering a special on Botox, a two-for-one deal. You call between certain dates and paid up front. That should have been a clue, but like many women she wanted a cheap, quick fix.

It occurred to Suzanne to check the online reviews, but remembered the time she listed her house as a vacation rental. The site promised if she got a bad review, it would not print it...ever since Suzanne didn't trust reviews. Thinking positively, she had figured if the doctor were bad someone surely would have run him out of town by now, right? Counting on others to be the watchdog, she recalled an article in the newspaper—a doctor in Beverly Hills performed boob jobs on young, Korean women. The procedure was so cheap they flew over by the planeloads, but got nailed when Medicare questioned his charges for so many twenty-year-olds receiving breast reconstructions. Even after reading the article, Suzanne believed someone else with more time and money would take care of the bad guys.

She called making the appointment for the two-for-one deal.

Paige had a fit. "You can't go to just any doctor!" She made another appointment with her dermatologist—once again getting Suzanne in for an immediate appointment.

The office was upscale, chic with the cleanest lines in furniture—all white. Suzanne liked this guy already. Within minutes she was reclining in the padded treatment chair as Dr. Harry Rosenfeld prepared a Botox injection.

Squeezing the arms of the chair—she waited for the needle.

"Look at any actress in her thirties. You think they got that great look without help? It begins in your twenties. It happens slowly...then surprise! Celebrities nip it before the camera captures it!"

Squirming in the chair, Suzanne anticipated Dr. Rosenfeld injecting the first needle.

"*Ouch!* That numbing cream isn't working!"

Ignoring her complaint, Rosenfeld continued his chatter, "Why should you not be timeless? Here comes a little p-i-n-c-h."

"*Ouch!*"

"Everyone's doing it. Even men. Fifty is today's forty."

Then came another injection.

"*OUCH!*"

"Finished."

"Thank God!" Suzanne meant it.

"Was there one reality TV show that didn't disgust you? Tell me, who wants to look at ugly people?" Rosenfeld queried.

"Whatever happened to a face with character?" Suzanne asked.

"That starts at eighty."

Dr. Rosenfeld handed her a mirror. "Can't do much for that double chin, neck cords are showing...need a plastic surgeon for all that."

Suzanne looked closer at the fat under her chin and the lines on her neck. Rosenfeld wasn't exaggerating.

"You mean a...*facelift?*"

"Better sooner than later. The best investment you can make is in yourself. When you look more attractive, you feel better, perform better becoming more engaging…friendlier. People want to know you. They want to be your friend. Zuckerberg had the right idea when he called his social network *Facebook*. It's all about the face, my dear!"

His rapid thirty-second repertoire got Suzanne thinking. Rosenfeld was able to totally convince her. Must be the numbing cream—actually he made good sense. Suzanne hated to admit.

"I get it, but it's expensive to have filler and Botox treatments. Forget a facelift?"

"Actually if you think about it, women spend a fortune on clothes. Why? To look good. It's the same with your face. After a facelift you can wear *rags* and look terrific!"

In front of Suzanne stood a man who was perfectly groomed, well educated, loving his job. Dr. Rosenfeld was winning her over—Suzanne's next BFF after Rosemary.

"You can get ten years out of a facelift…it's a bargain…you will look years younger. But meanwhile fillers are a temporary fix."

"It's a huge chunk of change every few months…it doesn't last."

"Think about what's spent at Starbucks? …$2,000 a year!" He didn't stop there. "That's why women carry charge cards because their man wants them to be beautiful."

Now, Suzanne really thought Dr. Rosenfeld was pushing it!

"You're single, dating, am I right?"

"They're going to have to take me as I am—the good, the bad and the ugly!"

"Aren't you a local personality? People watch you."

"I do radio, Dr. Rosenfeld, *no* one sees me."

And then the clincher—"Do it for yourself!"

"Don't think it's bothering me…at least not today," Suzanne answered.

"May I suggest, just as a temporary measure…." Handing her a mirror, "…a laser peel for those lines around the eyes? Once I remove those fat pads underneath, you will look younger. Also add a little filler… maybe more than a little, but we'll see…to smooth out the smile lines."

"Isn't that why they're called *smile* lines?"

"You've got great lips. Won't touch them. Not a smoker, right? Yep, great lips."

Putting down the hand mirror, Suzanne felt claustrophobic in the tiny treatment room and anxious to leave.

"This is enough for today. Besides, there are other parts of my body that need fixing."

"Feel free to call me *anytime*." He said as a grin swept across his face.

She lifted her brows and they moved. She picked up the mirror again. Sure enough, her brows moved—the lines still there.

"It didn't work." Suzanne wined, not pleased.

"Oh, it takes a few days to take effect," Dr. Rosenfeld reassured her.

"So, I wake up one morning and my face will be frozen?"

"That's exactly the result we want." He beamed.

Suzanne walked through the reception area. The walls were mercilessly mirrored, capturing her reflection everywhere. Leaving, she opened the office door finding herself up close to a mirror. Sucking in her cheeks pressed her lips together, as if to be kissed. —*Great lips!*

———

Walking to her car Suzanne thought about Rosenfeld. —*Wear rags and still look good? Ha! Never going to happen!*

CHAPTER 26

Skinny Jeans and Stilettos

Wearing new skinny jeans and stilettos, Suzanne sat at the monitor in the broadcast booth with two cups of coffee. Her face covered with this *smart-ass* grin. She handed Paige coffee.

"Where're you going?"

"To the *supermarket.*"

"Go girl go!" Paige gave her the thumbs up.

Suzanne leaned over to show Paige the tiny red spots on her forehead, the Botox clue.

The blinking red broadcast light changed to green. Suzanne grabbed the microphone.

"Good morning, all you computer geeks. #680 is moving along... good news, especially for a Monday. The #101 at SFO is also looking... good! The #380 interchange to the #101 north, also looking good! Could this be a Monday to tell your grandchildren about? Then, again it's early, so hang on to your hats! Easy, breezy, cool and foggy San Francisco can change in a second, it's always full of surprises."

At that moment as the sun peeked over the Golden Gate Bridge, a farmer's market truck came to a sharp, quick stop. The lock on the back door snapped and the door sprung open. Seconds later, loose crates of produce slid out smashing to pieces as they hit the pavement. Flying tomatoes, cucumbers, carrots, watermelons and fresh-crushed ice covering wooden boxes of fish spread over the south bound lanes of the bridge. Cars trying to avoid the produce came to a dead stop. Others slid on the slippery tomatoes…now sauce…did their best to avoid hitting other cars.

Luca with his usual dark glasses and racing cap with some logo sat in his Ferrari, stopped in the middle of the bridge, worried about the fish pieces splatted under his carriage. His radio tuned to the morning traffic heard the voice of the traffic reporter, "All in all, a good morning…even the Golden Gate Bridge is clear." The happy voice—even though Suzanne had been mistaken—rambled on, "Yes, folks, it's *clear as a whistle.*"

Luca's face turned a deep, explosive red as he listened to the traffic report. Livid, he pressed the radio station's pre-programmed number in the car's Bluetooth.

———

The assistant held the note up to the glass panel. Suzanne's eyes read—Luca/GG Bridge.

"Hold for a caller in a jam! Luca how is it out there on this gorgeous day?"

"Ms. Robins, the bridge is not *clear as a whistle* as you report." Actually the words in Italian cannot be repeated, but go something like this— "The bridge is an *insalada di mare, pomodori,* zucchini, minestrone, linguine, *baccalia!* Putrid *pesce! Cioppino!* Can't you see the mess from your helicopter? Are you *blind?*"

"Sir—"

"*Luca!*"

"Luca…I don't see the bridge…I'm reading from a monitor," Suzanne tried calming him.

"So! Your information is false?"

"We have helicopter reporters calling in the trouble spots."

"Well then, where are they?"

"Oh, they're out there."

"I'm looking up…I'm listening…no helicopter overhead…don't see them…don't hear them."

Suzanne eyed the station clock, it wasn't moving fast enough, if at all.

"Folks, hang on…there appears to be a major problem on the bridge—just reported. We're on standby, waiting for details."

"Are you making it up?" Luca insisted.

Impatient, Suzanne checked the clock, again. It's only seconds to the weather. —*Is this guy living in the 18ᵗʰ century?*

"It's all a lie!" Luca added a few angry Italian words.

"Luca on the Golden Gate Bridge, stuck in traffic…" she wasn't going to allow his ranting get to her. Suzanne took a deep breath and exhaled slowly, "…turn to *music!*"

"*Music?*"

"Relax and enjoy the moment. Hang in there, folks. We'll check this out. *Cioppino* for lunch, anyone? Weather…next."

The broadcast light changed from blinking green to red.

Turning to Paige Suzanne shook her head. "Is this guy for real? What is he drinking?"

Just as the two-minute commercial break began, the door opened. A young, teenage girl quietly stepped in.

Paige looked surprised. "Sasha, sweetie, you OK? Don't you have school?"

"Teacher conference day. Mom's waiting in the car."

"I've been calling. What's up, sweetie, tell me what's up?"

"I just want to tell you, that…"

"Oh, sweetie, I love you." Paige couldn't hold back and hugged her daughter again and again, but Sasha did not hug back, instead pushed away.

"…Dad. I want a real dad. It's not like you're sick or dead. You're alive, and it's just not fair. I know we've talked about it a million times. I don't like what you are doing to our family. I *don't* want you to do it."

Too soon for what was going on, the monitor light began blinking red.

"Oh, sweetie, I know this is awful for you. As a boy, I screamed when they cut my hair. I was always different. Sasha, I'll always be there for you. I will always love you. I'm sorry it's so hard."

"You don't care about *us*. You only care about what *you* want." Sasha pointed to the blinking light.

"I'll text. We'll talk more, do a movie." Paige was afraid of loosing her.

Sasha stood there, eyes filled with tears. With her head down made a small wave to Suzanne as she left, not looking back at the person who used to be her father.

Broadcast blinking red went to green.

Paige choked up as she struggled to read her report: "A low…pressure system off the Pacific…Coast…."

Always the professional, Paige finished her report, but could not hold back the tears.

CHAPTER 27

"Dating anyone yet?"

———

"Dating anyone yet?" asked Patti.

Dianne in her signature Jimmy Choo's finished putting foil wraps in Suzanne's hair. It seemed like yesterday she was here…root maintenance drove her nuts. Yet the results made a huge difference in her appearance and of course, her confidence zoomed.

At first Suzanne was blind to it. But in the elevator after the last visit to the salon, a man complemented her on her sneakers. And it wasn't until she got home she realized, "He was hitting on me." And then a few days later, this guy in the supermarket…at the time she didn't know it's the best place for meeting men…asked, "What's the best onion for salad?" After she told him how she preferred the long skinny green tipped onions, "Chopped, very fine." She moved on to the beets. Totally clueless, Suzanne missed two good opportunities to meet a man. She didn't see it coming.

Holly was soaking Joyce's toes while Joyce read the *Enquirer*. Harrison put Patti in his chair and Margie under the dryer. Patti spied Suzanne's red dotted forehead. Hiding herself in the travel section of the newspaper, the dreaded question felt like chalk scraping on a classroom blackboard.

"I'm…starting to get out," Suzanne finally replied, slouching further down in the chair.

"Not with Paige? Men will think you're like her." Joyce put aside the gossip paper.

"Paige looks great." Harrison picked up the conversation when his ears heard Paige's name. "Fantastic dresser. She's got the walk. She's got the talk!"

He looked over at Suzanne, "Has she...?" Lowering his hand to his crotch made a gesture with his fingers snipping like scissors. "...done it yet?"

Suzanne shook her head. "Not yet."

Suzanne moved the conversation in another direction, "I've been thinking of the internet...online dating?"

"How can you be sure about those guys? Look at Paige. Who would know?" Joyce crinkled her face and shook her head.

"Remember Monique?" Patti cautiously jumped into the conversation.

Harrison stopped cutting...her physically animated gestures drove Harrison crazy...now Patti could tell her story.

"Monique liked chatting with this Utah guy, Adam. You know, on one of those dating hookups you're talking about. Good-looking guy...I saw his picture. They emailed. They talked on the phone. After two months, it's time to meet...she's falling for the guy. This man of her dreams—never married, no kids. And Monique's not getting any younger! He agreed to fly in so they can go to dinner, then the next day the Legion and lunch at the ferry building...*big* plans. Monique offered to pick him up at the Santa Rosa airport."

Harrison found it impossible, but was anxious to finish cutting Patti's hair. "You can talk, but you can't look at Suzanne. You've got to keep your head and arms still," he warned Patti.

"OK, OK." Patti sat on her hands and continued, "Everyone comes off the airplane. He's not there. Now this was Santa Rosa. It's not like SFO..."

Harrison, frustrated gave up. Impossible for Patti to sit still, he let her ramble.

"...you have to come down off the plane using the outside portable stairs...Monique was in the waiting room outside security, looking through the glass. No one else came down those steps. She checked her cell to see if he's called, but no message.

"So?" asked Dianne, listening anxiously.

"She likes the *drama*." Margie slipped in.

"Let her finish." Dianne shushed Margie.

"So...she's going to leave when she sees a wheelchair being pushed over to the airplane's roll-up stairs and a security guards took it into the plane."

Patti kept milking the story, "Down come the four guards, lifting a three-hundred-pound man in the wheelchair. That was *him* all right!"

"Adam?" Suzanne asked.

"Yep! It was her Adam." Patti repeated.

"But he sent her a picture?"

"Yep! He did...several good-looking *head* shots!"

Harrison finished Patti's hair and helped her out of the chair.

The Golden Gate Girls gathered their things. Margie added a little red lip rouge and Patti was squishing her wet hair to make the curls pop. As Joyce changed into her heels she looked back at Suzanne, "Just masturbate!" and giggled like a teenager.

Patti looked shocked.

"There's no age limit." Joyce answered her look.

Dianne couldn't help but laugh. The Golden Gate Girls meandered out the salon, each one checking to see if anything got left behind.

Suzanne found an article in the travel section of the *San Francisco Chronicle*, and tore it out. This was not the first time she read an article about some great escape—a Himalayan retreat, or an Eastern European city still untouched by gawking tourists. She saw vacations to secluded beaches with palm trees and placid waters, where you walked out for miles in clear blue water and did not get wet above the knees. Never going to happen! These were places you only go to with a man!

In fact, Suzanne had a section in her closet—before Paige's de-cluttering—with this stash of south-of-the-border type dresses, shorts, matching sandals and great, straw hats. She saved the magenta dress for just such a vacation. "And now look where that's going...south, but not to Mexico." Confirmed her inner self-dialogue.

Still, traveling to some ancient undiscovered city was a possibility—especially if it had anything to do with food. Drawn to regional cooking...anything rolled in herbs worked for Suzanne. Maybe her body was telling her something. Rather than hot night sweats and panic attacks, it was looking for cool patio evenings with the scents of basil, oregano and rosemary.

"After we give up men, we get into cooking."

Or was it that our bodies have become fat and no man wants us. Suzanne had this theory—the fatter women got, the more basil, oregano and rosemary women desired. Because cooking satisfied other senses, women forgot about men. If she threw in a day or two in Florence or Paris, Suzanne could certainly make a cooking school trip happen.

Dianne read her thoughts, "Go with a girlfriend."

Suzanne nodded thoughtfully, "I do have several girlfriends...it's a thought."

While the foils wrapped her hair and cooked under the dryer, Suzanne mentally cruised a list of possible travel companions.

Suzanne first thought of Sophia a New Yorker, who she met years ago in L.A. and had remained great friends in spite of the distance. Suzanne thought she might be perfect. She had spousal support and was single with no obligations—not even a dog or cat. "I love Paris, London and Florence with the boutiques, theaters, and great restaurants." Suzanne heard her comment. She also had the pocket book to go with it, "The Ritz...the only way to travel."

Suzanne was more laid back. She liked to explore old cities, rummaging through dusty, local street shops. She didn't mind struggling with cobblestone alleys, and staying in smaller, charming, boutique accommodations. Sophie's stilettos kept her off back streets and her morning *toilette* killed half the day. Then, there was her New York driving style forcing Suzanne's passenger foot to continually stomp an imaginary brake.

Sophia also traveled with a lot of baggage...the overstuffed suitcase kind, so they would need a private driver. Bottom line—they both would be miserable. Traveling abroad with Sophie didn't work unless there was an unlimited amount of time and cash.

Suzanne's credit card and self-control would certainly run out. She loved their uptown outings in Manhattan, the theater, and galleries, but she guessed that was what they did best and will be staying good friends forever.

Maybe Jenna? Suzanne and Jenna took many trips together as single parents and have shared lots of late hours hanging out at the bars, skiing, dancing. That was in the old days right after both divorced...yep, some amazing wild romps. But Jenna was married now. Although they could still take a trip, Suzanne sensed *married* Jenna wouldn't be the same as *single* Jenna. Suzanne still enjoyed going out at night, searching for a jazz group, or having a dessert wine at some local bistro. She also liked to sit at a bar and talk to the night people.

Married traveling companions seemed to savor a five o'clock cocktail hour, early bed, and spent hours making frequent phone calls home. Suzanne attended wonderful dinner parties at Jenna's that included all the A-list couples from Napa and Pebble Beach. Sure, she always had a great time and got a lot of attention. That's one of the perks of being even a second-class celebrity. She delighted in going, until one time Jenna made the comment, "You need to bring a date."

It seemed the wives of the dinner guests didn't relish having a single woman around, especially after Suzanne became a blonde. It was true she mused, remembering how the wives were in a corner chatting, and the men would be in her corner chatting. Suzanne and Jenna do lunch at the lodge. Their lives have changed too much to travel together.

Heidi! Heidi might be the one. Suzanne lit up at the thought. Heidi was still single and passionate about traveling. That was the way to go... travel with Heidi. With her Nordic background, long braid, and adventurous spirit, it would be only seconds after hanging up she'd call back saying, "I'm packed and ready". Heidi was a little overweight and dressed to trek...researched every museum for the free day, local cultural attractions, walking trails, free beach and campgrounds. She also scoured the world for the best deals…standing room only at the opera in Rome would be a coup for her. Climbing Kilimanjaro and hanging out with the tribesmen in Africa? Heidi called that heaven. Globetrotting for years, Heidi was wonderfully easygoing, loved people. She met all her male companions at sporting goods stores, or Costco…with a name like Heidi and those braids, how could she miss? She never panicked, and as long as she had her sleeping bag, she was a happy camper.

Suzanne on the other hand, would be miserable. Living as a part-time gypsy didn't strike her as fun, even if it was only temporary. She didn't feel she had to see everything in the guidebook. Suzanne did not camp. Besides, Heidi snored. Nope, they would not be a good traveling match.

Suzanne didn't forget Stacy. Actually, Stacy was a couple years older and might be a real possibility. She was not too highbrow, traveled light and loved art and music. She dressed casually in Hilfiger. Lived in an expensive home in Beverly Hills, belonged to the elite Beverly Hills Tennis Club. Her divorced husband had remarried living around the block in a house backing up to hers. He moved there to be close to the kids as they grew up—the kids only had to jump the fence. They all got along, kind of. There was a strong possibility here until Suzanne remembered Stacy saying, "Now that I sleep alone, I lay on one side of the bed one week, and on the other side the following week, to save laundry— I have rent to pay and club dues. I can't take out the trash without my makeup!" Keeping up appearances topped Stacy's priority.

On second thought, traveling and having to worry about every penny didn't appeal to Suzanne. In spite of the fact Stacy had the most entertaining sense of humor…telling stories about unsuccessful *male encounters*. Life was always half-empty. A very attractive woman, she would see only the other woman, and not how pretty she was. Suzanne loved her alarm code—0055, a reminder of the age Stacy told everyone.

Although Stacy was witty and fun, she wore on Suzanne's patience when some of her stories became reruns. Best keep the friendship as it was. This way they can still laugh at the personal sagas even the repeats.

Besides, Suzanne liked to meet and talk to the locals...with Stacy, it would be hard to do that.

What might have seemed like a solution would be a tour group. But Suzanne had never been the type to go on a tour. The forced schedules, waiting around for that one lost person didn't work for her. She liked making her own plans. If she wanted to sleep in, she slept in. She didn't have to see every museum or art show or famous attraction, leaving something for the next time. Suzanne liked the adventure part of travel with the excitement of discovery—a new, old village became a instant lunch stop, or accidentally discovering a local deli or bakery for breakfast. She loved helping a child tie her shoe or practicing English with a school kid. Strange, but she enjoyed talking to the local pig farmer, or gamed stealing fruit from an orchard...child-like stuff.

And then...there were the clothes. Suzanne had no baggage—the only place in her life she could say that honestly. She kept it to one carry-on. She packed thoughtfully squeezing plenty inside...one sexy silk dress and stilettos worked for dinner anywhere!

The fear of a personality clash with a girlfriend...longer than a girls' night out...kept Suzanne tearing out articles about places to escape, but ended up never going.

Suzanne had second thoughts, "We're not in college any more. We have our own ways. You know the old saying, about how you find your worst faults in other people? There's always something you end up squabbling about."

Suzanne held the travel section up, "Ever been to Italy...a cooking school? Don't ask me why, but I keep thinking, I'd like to do something like that."

"Awesome, Suzanne. You should go with Paige."

"Actually, Paige would be great to travel with, but one of us has got to do the morning reports."

"I'm going river-rafting. Come with us," suggested Harrison.

"River-rafting?"

"Yep, three days on the rapids!"

"Camping? Cold water? Mosquitoes?"

"We're protesting river pollution. It's for a cause."

"Italy's more Suzanne's style. Go solo, Suzanne! Italian men! Yep... London's too foggy, German men too cold, and the French too arrogant! Italian men? *Hot* and awesome!" Dianne answered for Suzanne.

Dianne washed Suzanne's hair. The water ran through it. She felt the wonderful head massage...Dianne's invigorating fingers scrubbed Suzanne's scalp waking up all the blood vessels, and putting them to sleep at the same time.

"I used to be passionate about causes. Now what do I do?"

"You have a very personal passion—man-hunting. You should try going out alone...a nice bar after work. Sometimes a single woman is more approachable than with a girlfriend," Dianne prompted. "You need to try new things."

Dianne's long fingers massaged the worries away from Suzanne's scalp.

"Sex in the bathroom." Dianne whispered.

"I thought the same thing, Dianne. So I decided to do it. Not the sex, but a drink. I got off work early in the afternoon, went home...took a nap. Refreshed, I got dressed as if I just got out of work...drove back into the city heading for an after-work drink at Spruce in the Pacific Heights district—bistro food. You know it? It's got a great after-work networking crowd. I drove around looking for a parking space...circling the restaurant at least four or five times, praying to the parking fairy...nothing became available. Every time I passed the entry to Spruce, I could see men in suits pouring in as if a Google bus dropped them off. The place was alive, the aroma from the kitchen, delicious. They even valet."

"So what happened?"

"I went home."

"You drove all the way back over the Bridge, to go home? Why didn't you just valet?"

"I couldn't give my car to the valet guys."

"Oh! Expensive?" asked Dianne.

"No. It was complimentary. I just couldn't walk in *alone*."

Dianne finished shampooing. Suzanne wished she would never stop. The smell of the shampoo and the scalp massage relaxed her...if only for a few minutes.

"You know, Suzanne, I have a new client...single, older, newly divorced."

"Another blind date?" Having struck out, she hesitated.

"You gotta kiss a lot of frogs before you meet Mr. Right. Besides, can't waste any time. Just do lunch. He's got money."

"Dianne, newly divorced men want the twenty-two year olds."

"Age is only a number, Suzanne. Sixty *is* today's fifty." Dianne combed out her hair.

Paige's *fucking-real-self-faking-it-theory* popped into Suzanne's mind. — *Your date has no idea how old you are. It's usually understood the woman is younger unless someone tells. So, Paige is right. What they see is your persona and it's that first seven seconds that steals their attention—that's the hook.*

"He's recently split...a new guy on the block. You got to get them while they're hot!" Dianne insisted. "In fact, do dinner! Women always look better at night...lower cut dress, softer lighting, a touch more makeup...."

"OK! OK! My real-self is going to fucking-fake it."

CHAPTER 28

Jason

———

After a phone conversation and several texts, Suzanne's mood changed. Hyped, she let Jason pick her up. It was his suggestion, as it seemed fruitless for both to drive in traffic—which Suzanne knew all about. Jason Katz was fifty-eight, not a tech geek but the preppy type.

He pulled up in a classic 911 Porsche just steps from the front door of D'Angelo's in Mill Valley, an upscale eatery in an upscale Marin town. Removing his leather driving gloves, he pocketed them on the dash. Exiting the Porsche, Suzanne watched him duck to allowing room for his wonderful six-foot-two frame and full head of tasseled gray hair.

Nicely put together with a casual Armani blazer, tie-less white dress shirt, and faded jeans down to his sockless classic sandals, was he for real or just some *GQ* ad?

Watching, her mind sizzled—P-e-r-f-e-c-t.

Why would any woman give up this guy?

Jason closed his car door and without glancing back, headed straight to the restaurant.

It was not an afternoon visit to the local farmer's market, but an upscale restaurant, a Saturday night, and Suzanne was in a trendy outfit that survived Paige's de-cluttering.

She quietly waited for him to open her door.

Inches from D'Angelo's. Jason turned, seeing Suzanne still sitting in the car walked back to the parked Porsche. Standing curbside with his arms folded, he rolled back on his heels eyes fixed on Suzanne. Who was looking out the passenger window, following every move he made.

"I'm divorced now." Cocking his head, spoke through the closed window.

Gliding her seat back, Suzanne folded her arms and crossed her legs.

Jason shook his head and mouthed—NO.

Suzanne could see he was serious...this was not a joke. She shook her head—NO.

Another painful sixty seconds passed before the newly liberated Jason expressed mental suffering and moaned, "I'm divorced and don't do that anymore."

Then with agonizing facial expressions, grabbed the door handle swinging the car door open.

Suzanne bit her lip so not to laugh, ignoring what just took place.

————

D'Angelo's was happening. The kitchen smelled delicious. The crowded bar...bodies deep. Immediately after being seated Jason selected a fine bottle of wine, unwinding after enjoying the first pour. And when he was ready to order, consulted Suzanne first. She liked that. He suggested the beef *carpaccio*...sliced, surgically thin, local greens with watermelon radish and chives, as well as two pasta dishes—homemade fettuccini with garlic and mushrooms, and homemade ravioli stuffed with lobster served on a puree of lobster and wine. Both dishes had excellent presentation and tasted delicious, which got Suzanne thinking about cooking school in Italy. The service reflected Jason's frequent patronage...it was excellent.

Initially acting distant, after being pissed at being out-dared at the curb, Jason became mellow, loquacious and genuinely friendly. His quick-witted conversation pulled Suzanne in and she became engrossed in his company—totally. The evening went well...maybe Dianne was right. —*Meet them early in the dating game.*

The *real-self fucking it* was working, too! Oops, Was it *fucking-real-self faking it?* Whatever! Suzanne was not shrinking away playing the 'yes' game. Instead, she was opinionated and feisty having a hunch it had something to do with the earlier event. Or was it the blonde?

Jason savored the wine and pulled apart the warm sourdough bread dipping it into spicy olive oil. He dove into the *insalada di mare*, which Suzanne couldn't remember him ordering—didn't matter. And between bites, he generously opened his backstory and past relationship.

Sliding off her heels, Suzanne rubbed one foot against the other.

"Yeah, I got the Porsche the day it was final…a present to myself. I was heartbroken. I really thought…" pointing to his finger with the missing wedding ring, "…my ex loved me." Pouring more wine into the glasses, ordered a second *carpaccio*.

Jason's monologue freely expressed his feeling about his ex-wife. However, every time he mentioned her, Suzanne noticed he pointed to the missing ring on his left hand. Obviously he couldn't get her out of his mind, and considered himself still married. He kept checking to assure himself, the wedding band was gone reminding him he was no longer married. Whatever the reason, Suzanne ignored the really annoying gesture.

"I couldn't believe the ex…." pointing to his missing wedding band … again, "…filed for divorce. I can talk about it, can't I?"

"Hey, it's good to talk about it." Suzanne encouraged, helping herself to a little more of the *carpaccio*. She noted to herself, that she liked the way he shared the pasta and didn't wait for the wine in her glass to reach the bottom. This evening gave her even more reason to think about a trip to Italy…and him.

"The ex…" he said pointing to his ring finger, "…had the gall to hire my partner to handle her side of the divorce. Would you believe?" He paused for a second looking at Suzanne and caught her eyes looking at him. He smiled back. She noticed he had great teeth…maybe this guy would work? He was open and communicative, good vibes. Suzanne liked him.

"You can be my therapist," he said softly—again that smile and eye contact.

"Sure, I'll be your therapist."

Jason laughed, "I'll bet you'll be even better!"

Then his tone turned serious, "You see, we made a lunch date and I was to meet the ex…" pointing to his empty ring finger, again, "…after fourteen years of marriage, a totally devoted mother to our three little kids…lunch dates…well you understand…lunch dates were rare."

Jason sipped from his glass and shrugged, "I completely forgot."

"Your ex…" Now, Suzanne pointed to her missing wedding ring finger, "…divorced you because you *forgot* a lunch date?"

"Yeah…I forgot to lock the office door."

"OK. What happened then?"

"Yeah. It was lunchtime and the ex…" pointing again, "…barrels in just as I was coming! But I'm over it!"

"You were…*masturbating*?" Suzanne's voice rose on that last word.

"Oh, no! My assistant was on her knees giving me a blowjob. It wasn't romantic sex! I don't get it. Every guy is doing it!"

He had to see her cringe.

"Doesn't make it right. Sounds like the ex," pointing to her ring-less finger, "…is a nice lady."

"She never forgave me. It was only a blowjob for God's sake! But it's okay…I'm over it! Yeah! I'm over it." Jason looked at Suzanne…eye contact…again that sweet smile.

They finished everything. They laughed as they caught each other wiping the plates fighting over the last bit of sourdough. The food was incredible and Jason had a good nose for Italian reds.

Requesting the check, Jason took his iPhone and calculated.

"Eighteen percent? Service was good. What do you think?"

Suzanne agreed, liking how he included her in his decisions.

Jason drained the last drop from his wine glass. "Yeah, very good, so if we round it off…that's eighty-five…each."

Puzzled Suzanne stared at Jason. Did she hear correctly?

"I'm divorced, only go Dutch," shaking his head agonizing again as if it would kill him to break his new rule.

"When someone is invited out to dinner, it's the person issuing the invitation—you—who pays for the invitee—me. Unless..." she said in her defense, "...it's discussed before the date."

Suzanne struggled to find her shoes.

Jason pouted like a spoiled child...he wasn't buying it.

"Actually Jason, you owe me two hundred bucks."

"For what?"

"My hourly fee for being your therapist.

———

Out front, just about to call Uber, Suzanne lucked out and grabbed a taxi pulling up to drop off three young trendy gals. Getting into the cab, she saw Jason sliding into his Porsche.

"Get over it! Yeah! Get over it," she muttered to herself, painfully pissed.

Inside the taxi on her iPhone, Suzanne put Paige on speaker. "How many dates do I need to have to accept the fact I'm going to die alone?"

Paige laughed so hard, she snorted. "Darling, you've just started!"

———

By the time Suzanne got home, she was beyond pissed. Storming into the bedroom, grabbing the shoebox from the closet screamed the words as she carved them on the notepad left in the box: ARE ALL MEN JUST PLAIN ASSHOLES?

She shoved the note into the shoebox. Slamming down the lid, she threw the shoebox back on the shelf.

"I can't do this!" Suzanne's shouted loud and clear into the empty room. But the stress caused a panic attack. Suzanne's chest became tight. Her breath stuck in her throat. She couldn't swallow. She ran into the bathroom and soaked a bath towel, returning with the wet, cold towel wrapped around her face and neck.

Suzanne crawled into bed, clothes and all.

Later that night, the alarm clock sounded.

Bob *barked*.

In the dark Suzanne shut off the buzzing, coaxing Bob into bed with her.

"It's OK, Bob. Just checking…I'm not dead."

CHAPTER 29

Miserable

———

S uzanne arrived late.

"You have ten seconds to tell me what's wrong." A negative tone ran clear in Paige's voice as she reached for the half-bagel in Suzanne's mouth that was oozing cream cheese.

Suzanne felt as if she was heading a dozen steps backwards. She grabbed the headphones.

Paige stared waiting for an explanation of why she was wearing pajamas to work.

"You cannot teach an old dog new tricks!" Suzanne barked reacting to her look.

The broadcast blinking red light turned green.

"It's a dark and cloudy day. It's the fing slog!" She almost said it! "Whatever you want to call it…." And so Suzanne started the morning.

Paige mouthed, "*What's a fucking-slog?*"

"Get ready for the day of all days. Heads up! At exactly nine this morning, the Golden Gate Bridge will drop to one lane, each way. *Merge.* Ladies first! Gentlemen don't ever forget common courtesies. Moist pavement remains on the #92 overpass west, possible hydroplane effect. Looking for fun…head on over there…."

Eyeing the monitor, Paige mouthed, "What are you reading? Where are you going with this?"

"Bay Bridge, slow…nothing new there…but look at the amazing cloud cover. Tricky to look up and see the road at the same time, but

I know there are those out there who always drive that way. Just in folks, the best news yet…the ferry from Sausalito has mechanical problems… expect a ninety-minute delay to the San Francisco financial district. Stuck on the ferry? Not to worry. You're in the best place to be…forget morning coffee! Open the cocktail bar. It's five o'clock somewhere in the world."

Waiting patiently for Suzanne to finish, Paige attended to her nails and quietly sipped her coffee letting Suzanne have her way with words. She can be really funny when pissed and mostly it was harmless.

The assistant held a note against the glass of the broadcast booth window—Luca/GG Bridge. Reading the note through the glass, Suzanne winced. But then with a burst of energy, took him on.

"A caller from the mighty Golden Gate Bridge…good morning, *Luca*. What's up?"

"The bridge is impossible, complete chaos!" Luca poured forth his latest analysis of the situation, and as always in Italian except for those words he wanted to be clear about.

Translation went something like this: "A stupid tourist, of course a *woman*, stopped her car on the bridge to take a photo! And her little dog got out the window! Can't you see that? We have a dozen people getting out of their cars chasing the mutt across the bridge in the dark. The creature is so scared, and keeps running farther away! I can't believe you don't see this. Every lane was stopped. There's going to be blood! *I need to get off.* Are you blind?"

"My eyes don't see the bridge, Luca." Suzanne needed to take a deep breath, to calm her nerves. "Didn't we discuss this before? The bridge at sunrise is gorgeous, I can't blame the woman."

"I don't get it. How do you report traffic when you don't see it?"

"I have helicopter eyes, Luca."

"Your helicopter eyes need glasses!"

"Well, that happens when you get old. You have no control over things. Old age just creeps up on you. You can't stop it. Then it's too late and you've missed the boat!"

"What do you expect me to do? There is no boat."

"Luca, when you get old and your eyes go and wrinkles appear—it's just the process of aging. Think about it. You become wise, but lose your mind. Win some, lose some."

"What does that have to do with the fucking bridge?"

"Sorry, what's your problem again?" Suzanne was totally off-track.

"How do I get off this bridge?"

"Oh, I get it, you want to get off the bridge? Don't worry. The time will come…like death…it will happen."

"I can't wait. I'm late. I need to get *off*!" Irritated, Luca wanted answers not a verbal discussion.

"You're late? But it's not even 7:00 a.m. Have a *hot* date?"

The green light blinked, seconds to red.

"OK! You want to get off the bridge?" Suzanne repeated. "Just jump! Luca, just *jump*!"

Those words hit the microphone at exactly the same second the blinking green light turned solid red.

Suzanne took off her headset. "At least he won't die alone!"

"OK? What's up?" Paige could see the old troubled Suzanne was back.

"Doesn't this jerk realize the traffic can change in just one *fucking* second? Why is *he* the only one who complains?" Suzanne was livid. Then it hit her, "Oh my God! I told him to *jump*."

Oops. Not smart. Could lose my job over that remark. Then again, didn't he deserve it?

"Did it make it to the air? Maybe it didn't?" asked Paige.

"Who's up at this hour?"

"Probably only the President of KABC radio. I'll explain to him how you're writing your obituary." Paige wasn't funny.

The engineer waved his arms as he replayed the last few seconds of Suzanne's traffic report. In a moment they'd know.

Suzanne and Paige both watched as he carefully listened to the replay, but then he smiled as he gave a thumbs-up.

They gave a thumbs-up back.

"I don't know what got into me, Paige? Maybe I'm incredibly angry with myself. Maybe I have to accept the blatant fact I'm going to die alone!" Suzanne's chest pounded and her body poured sweat. She wanted to take off her pajama top, at least peel it away from her body.

"Nothing seems to be working. My life is going downhill! I'm going to die with my medical alert tag around my neck."

"A phobia doesn't disappear overnight," Paige reassured her.

The red broadcast light started blinking, going to green.

Paige reached into her bag frantically searching for something.

"My obit's going to read: Suzanne Robins died alone because she sucked at dating and failed therapy."

Paige handed her a business card with a tiny gold embossed airplane.

"Suzanne, you need a break. Take ten days. I'll cover the traffic for you."

Paige put on the headset and took the microphone.

Red blinking light turned green.

"Fifty-five degrees, thick clouds over SFO flight delays. Sprinkles reported on Woodside's #92...."

Suzanne looked at the card, read the name: ITALIAN SPECIALTY TOURS.

Paige covered the mic with her hand and whispered, "Don't even think about it. *Go!* Before you really screw up!"

CHAPTER 30

Traveling Solo

———

S uzanne packed light. Traveling solo she had no big plans. Pulling her carry-on suitcase to the Alitalia Airlines check-in at San Francisco airport, she was hot and uncomfortable, yet wasn't over dressed. She was anxious. It seemed as if everyone traveled with someone—families, senior couples, college students. An occasional businessman traveled alone—married...she could spot a wedding band a mile away. And if not, he was married to his iPhone, which still counted as a couple.

The line crept along.

A young girl, not more than fourteen and by herself, wore a short mini with high, heavy, black boots...texting...not a scared bone in her body. Suzanne watched her move up the line, check in and walk towards the gates without ever lifting a finger off her iPhone.

Finally Suzanne reached the head of the line and rolled her carry-on up to the check-in counter. The attendant...very young, super efficient... checked her passport.

"Traveling 'lone, *Ma'am?*" he asked with a heavy southern accent. This threw her off. Everything else around was Italian. —*He must be a temp.*

"*Ma'am?*" Suzanne gave him the evil eye. "If you're referring to the fact that there is no man in my life? Yes...and for your future information...I might die that way."

"Just try'n to find a seat assignment."

"In that case, put me next to a sixty, good-looking, single, straight male."

"Sorry, Ma'am, computer doesn't work that way."

"Well, it should. Every other computer-based company can do it. And here it could count…in fact this is a perfect place for an on-plane, matchmaking, dating site. Think about it…a gal's stuck for hours next to some guy and it's either love or hate at first sight!"

The attendant thinking Suzanne was either loony or just plain lonely handed her her passport and the boarding pass to Milan. Then with her carry-on and over-sized backpack, she marched on to security—piece a cake!

Checking the time, Suzanne took advantage of the few minutes she had to kill before they announced boarding. As she walked down the corridor, she felt excited to be on her way, as every person and every shop in the Alitalia terminal was Italian…kids crying in Italian sealed it. Then she spotted a Starbucks, the only non-Italian eatery in the Alitalia area of the International terminal. "It should at least be Starbuccio," she chuckled as she searched the board for a specialty coffee and something sweet. Being anxious, she craved carbs…a muffin. No, chocolate, eyeing the brownie.

Rolling her carry-on up to the counter, carrying her handbag heavy with reading material, she wore the backpack stuffed with socks, a sweater, a scarf, neck roll, nuts, toothbrush, and anything else she just might need on the plane for the eleven-hour flight. She dreaded being unprepared.

Struggling with the shifting weight of the heavy backpack, Suzanne searched through the handbag for her wallet. Juggling her possessions and the hot coffee, she tried to escape from the backed-up line of anxious, Italian businessmen…impeccably dressed clones with ties, attachés and baldheads…which she created as she searched for her money.

Quickly swinging around and with perfect timing, she accidentally *smashed* her backpack into the Italian man behind her as he approached the counter, thus jolting Suzanne's hot coffee into the air and on to the front of this man.

"*Whoops!*" Suzanne so surprised, shrieked.

The hot black coffee drenched the man's white shirt, tie, and suit jacket. It happened so fast he stood there looking her straight in the eye with a what-the-fuck expression.

"OhmyGod!" She said, wishing that she could disappear. "I'm so sorry!"

Taking a napkin Suzanne blotted the hot, black coffee from his suit and frantically grabbed more paper napkins from the counter to finish the job. In the excitement, she swung around accidently hitting the same man in the chest with her backpack *again*! This was not slapstick comedy. This was for real.

"I'm so sorry! I didn't see you. Look…I've got a plane to catch—Milan." Searching her purse for a business card and pen, Suzanne dropped things making a scene, but she couldn't help it.

The man looking down at his shirt assessed the damage.

"*Basta cosi!*" Waving her away, wanted nothing more to do with her, clearly afraid of what she might do next.

The Italian practice audiotapes spun in her head with all the versions of *sorry* she could think of. "*Scusa! Scusi! Scusate!*

"Please, take my card. I'll be back in ten days."

Gathering her stuff, Suzanne kept apologizing in English and Italian as her eyes avoided the sinister stares from the coffee line stepping aside avoiding her as if she had the plague.

Pointing to the card, "I wrote my cell number on the back. I'll pay the cleaning bill. *Scusi!*"

The man refused the business card.

"Please! I must pay for the cleaning."

Waving her away again, mumbling in Italian…probably swearing…it was clear he wanted nothing to do with this woman.

Now, Suzanne heard the boarding count down for Milan announced over the speaker. She had to get to the boarding gate. Then she realized—he didn't understand English. So she spoke very slowly. "P-l-e-a-s-e…t-a-k-e…it. In case y-o-u c-h-a-n-g-e y-o-u-r m-i-n-d."

"*Una povera vecchietta!*" He scowled grabbing the card.

Suzanne walked towards the gate scrolling through the Italian Dictionary iPhone app. She found the words he called her—a *helpless old woman*. That pissed her off as it hit too close to home, he was right.

Speed walking down the corridor, feeling guilty, she stopped to look back. The businessman was staring down at the massive coffee stain. Then, Suzanne watched as he reached into his pocket and read her card.

Shaking his head, she read his mind—*tourista*.

CHAPTER 31

Villa Alessandria

———————

The large iron-soaking tub with four gold-painted feet placed in the middle of the bedroom threw Suzanne off. Unpacking, she hung clothes in an old fruitwood armoire at Villa Alessandria. Then she collapsed on the bed looking up at the high ceiling painted with a scene of the heavens. You could pretend you were lying in a meadow and looking up at the sky—just what Suzanne needed.

But she couldn't resist pushing open the shutters. The fresh air and a magnificent light filtered the view of hills, vineyards, sheep, goats and cows. In the far distance many other four-legged creatures living in the wild. She heard a rooster and took in the smells of fresh cut grass in the pasture. The brochure didn't lie. It was at this gorgeous villa in the countryside outside of Florence where Suzanne would immerse herself in Italian cooking for six days—her dream. She did not read or bring *Under The Tuscan Sun*. Nothing worse than coming with grandiose expectations. This will be her unique experience...she came to cook.

There were nine students in the class. Yep, Suzanne was the odd number. They sat on high stools around a large, u-shaped marble worktable, each receiving a handbook and pencil. Standing in front of a massive eight burner commercial gas stove was Giovanni Vicente Giustiniani—mid-forties, with dark skin, thick curly, black hair and amazing light blue eyes.

Suzanne opened her handbook and wrote, *Awesome!* —*young, but awesome.*

"Call me Giovanni! I am from Calabria, that is why I am so good looking."

Suzanne gasped at the egotistical self-introduction. His English was clear and his attitude—vain Italian style. She secretly laughed ignoring his grandiose self-flattery. —*Oh my God! I'm just going to force myself to be nice.*

Ages ago Suzanne read in one of the Italian guidebooks the southern region of Italy had been heavily influenced by Greece and Africa. The men in particular had dark skin, shinny curly black hair and light, blue eyes. The women? How come they never mentioned the women in these guides? Maybe because they worked the fields when these guidebook authors dined at the cafés, socializing with the men?

Suzanne ignored Giovanni's self-absorption, yet loved his accent and his spirit. She decided, "Just go with the flow," careful not to be overly critical wanting this to be a true vacation with nothing holding her back. —*If I want to sleep in, I'm going to—it's my vacation.*

Suzanne should have known better as the instructions were clear and simple: Arrive at 9:00 a.m. to prepare the midday meal. In Italy it was the main meal. —*Oops, there goes sleeping in!*

Then Giovanni and his assistant, Romeo, served this main meal, which Suzanne referred to as lunch…outside on the patio. It would be the food the class prepared along with wine pairing for each course. Later in the week would be truffle hunting, olive oil tastings, a trip to a vineyard and a local market to experience what fresh seasonal fruits, mushrooms, spices, herbs and local cheeses were really about.

Romeo explained, "We'll make fresh, homemade pasta and gelato every day."

Both items Suzanne knew she would never attempt again back home, but this was her dream vacation…a birthday present to herself. —*I'm going to suck it all in, even if I never make one dish back in my kitchen. Now, at least when I go to Ferrari's deli I'll know the language. All I need is to learn a few Italian tricks and my real-self can always fake the rest.*

Romeo rambled outlining a typical day. "After the mid-day meal, you have a one hour break…nap, computer time, text, selfies, whatever.

At 4:00 p.m. we meet back here for the evening meal's prep." This meal at nine—very Italian—was served again by Giovanni and Romeo.

After the announcement of the daily schedule where Romeo playfully switched between English and Italian, Giovanni shifted to chef posture.

"We partner up!" Giovanni said with enthusiasm and put together groups of two—mother and daughter, husband and wife, two gay guys, and two elderly sisters.

"You, Suzanna, no partner?"

An eternal pause drawing attention to her solo situation, Suzanne wanted to crawl under the marble table.

"*You* are a lucky girl, you will work with me," Giovanni said seriously, that is if you ignored his grandiose gestures.

Turning back to the group he announced, "Today, first day, we do *pesce!* The first meal of a new year is always *pesce.* It brings good luck."

Giovanni slapped down a whole sea bass…head, tail, guts dripping with seaweed…on to the marble worktable and in front of each student. No question it was fresh as the ocean fresh aroma filled the room. Then Romeo passed with a large tray of knives all exactly alike. Each student selected one acknowledging its sharpness. Following this ceremonious gesture came the passing of aprons and the pouring of chilled Prosecco—it was 9:30 a.m.

Suzanne made note of the word—*gourmet.* Sounding savory, delicious and upscale, she planned to use it in her obit. Markowitz would be pleased.

"We begin like-a-this," Giovanni said. Yes, those were his exact words. And as if on cue, he gutted the guts and demonstrated scraping the scales. Then in a surprising grand gesture, grabbed the fishtail and slapped it down in front of Suzanne. Holding her breath, she tackled the scraping. Flying scales landed into her hair, onto her face, and sucked up her nose. —*Was this not what I came for?*

Being strict in the kitchen, Giovanni meant business. In the back of his mind the thought of anyone loosing a finger…with the free flowing Prosecco…was pretty scary.

After having spent ten years working under big names in Canada and at upscale New York City eateries, Giovanni developed into a talented chef. But Suzanne suspected he didn't work hard on his English realizing early on his accent charmed patrons making his food taste even better.

Eventually Giovanni got homesick and decided to return to Italy filled with stories about his early days on cruise ships. It seemed young Italian chefs got their first jobs on the very large ocean crossing cruise vessels. Because he was new and young, his first assignment was to serve the midnight buffet. He chuckled while recanting a story about an older American woman coming to the buffet specifically to see him asking provocative questions. She even asked for his room number. He politely avoided her, but she kept inquiring about his sleeping accommodations. After several nights at sea, he told her honestly—as honest as any Italian man could be with a female—"The captain sends me home to be with my mother." Adding to the story, told the woman, "The captain flies me home in his helicopter." Then Giovanni continued, "The next day, the captain approaches me and says, 'I do hope your mother appreciates my generosity.'"

Laughing, Suzanne couldn't help but like the man. He was interesting and entertaining. When it got to be routine, he looked for creative ways to break up the day like a trip to the outdoor market exposing his frisky side, a complete change from the lessons in the kitchen.

Giving the impression of being aloof, Giovanni was challenged by Suzanne's unimpressed attitude. Unlike most single American women who came to Italy, drank too much and acted eager to hit on the young Italian chef, Suzanne didn't get caught up in Giovanni's arrogance. She wanted to learn Italian cooking. Sex was not on the menu...not sure she even remembered how all the forbidden parts worked. Besides when it came to sex, Suzanne wanted everything to be just so. Like the scenes in a romantic movie—perfect body, perfect lacey nightie, etc., etc.

Giovanni on the other hand, made himself her personal tutor, determined to loosen the uptight persona. Feeding Suzanne samples of bread dipped in flavored olive oil was only the beginning. Taking a large, ripe, black fig cut with his pocketknife into very thin airy slices, then adding paper-thin slices of a local, aged, dry Italian cheese. He enticed Suzanne with the delicious aromas offering her this beautifully served fig. His blue eyes played as he smiled.

"This is incredible," giving herself away.

"It's the thin, sheer slivers that make this so amazing?" she questioned. "I can't figure out why such a simple thing as this, can be so succulent and delicious?"

Giovanni savored a bite of the delicious fig and while slowly chewing explained, "The thin slices allow the air to activate the sugars of the fig, and air brings out the unique flavor of the aged cheese...*Americano mancanza tutto grossi pezzi.*" He replied wiping his mouth with the back of his hand.

"Bigger is not better!" he smiled being quietly flirtatious.

Peering behind sunglasses Suzanne scrutinized Giovanni...he had absolutely no belly fat. Maybe she expected all chefs to be a bit rounded, but she had to admit this man looked great in a T-shirt and *tight* jeans.

Giovanni, approaching Suzanne whispered coyly, "Bigger is better in only one place."

Suzanne pretended to ignore the comment, but secretly found it hard not to laugh. She knew she had wet his appetite.

Wondering the farmer's market aisles, Giovanni picked up a fresh carrot with its lush greens attached and leaned into the fountain to rinse it. Suzanne saw that his jeans were faded and frayed under his butt moments away from tearing. She found this sexy and snapped a photo.

Ambling from stall to stall, gesturing and pointing to the fresh produce, Giovanni handed Suzanne the wet carrot. Suggestively she put it in her mouth and sucked it like a deliciously sweet popsicle. Drawing it slowly back and forth, in and out of her mouth, she teased him. She couldn't help herself as she became totally smitten by his playful behavior.

Giovanni discovering Suzanne's unique prankish humor reciprocated with a gentle pelvic thrust.

Suzanne countered by biting off the orange tip.

"*Ouch!*" Giovanni pretended pain, grabbing his crotch.

————

Later the class wandered in the vineyard to pick grapes with the wine-maker's crew. Giovanni led Suzanne to the sunny side of the vineyard where the vines were laden with dangling fruit. Under the heavy, grape layered arbor...with his private pupil...he demonstrated how to judge the ripeness of the fruit.

"Suzanna, you pick one grape, squeeze it gently between fingers to break the skin, then suck the fruit tasting the level of sweetness." After several attempts, he found the perfect bunch and passed a grape sensually from his mouth to Suzanne's.

Feeling flirtatious Suzanne accepted his invitation.

Sensing her openness and safely hidden under the arbor, Giovanni adroitly unbuttoned Suzanne's shirt and caressed her breasts, licking and kissing them. He slowly worked his way up her neck lifting her hair and gently kissing the back of her neck.

Suzanne's body gave in in response to his lead.

The dried leaves fell from the vine into her hair. She heard the crunch of dead twigs snapping under the weight of her body as she found herself on the ground, rolling in the crusty leaves under the vines, and shielded from the world by the rich abundance of ripe grape clusters.

Suzanne could not recall the last time she experienced such a thrilling moment of unexpected foreplay. Unzipping his jeans reached inside and touched him.

Falling into place, it felt so right. They kissed again—more open, deeper.

Giovanni wanted more as Suzanne fondled him. Kissing her breasts, she arched her body into his. Just as Giovanni slipped his jeans down to his knees, they were interrupted by the three beeps of a truck's *horn*.

The class gathered. They were leaving.

CHAPTER 32

Late Afternoon

The late afternoon light from the Villa's window view was an artist's dream. Nude in bed, Giovanni gently massaged a rosemary-scented olive oil into Suzanne's skin—one hundred percent Italian style.

After years without an intimate relationship, Suzanne thought when the time came it would be sophisticated and nonchalant. She would have been sipping a glass of wine or two, or something stronger like a martini to unwind her buzzing brain. She relaxed now, but thoughts were running in her head. Like Harrison said, it's been years since she had been laid!

Sex? Suzanne wanted someone really *hot* to turn her emotions on unplugging her brain—both at the same time. And it would not be just a good-looking face. No man turned her on with weak shoulders or a potbelly. She never understood why fat men didn't get it. Do they think because they were financially successful or are tabloid famous, they can let their bodies go to hell? She guessed there were always be women who didn't care as long they saw dollar signs. Those wife players were good at that...so were desperate women.

A single mother, whose daughter went to school with Lucy, stayed as a rich man's mistress for some sixteen years. He was short, fat and bald. When he died from a heart attack, she got nothing and couldn't even be at his funeral...her young, dating years wasted. Starting over in her late fifties—deepened wrinkles, thinning gray hair, menopausal hot flashes—shocked her.

Another gal, a nurse, spent twenty years a girlfriend to a successful older doctor who had homes all over the west including one on the beach in Malibu. When he turned seventy, she was fifty and realized he had no intention of ever marrying her. After giving twenty sexual years to the doctor, she had nothing to show but videotapes, selfies and tons of sexy tweets. Back in her mid-west hometown, she hoped to find a divorced high school boyfriend looking to marry again.

Not seeing herself in either group, Suzanne's problem...and she did have a problem...was a lack of sexual drive. Flat Lined! Sexually Stale! Dead in the Water! Zero! All those terms hit the mark.

Maybe it was because Suzanne had wanted different things for herself. She never experienced big-house fever and preferred a cottage. Nor, did she like to endlessly shop for clothes—or anything else for that matter. Wait! Shoe shopping at a small boutique worked. Malls nauseated her having thrown up in their parking lots. She felt very close to her old clothes and wore them until they fell off her body. She liked how soft her T-shirts got with age. PTA meetings disgusted her, as well as any women's movement preaching females were better than males. She preferred to see them through another view, "Women aren't better. Women are different."

Small dinner parties and intimate picnics were OK, but Suzanne shied away from big events. She admired small, beautifully crafted deco jewelry to be worn around the clock, because she'd forget to put it on. The same with makeup and perfume—she just forgot. She liked a good laugh, the kind of laughter that hurt her side and took her breath away. Suzanne knew she was far from perfect—she burnt toast.

Paige was right. It was not going to be easy to find a man who would appreciate her individuality, her quirkiness. Paige also reminded Suzanne about dragging lots of very old baggage around that didn't fade with time. With Paige's coaching, Suzanne was working past it. Still, she could not jump into bed with just anyone. Listening to girlfriends tell of their sexual play-nights with guys they picked up at a party or a bar, she'd laugh. "That's never going to happen!"

Sex was a big deal for Suzanne.

Concerned with preparing herself for that moment: vaginal lubrication and having everything else just right—hair washed, sexy underwear, Chanel No. 5, music, mints, candles and fresh flowers. She added to that, clean linens sprayed with lavender water, sweet smelling massage oil, the latest bestsellers lying around on a pile of DVD foreign films suggesting her good taste and of course, the chilled wine. That was just for starters. There were other must-haves like butter croissants from a French bakery with great fruit preserves such as strawberry-rhubarb, or tangerine marmalade...in case he stayed over for morning coffee.

More—Suzanne dreamed of the right romantic setting. She wanted that memorable moment and was willing to plan the perfect scene—clean towels, no dirty dishes in the sink, no rotten food in the fridge, no dog poop on the lawn, the car has been washed, anti-aging creams hidden, the night table drawer had three sizes of condoms, the laundry hamper emptied, her closet organized especially the shoes, the toilet seat scrubbed and bleached, Fiji water at the bedside along with the one-size-fits-all terrycloth *guest robe*. Of course, there would be plenty of toilet paper readily accessible and a clean shower available.

God forbid Suzanne would be taken by surprise!

And then her worst fear—will he put the toilet seat down?

On this late afternoon in the Villa's room with a view, all that post-menopause stuff about vaginal dryness and lost libido just got left behind in the good ol' USA. Suzanne panicked for a second, but immediately got over it.

"*Quest'olio, fantasticoa per capelli e meravigliooa per la pelle,*" Giovanni said with his charming, seductive Italian accent as his gentle hands kept rubbing the sweet-scented oil onto her warm body. Suzanne didn't care what he was saying as long as he didn't stop. Dried pieces of grape leaves fell from her hair onto the sheets. He turned her over and gently massaged her breasts, making sure he gave equal time to each, treating them like little princesses—crowning them with a gentle suck on each nipple.

His hands. Oh my God, his hands were magic. He knew this turned her on. He had done this before, for sure. Giovanni was into sex.

Sweaty and dusty from rummaging in the vineyard, Suzanne could smell her own body. Her feet were dirty from walking in sandals. And she was sure she had garlic breath.

Giovanni was tan from working shirtless in his organic garden. He had healthy muscles, and a strong back. Suzanne's eyes took it all in. She chuckled at the sight of his tight white butt next to hers.

Giovanni's gentle hands rubbed her thighs, spreading her legs. His light touch was sensual as he kissed her inner thigh. Working in slow motion she sensed the pure sexual enjoyment it was giving him.

Watching him turned Suzanne on.

His body was moist, sweaty. He smelled delicious…a savory aroma. She wanted to lick him. She wanted to taste him.

He continued to kiss her inner thigh until she let his tongue in. He didn't let up until he came down on her completely. His face smothered in her wetness, the wetness she thought she might never have.

Loving it, she gently held his head and pulled him up. She wanted his wet lips on hers.

Giovanni kissed Suzanne, secretly slipping inside her wet body. She was so ready.

Suzanne's body moved with his rhythm, the natural performance of wanting someone to be as close as physically possible, fitting perfectly, thrusting deep.

His eyes told her he loved it.

How can I not want this? What have I been missing? How could I have been wrong for so many years? Was this guy too young for me?

———

The next day was the departure day from cooking school. Taxis waited for the students as they said their goodbyes giving each other one last hug. One by one taxis drove off to catch the train to Florence and then on to Rome.

Embracing Italian time to its fullest, Suzanne found herself without a taxi.

Seeing a small Fiat slowly leave the driveway, she waved it down.

Giovanni waved back, stopping to help her put her bag into the trunk. Suzanne quickly climbed in and they continued down the driveway. When she heard the sound of a baby's cry, she turned to the back seat seeing for the first time, a woman nursing.

Turning back to Giovanni holding out her left hand, she pointed to the wedding ring finger.

"*Sei sposato? Il tuo bambino?*" Suzanne managed to whisper with a false smile.

Giovanni nodded.

"***Stazione!***"

CHAPTER 33

A Rusty Iron Gate

———

Suzanne ached. There was no question she felt sore. But excitement lingered throughout her body. Yes, it was the sex.

After a week at the Villa Suzanne took the train to Florence. The fact Giovanni was married didn't sit well with her, but she got over it pretty fast. Being miles away factored in a big way. But his gastronomic advice Suzanne took to Florence. She had a mission—the perfect Italian dining experience.

Approaching Marco's, Suzanne followed Giovanni's theory on finding authentic Italian cuisine. She spotted a simple, quaint unpretentious entrance—a good sign. It was so simple…a rusty iron entry gate from some recycled villa, green ferns in cracked ancient stone urns, hanging dangling fuchsias. The interior décor appeared more patio than luxurious. Looking closely, she realized a canvas roof stretched from one exterior side of a building to the exterior side of the building across the alley. The interior walls were the stucco exteriors of these two structures. In fact, the restaurant was actually a canvas-covered alley that sat between two buildings. She liked it. Closed until evening, she studied the posted menu scribbled in Italian—another part of Giovanni's theory.

After her nap during an Italian rain shower, Suzanne walked back.

Checking the space and amazed again, she recalled how locked-up the place appeared in the afternoon …now with white linen covered tables and wood slat chairs…no hint of its true beginnings.

"It's all a front! These Italians!" Suzanne chuckled shaking her head remembering Giovanni's helicopter story.

The small, compact kitchen from the lower residential unit of one building served as the kitchen for the restaurant. The kitchen window acted as the pass through. The wine bar was but a cart on wheels. The host became a walking phone booth making reservations on his iPhone. The waiters were young, good looking Italian male clones. She hit the jackpot.

Suzanne's sexual escapade was short lived. She was now into food. And as she had always felt, if it isn't sex, it's eating. Famished having walked for miles engrossed in magnificent classical Italian art, and then hours more cruising incredible boutiques trying on one-of-a-kind upscale pieces...atypical for Suzanne. But the boutiques in Florence were not only tiny holes in a wall, but uniquely amazing. She went as far as collecting their business cards for Paige.

Not understanding English...a very good sign following Giovanni's theory...the host escorted Suzanne to a small, unassuming table in the rear. Delighted, Suzanne preferred it, as it was the perfect spot for people watching. Although the host handed her a menu, Suzanne already knew exactly what to order. When she discovered Marco's, she checked her Italian dictionary for anything she didn't recognize. Yes, she cased the place not wanting to look like—God forbid—a tourist!

"In many restaurants in Europe, bread is an additional charge. Here the olive oil was extra, but the bread was complimentary. Most Italian bread was made fresh each morning and by noon it's dry and crusty because it's made without yeast."—Suzanne remembered Romeo telling the class in cooking class. He was right. She never found Italian bread to be as good as San Francisco sourdough or anything made by the La Brea Bakery or Mollie Stone. No matter, Suzanne was not going to have carbs unless it was homemade pasta, and repeated to herself Paige's mantra— "If you want to maintain your desired weight, cut out carbs from your life!" Paige's words were glued to her brain. Suzanne could not stand belly fat especially her own...she followed in Paige's footsteps. —*Only wish I could grow long legs.*

Settling into the corner, Suzanne realized no one in the restaurant actually spoke English. Well, maybe a word here and there. Using limited Italian, Suzanne questioned the waiter who apologetically struggled with the English translation.

"*Branzino aromatizzato al forno.*" Together they agreed on the choice.

Feeling devious she ordered the *calamari ripieni* as an antipasto to test the kitchen. She had been obsessed with cooking squid. They prepared octopus in class, but she passed. Instead requested *carciofi in umido*, which she knew would be delicious on top of a little homemade linguine. But trying to ask if the pasta was homemade stalled the verbal flow, so she managed to have it on the side...at least she thought she did.

"Prosecco. *Perfecto!*" The waiter expressed relief when she pointed to the wine list.

First day out of cooking school in an authentic Italian restaurant, Suzanne ordered from an Italian menu in Italian. Sipping Prosecco she was totally into it, yet felt out of place. —*Was it the language or the fact I'm the only solo female?*

Trying to be inconspicuous, she took out her iPod. Leaning back in the chair, careful not to catch her new cashmere sweater on the chipping stucco, she hated behaving like a tourist.

"There must be something about tonight I can use in my obit." She said chatting with the waiter when he pointed to her iPod.

"I went to cooking school and I'm writing about it for my obituary. It would great if it got into *The New York Times*...but more likely end up in a local California newspaper."

"*Scrivere per un* **giornale**?"

"*Si, un giorno*...reporter, not a journalist...at KABC."

"*Celebre* at KABC?"

"I'd like to think I am!" Joking, Suzanne gave an approving smile.

The squid arrived. She tasted it chewing slowly to let the first morsel's texture and flavor reach its peak, "P-e-r-f-e-c-t-o." She mumbled to herself.

With broadcast precision timing, the grilled sea bass arrived...gorgeous. But as she checked the olive oil on the table to add a moist flavorful dribble, she waved the waiter back.

"*Per favore, quest'olio d'oliva...molto aggressivo.*" Not wanting to make the waiter feel inefficient, apologetically Suzanne explained, "You see in my cooking experience, I learned about food pairing. And the *olio d'oliva* is just as important in bringing out...." The waiter looked confused and motioned for her to wait. Then immediately returned from the kitchen with the chef.

"I Marco." The chef said in not-so-perfect English. He had a tray of cold pressed olive oils of different flavors and labels from various areas of Italy.

"Marco! Of course, this is your place. *Mi chiamo* Suzanne Robins. I'm from California. I'm on a break from my job at KABC. I finished an incredible experience at a cooking school and..." rambling on a mile a minute, she copied Giovanni's gestures, "...I learned that *quest'olio,*" pointing to the bottle on the table, "molto aggressivo for the *pesce.* I'm looking for something lighter?"

Analyzing the oils on the tray Suzanne carefully smelled some, put a drop on her finger and tasted some setting aside the ones she liked. Then as if on stage, selected her choice holding it up to Marco.

"*Questo!*"

"You...you food critic. *Televisione.* ABC!" Excited, Marco now had the attention of all the customers. Gesturing with open arms he introduced Suzanne, "Tonight we have celebrity! She do food show on ABC *televisione.* California...*HOLLYWOOD!*"

"Oh no! You don't understand!" Suzanne tried to correct him. "I went to a cooking school. And before that, everything I know about cooking I learned from those cooking shows on television. I do work for ABC, but radio...I'm a traffic reporter."

Marco didn't understand, but selectively picked the facts he did. He called for more wine and sang out in Italian to the kitchen to bring more small plates, *per gusto.* In his excitement he explained to his patrons, several times…going from table to table…they had a very famous food critic visiting from Hollywood—ABC television to be exact.

"*Cavolfiore fritto, funghi arrosti, finocchio, peperoni!*" Suzanne said in her best Italian. And by now the table was completely covered with Italian delicacies. So much so, Suzanne searched for her fork.

"No rush. No traffic." Marco smiled.

"That's the only fact you got straight," she smiled back, but of course he didn't understand that either. She let it go.

Marco apparently felt this was his only shot at making a television debut. "*Mangiare!* I honored to have a *bella donna* come to my kitchen. Here, my specialty—*trippa."*

There was no turning back as Suzanne recognized the raw tripe. She saw it served with a squeeze of lemon at the local market with Giovanni—not her thing! But she followed a small taste with a large gulp of wine quickly washing it down. She didn't want to blow her cover—the first genuine fun in years.

"*Superior lo chef…*Marco!" Suzanne made a toast.

The patrons stood and toasted Marco.

Now one big party, people were eating, drinking, talking and laughing, even teased Marco that he was on the road to his own TV show. They came up for selfies with Suzanne and Marco, documenting Marco's night of discovery. Suzanne looked around the restaurant. It was a night to remember. —*My fucking-real-self is having a fucking ball!*

This man had been working in his restaurant for years, building up a clientele and keeping pace with all the new younger start-ups. Looking at the exterior stucco walls, removable canvas roof, and peeling paint on the windowsills, Suzanne pondered on how clever it was to make use of this back alley space. —*I can reinvent myself, too.*

Marco would be waiting for some sort of restaurant review. He probably wouldn't understand the description of him in her obituary, but she could write a review on KABC stationery and send it to him. What harm would that do? She could say it is what she would be submitting.

No promises. Maybe Paige could get it to one of her friends at the *Chronicle*. Marco's food was fantastic and the man deserved recognition.

Suzanne called Paige and found her at a Poggio street-side table in the sun having lunch with Zach...all Paige's men were good looking and friendly. Paige ignored his kiss on her shoulder, and removed his petting hand from her thigh as she answered.

"Paige, I'm in Florence!"

"Did you shop?"

Suzanne heard Paige explain to her date, "My best friend is in Italy and hates to shop."

"Yes, and I got some incredible things. Love Florence. Paige...everything looks so good on me! I mean *everything*." As excited as she was, she didn't chat long as international cell minutes were costly.

"Meet you curbside...text details. Do I need to bring a truck?"

Then as in any Italian film, as the wine flowed so came the tragedy. Marco's mother dressed in an ankle length black dress, wiping tears, shuffled into the restaurant. She kissed Suzanne on both cheeks.

Suzanne was convinced that when Italian women turn sixty, they all wear black dresses. —*That could be me in a month!*

"My mother, Maria, is happy for me," said Marco. Then in an operatic tone, "But her heart is sad...today she buried her cousin. But tonight you bring her joy."

"*Piacere di conoscerti.* Maria, please join me."

Not only do all the elderly Italian women wear black, they were called Maria.

Maria recanted her tragic story—"I found Anna on the kitchen floor. *Morto....*" In Italian she dove into the family saga and Suzanne understood almost every word, especially *morto*.

"You found her, *morto. Solo?*"

"*Si. Forse due...o tre giorni*"

Suzanne took a deep breath letting it out slowly. Grabbing the pitcher of ice water from the table, she put it next to her preparing for a panic attack. She repeated the breathing technique.

"*Mi dispiace davvero...*two or three days, she must have looked terrible." Suzanne wasn't sure she was using the right words, but she was sure she got it right...Maria's cousin had been dead for two or three days.

The deep breathing must have worked. She poured Maria and herself a glass of wine from one of the many opened bottles on the table. Surprised, she didn't feel a panic attack. No racing heart beat. No clammy palms. No sweaty neck.

Strolling musicians from the big alley meandered into the festive scene. Was this not a perfect Italian vacation—widows in black, crying over a death, surrounded by great pasta, red sauce and jugs of red wine with live, opera music in the background? What's missing? Oh, maybe a mangy dog enjoying scraps from under the table.

Suzanne was sure if she looked, she'd find him.

CHAPTER 34

SFO

———

Suzanne strutted along the Alitalia corridor of the International Terminal at SFO. Afraid of losing baggage, she strapped the backpack to the carry-on and wore most of the Italian purchases. She had second thoughts about being searched; still she felt it would be less traumatic than having her baggage somewhere over the ocean on another plane, going to another continent possibly lost forever.

To lighten the load, Suzanne ditched her old clothes.

Fortunate to experience Italy's fashion week, the boutiques were open evenings. A *fashionista* experience that made you feel special…staying open just for you. The sales assistants' impeccable taste and attention to detail took their talents to the level of a private shopper…matching eye color to a cashmere sweater.

"Make sure it's an outfit. Don't just buy a bunch of sweaters in a million colors." Suzanne glued Paige's words to her brain before leaving.

"You'll never see this back in the states. What if you change your mind, you'll be six thousand miles away. Just get it now, Suzanne! Remember your closet, Suzanne? It's empty!" Suzanne mumbled as she shopped. Not a saint, she couldn't help but make purchases way more expensive than her budget forcing a mental debate on the spot.

Landing in San Francisco, Suzanne knew she could only carry out the new persona if she acted like a pro—that Paige walk, that posture, that attitude. Her 5' 4" spine stretched six inches. Her *real-self-faking it* percolated to the top.

She scrutinized her appearance in front of the restroom mirror before stepping out into the public area of the International Terminal. Working eyes upward, she was grounded in the shoes…a Paige rule…a stunning pair of Brunello Cucinelli leather stiletto sandals. Then a short Dolce & Gabbana skirt with a tiny print. The fabric was light enough to gently sway as she walked, *á la Paige.* The Prada cashmere cardigan was cinched at the waist by a fantastic leather belt detailed with a handmade, oversized Gucci silver buckle—a good chunk of change. The Armani white silk blouse has just enough gentle ruffles to hide the fact that she slept in it on the plane.

The jacket was a coup—a simple, Ermenegildo Zegna, 1920's classic. The linen texture and natural color gave it a totally new look. It reeked of style. Yes, expensive and came from a men's boutique. Not wanting to clone Paige, yet ecstatic to have the guts to make such a wild purchase… she owed the look to her.

The whole enchilada topped off with a dark stained Panama and an enormous Balenciaga leather bag. Suzanne justified the purchases by thinking like Dr. Rosenfeld—"If you use it every day for the rest of my life, it barely costs a penny a day." She began to look at all her purchases that way. *—If it's classic, it never goes out of style. Isn't that what Ralph Lauren figured out years ago and keeps recycling designs? Didn't my mother tell me that?*

Stretching her neck, flaunting along the last leg of the SFO International Terminal, Suzanne appeared to have stepped straight out of Euro *Vogue*—her *real-self-fucking-faking it* attitude at work.

A suited man with a quick stride raced toward the Milano departure gate located behind Suzanne. As he approached, she caught his eye. He checked her out from stilettos to Panama.

Suzanne stared back

Recognizing her he was blown away and stopped dead in the middle of the corridor. His eyes bored into Suzanne, so focused they penetrated through people as they passed.

As Suzanne approached, she kept walking.

"Milano?"

Hearing the familiar voice, Suzanne stopped. —*Yep! It's him.*

She didn't panic. She knew he wasn't seeing a helpless old woman with the giant backpack. The man was seeing an incredible chic woman—racked, fearless, and unforgettable. Yes! All of the above! The seven-second rule was working. And Suzanne felt this energy.

"*Si, Fantastico! Firenze. Venezia*...not enough time." She said nonchalantly, but blushed.

"Never enough time *per Italia!*"

"The suit?"

"*Perfecto!*" Holding up the suit carrier, he smiled and slowly paced backwards toward the departure gates.

"Let me know what I owe you!"

"Later...Ciao!"

Spinning around, he pointed to the sign marked Milano and walked briskly toward the gate.

Suzanne stayed fixed on him walking away.

Just as she was about to leave, he turned around and while walking backwards, waved.

"*Ciao!*" Suzanne shouted waving back.

Suzanne captured a smile as once again he continued to the departure gate.

"HEY! You have a name?" She called, but it was too late. He became one with the crowd.

CHAPTER 35

Thirty Days Before B'Day

———

"**O**hmyGod! *Ten thousand dollars?*" Astounded, she shouted. Scanning the letter, "Aunt Blanche, having no children...."

Aunt Blanche was not a blood relative. She married Uncle Pete during the war. They were pen pals. Aunt Blanche, an attractive party girl, wanted a stable family, but she was tall and worried about finding a tall man. Uncle Pete was shy, and Suzanne couldn't see him being anyone's pen pal, then again with computer dating many shy men have become gregarious behind the computer screen...so maybe it was the same for Uncle Pete. To Aunt Blanche's delight, Uncle Pete stood 6'3". At the end of the war and hundreds of letters later, they discovered they were the perfect match.

Suzanne loved their story. Even in her eighties, Aunt Blanche was a feisty modern woman with contemporary opinions...she liked Aunt Blanche.

Suzanne immediately informed Paige of the inheritance. "She died seven years ago. It's from the probate office. I guess it takes a while...am I OK? You mean with the death?" Suzanne stopped, took a deep breath. "Not getting a panic attack." She realized she had not had a panic attack in weeks. "No. Don't feel sweaty. Or even hot."

Just then, her iPhone rang.

"It's Lucy, I have to take this...just come over."

Switching phones, Suzanne settled in for a chat with her daughter. "Everything is fine. Got home minutes ago, good timing. I'll send pictures of Italy as soon as I download them. And before you even ask, yes, I'm wearing it around my neck. Got a gold chain for it in Florence." She paused to check the medical alert tag. "Lucy, Aunt Blanche left me some money...what will I do with it? Investing comes to mind. Any news on the pottery analysis...." Then disappointed, the call got dropped.

———

Standing there with her sweater opened, Paige looked at Suzanne's sagging breasts.

"Why now?" Paige visually sized them up.

"It's something that's been bothering me for years. Why do I have to live with pancakes?"

"No, of course not. It's just...."

"See what I mean!" Frowning, Suzanne stuffed them back into her bra. "Come on Paige, of all people!"

Stepping back from the mirror, she pushed up her breasts and turned sideways. She liked that view.

"This is for me. My birthday present from Aunt Blanche!"

"I thought you were going to invest the money?"

"I am...in myself!"

"Actually, that's not a bad investment."

Then Paige made a call to one of her favorite plastic surgeons and got Suzanne right in immediately after Thanksgiving.

"They'll pop those implants in. You'll be as good as new!"

"Thanks! Paige you've done it again."

"But Suzanne, I want to warn you. When you die and your body decays, all that's left will be two balls of silicon gel. They are not biodegradable!"

"Who cares?"

CHAPTER 36

Back to Normal

W hy do things correct back to normal after you've returned from vacation?

"…Doyle Drive is closed this weekend for Caltrans to complete seismic repairs. Better we do them before we need to! We are in earthquake country, folks. We can glue down our china, televisions, and a lot of other stuff, but we cannot glue down the Doyle Drive tunnel. So this weekend at 11:59 P.M., that's one minute before midnight Friday, until 4:59 A.M., that's one minute before 5:00 Monday morning, when heading north or south on the #101, before the Golden Gate exit, detour signs will be posted. Go slow, follow the signs and you won't end up in the mud on Christy Field or fall into the Marina. The Golden Gate Bridge will be open and is unaffected by this roadwork. *Repeat*: the Golden Gate Bridge is fine, but you need to follow the detour signs. Sorry, but you will hear this announcement many times this week, that's because it's especially important for those who are asleep at the wheel."

To check she was not rusty, Suzanne added, "Today, anything goes! Like designer fashions in Milan. Beware! Driving over any of our San Francisco bridges, people are wearing miniskirts and tight bicycle shorts! Keep your eyes on the road, and not on those sexy legs! Good to be back folks, traffic again in ten minutes…time for my double-mocha-espresso-raspberry latte."

Blinking broadcast light turned red.

"What happened to Luca?" she asked.

Looking through the glass at the assistant in the broadcasting booth, she waited for a response. "I'd expect him to complain about sexy legs distracting his view."

"Maybe he slept in," said Paige.

"I think it was just my luck. A couple of reports came in late and he happened to be on the bridge...just luck." Then Suzanne smirked, "Maybe he jumped!"

Cracking up laughing yet holding it in, they knew this was not funny.

"What are you doing later? I'm drooling over your new outfit. You're spoiled by Florence, but I need to shop."

Red light blinked. Suzanne handed Paige the microphone.

————

Suzanne and Paige took off for Barney's and Neiman's at Union Square. Paige also liked to check out the smaller more upscale boutiques—Armani, Salvatore Ferragamo, Gucci, Hermes, Bottega Veneta, Yves Saint Laurent and a few more. It didn't take Paige long. She'd eye something on the rack and knew exactly how it would look on her. Seldom was she wrong. She wouldn't think twice about flying to New York just to shop at Bergdorf's—her heaven.

Once at Union Square, Paige dragged Suzanne to the incredible window display at Tiffany's. Sunlight bounced off the jewels turning little gems into masterpieces.

They're gorgeous," Paige whispered to herself, but Suzanne got it.

"Yep! They really are, but can't think about it."

"What do you mean?"

"I'd love for a man to give me one. Not one of those gaudy numbers..." Suzanne pointed into the window display, "...just a simple diamond. Isn't that every girl's dream?"

"Wake-up, girl!" Paige appalled, taunted, "Diamonds are rare, beautiful things and are meant to be enjoyed. What are you waiting for?"

"Buy myself a *diamond?*"

"Yes, damn it! Buy yourself a diamond. You're worth it!"

Suzanne pulled Paige away from the Tiffany window.

"Come on! The security guard will think we're planning something." Linking arms with Paige, "I can't get my *real-self to fucking fake it* enough to buy a diamond!" Then she corrected herself, "On second thought… that would make me feel less invisible."

Once inside Neiman's, since Paige only shops on one floor, the floor with her buddy, Oscar—Oscar de la Renta— it didn't take her long to select a few items. You would never find Paige wasting time flipping through the sale racks, not even at Saks. Paige figured if it didn't sell, why would *she* want to wear it? With but a few exceptions, she was right. Suzanne liked to check them out.

"How about that hot pink dress?" Paige reminded Suzanne.

"It's *magenta.*" Suzanne corrected.

The sales personnel loved Paige, especially at the boutique shops. They'd call if something really exceptional came up, like the day she got a great Prada butter-soft leather jacket, just minutes on sale. No doubt the jacket lingered on the rack because it was a size large. Paige, having a wider frame found it a perfect fit and now a perfect price.

Paige followed the salesgirl to a large dressing room beautifully carpeted with a three-way mirror, two large lounge chairs and windows to the outside…real daylight…referring to it as the Kardashian Suite. She hung up each item very carefully, pre-selected one item she's really liked and started to undress.

Hesitating, the salesgirl motioned for Suzanne to join Paige in the same dressing room. After all, isn't it what girls do? But Suzanne pointed to the next dressing room, although smaller she stepped inside.

"There's plenty of room in here," Paige called to Suzanne. Half dressed she came over to the smaller dressing room.

"Something wrong?" She confronted Suzanne.

"No. No. Thought you would like some privacy."

Paige stood there. She didn't move. "Is this what it was like when you were the first girl to get boobs, embarrassed to undress in gym class?"

Is my embarrassment so obvious? Are my true colors coming out? If I accept Paige for who she is, I have to accept her body. Yet, I am afraid to look at her.

Suzanne remembered the time she saw an adult male date come out of the restroom with his pants unzipped. She stood there and stared, mouth wide open. Shocked. He was not embarrassed. Suzanne was red as a beet. If that bothered her, she couldn't imagine how she would react seeing Paige with her male genitalia exposed even if it were tucked into her spandex panties.

"I'm sorry, Paige."

"You're afraid you'll lose it?"

"I know...I know. Of all people, I should be ready for this." Suzanne was embarrassed.

"Hey! It's OK. I'm the one who should be considerate, not you. I would have given anything to have been the first girl in junior high to have boobs or get blood stains on my panties!"

Now, Suzanne felt really bad. They've shared personal feelings... especially Paige. She gave up so much and was misunderstood all her life. Besides, she has been there for Suzanne whenever and wherever she needed her. —*Why can't I just look the other way?*

Maybe because Paige had been Paige for so long, Suzanne saw her as a real woman. Or maybe, Suzanne feared even a glimpse of her original body...nude...would be going backwards? And she would have to start all over. Or was it, that Suzanne was jealous of Paige? Who do you know who can start a whole new life, knowing what they know? What mistakes not to make, having the guts to change. Yes, Suzanne was jealous.

"It's just that...you look better than me! Men fall at your feet."

Paige understood she would have a hard time being a woman. How much can she tell before they think of her as a freak? She knew Suzanne was in her corner, defending her choice without question. They had an unusual bond.

"OK. I'll let you off."

"If I didn't love you so much, I'd see you as competition." Suzanne covered her embarrassment.

"Very funny! Thank God, I have you. Hey, it's OK! Enjoy your private dressing room." Paige teased, "Mine's bigger."

Minutes later, Paige came out into the hallway dressed in Dolce & Gabbana jeans and a tight tank top. Suzanne? Came out in Guess skinny jeans. They stared into the hall mirror. Looking *hot*! Linking arms, they high kicked into a Rockette stage routine. "One…two…three," and made one last approving back and front view.

Paige leaned in, "Suzanne, I'll be so glad when it's off."

CHAPTER 37

The O'Brians

———

A tall ladder leaned against the house. Having finished painting Suzanne's second story, Mr. O'Brian sat in stained painter's overalls on the front lawn with his wife. Those paint stains came from every house on her street. All these years they were Mr. and Mrs. Suzanne didn't know their first names. She thought Rose and his, James…but didn't want to be quoted.

Mrs. O'Brian made a lunch and carried the basket from their house across the street to Suzanne's front lawn…a real basket, not a plastic carrier…with a linen tablecloth and matching napkins. Suzanne bet those napkins were absolutely free of stains. She watched from the upstairs window as Mrs. O'Brian set up a lovely, old-fashioned picnic. Real china. And even from this distance, Suzanne could read a tiny floral print along the edge…real silverware, too.

"That's a nice touch," Suzanne silently complimented Rose.

CHAPTER 38

Comedy Night

———

Tuesday night was comedy night at a local theater. Suzanne and Paige squeezed past other theatergoers as they spied their seats in the center of the Throckmorton Theater, downtown Mill Valley. Entering the row from the left and working their way to the center, Suzanne found herself sitting next to an out-of-shape, ex-football player...mid-sixty... glad she was not on a plane with this dude next to her.

"I'd be meatloaf!" She mumbled under her breath.

"What was that?" Paige asked as they settled in.

"Oh, nothing."

Suzanne liked this theater, historic but small...any seat was a good seat. Paige didn't mind driving over the bridge, as the stand-up acts were good. New talent needed a chance for feedback and the audience was always honest, making it even more fun. Suzanne wasn't surprised to find a line outside when they arrived.

"Looks like a full house," said the out-of-shape, ex-football player smiling while looking Suzanne over. "Got here just in time."

Suzanne checked out the packed theater.

"I guess so!" she smiled back, not sure this guy had all his natural teeth. She got a good look, as his smile hadn't ceased yet.

"Did you ever see Robin Williams?" The big guy's salt and pepper hair curled up at the back of his neck. Suzanne noticed as he leaned into her.

"Yes. He was really great. Can't believe how he could take off on a subject for forty-five minutes," Suzanne gave a polite reply. "I miss him."

"Yeah, he lived in the neighborhood growing up, got his start here. I think of him every time I'm at this theater...walked these aisles, sat in these seats." The big guy rambled reminiscing.

Suzanne had a mini star struck warmth for certain celebrities. No, not a screaming fan, but has had a hidden crush on certain actors. Especially when they got older and evolved into more serious actor. Sean Connery was one such favorite. She loved catching those cozy interviews with famous people, thinking how great it would be to have dinner with one of those intellectual types—authors, artists. Suzanne would have a million questions.

One afternoon inside a parking structure in Beverly Hills on Camden Drive, Dustin Hoffman stepped into the elevator. He was wearing a tan jacket with a zipper, tan pants and a button-down dress shirt, maybe striped. No tie. He had brown leather loafers and socks. Suzanne remembered every detail, even the quality of fabric. He stared at the elevator door. She stared at the elevator door. They were alone descending eight stories before they reached the street level. Unlike her radio personality, Suzanne was totally speechless! Not even an "Hello" or acknowledging she was a fan.

The chatty, big guy noticed Suzanne's hands. "Paint? Thought that stuff washed off."

"It's oil paint. I'm doing the fence in my front yard."

"That stuffs lethal. Why don't you hire someone?"

"I have one of those two-story Victorians on Harrison. I have a painter doing the exterior, just thought I'd do the fence...no big deal."

The ex-football player smiled, smitten with her. Suzanne could tell.

Suzanne reinforced his smile, encouraging his friendliness.

"I grew up in an old Victorian on Sunshine Drive. It was a corner house across from the Sausalito's Women's Club. It had redwood shingles with white trim? Don't know how it's painted now. My parents let me take over the attic...great space for a teenager. Incredible views of the Bay, absolutely loved the space. I could hear the rain...each drop as it hit the slate roof."

He reached out to shake Suzanne's hand. She noticed how large his hands were...puffy. Glancing down, she saw how her hands had more definition and her fingers looked red and dry.

"Samuel Sandburg! SS—Social Security! Sammy Sand. Hamburg-Sandburg...just call me Sam."

He thinks he's funny—not good. Not-bad-looking—very good.

"Suzanne Robins. But, I'm not a Sue!" A little flirtatious smile went along with that stupid comment. But after his, she didn't feel bad.

"I know your house. It's in our historical section—walking tours, garden tours even kitchen tours. You need to check it out."

"Could I be so lucky as to find you single? Available?" Sam quickly cut in as the lights dimmed and the audience quieted down.

"Why, yes...I am," Suzanne whispered, surprised at his straight forwardness.

Maybe it was that *seven seconds of first attraction* Paige kept talking about. Or it had something to do with being blonde. If you try to analyze it, hair was the first thing men see. It was thick or had a cute cut or the color turned them on. After visiting Rosemary, Suzanne knew gray was not for her.

But Paige got it right. The bottom line was your persona. You had to live and breathe attitude...you never knew when someone could be watching...that unexpected moment, when you least expected it. To get over the hump you need to *fucking-fake it* until you've received positive feedback—like this guy next to Suzanne and the Italian man at the airport.

Suzanne silently convinced herself, the *fucking* word helped give it substance. Yes, your *real-self fucking-fake it* had become part of her life.

The theater lights faded to black. Sam now turned his full attention to a woman making her way down the row in the darkness, taking the empty seat on his other side just as the comedy hour began.

For the first minute before Suzanne got fully absorbed in the show, she pondered. —*Older, men wanting a second chance at love? Why not be open to more options?*

CHAPTER 39

Wet Paint

"Take a break?" Sam held up a brown bag surprising Suzanne. Minutes earlier that late afternoon a Mercedes slowly cruised down the street. Sam got out and crossed the street to Suzanne's house. He couldn't miss the house with a ladder leaning against the porch and a freshly painted white fence. Totally embarrassed was Suzanne's immediate response, but she quickly got over it, wiping the paint from her hands onto her old baggie sweats saved for yard work. That way, she just trashed them—one step ahead of Paige.

Suzanne soaked the wet brush.

Sam covered the unused paint in the can.

In the kitchen, Sam found the wine opener.

"Cakebread Vineyards, Napa…a very nice cab." Suzanne recognized the label and knew it was pretty pricey. "Nice choice. Thanks."

"Boy! I'm impressed with how much you've painted." Sam said as he pulled the cork, "Ah, there she goes! We'll let it breathe."

Wandering into the living room, Sam emptied his pockets—keys, wallet, loose change, and iPhone—putting everything on the side table. Then sliding off his jacket, threw it over a cherry wood side chair.

"Does he notice the leather club chair?" Suzanne questioned in a singsong tone conversing with herself.

"I hoped to find you home." He said.

After admiring the original chandelier in the dining room, Sam stopped and studied the etched glass panels in the front door.

Suzanne couldn't believe this guy...great taste in wine and appreciated antiques. And especially liked the fact he understood the hard work that went into restoring the house, which of course was her pride and joy.

"What a jewel of a front door." He said with a sincere voice.

That's it! Is this the man? Can older be better?

"Oops!" he laughed holding up his hand.

Sam had a really deep laugh. Suzanne remembered that laugh from the previous night's comedy performance. It was a laugh that made you turn around to see who's laughing...an unusual voice, almost to the point of embarrassing because it rang out above the crowd.

"Paint." He said staring at a stained hand.

"Powder room." Suzanne pointed in the direction of the downstairs bathroom, knowing it was in perfect condition.

"He's going to like the monkey-wood mirror...ebony-stained from the thirties!" another singsong dialogue with herself agreeing with his taste in style.

Then she wondered how long it would take for him to discover the Tiffany lamp. "Does he see the skylight beams light from three stories up?" In this running dialogue, she answered her own question, "He may not see that."

"Like the mirror!" Sam shouted from inside the powder room.

Suzanne knew it!

"I'll dig up something to go with that cab!" she shouted back from the kitchen. This gave her a second to do a quick hair fix and lip-gloss using the reflection in the glass front of the kitchen cabinet. She always knew this kitchen had more uses than just for cooking.

Suzanne liked the use of clear glass to display the glass and china collection. Even though she used the stuff every day, unlike her mom who saved the best for holidays. Suzanne's choice of china was nothing fancy…a white. Then again, the white was a brilliant white. Not off-white or dusty white or grayish white. It was snow white…that crisp, cold white that made all food look good. Suzanne liked to point it out to Lucy hoping some of her designer talents would rub off on her.

Suzanne had to admit black made food look really good, too. But she couldn't see herself using black for breakfast or lunch. And being practical, white became her first choice. The glasses? She had her favorites. Even though she didn't use the special ones every day seeing them behind the glass spelled—luxurious living.

Thanks to Suzanne's independence, she tried different things not having to fight over the design or choice with a husband. On second thought, —*Am I missing the part of marriage that makes marriage a marriage?*

Suzanne took a second to do a quick check in the fridge moving the pint-size blood bags to the back. She rolled the IV pole out of sight. It had been days since she thought of Jessica Markowitz, as she was stretching out the visits. She'd deal with the obit later.

Her keen eyes looked for something to put on a wooden tray—cheese or leftover duck paté? "Why is it I always have something to serve for just this kind of situation, except when the situation happens?" Suzanne mumbled.

"Did you say something?" Sam asked from behind the closed bathroom door.

"Just mumbling. Looking for cheese!"

Then she remembered, "Are you a doctor?"

"Nope. Commercial real estate."

"Oh…that's good," Suzanne felt better.

"It gets dark early these days, so when the office meeting got out early, I was dying to see the old street. After thirty-five years, what changes! I live on Nob Hill, in a condo…miss the village life." Sam and Suzanne were having a conversation while he surveyed the bathroom and Suzanne rummaged inside the refrigerator. Yes, he was still talking through the closed powder room door.

Suzanne heard water running, frantically searching buried her face inside the fridge.

Then Sam came back and poured the wine into two glasses—the special glasses. Suzanne got them as favors in the goody bag from the Pebble Beach Food and Wine weekend. Being a special invite, she saved the glasses for just such an occasion. Only great wine habited these special glasses, and since Suzanne didn't have a man in her life, it was usually a night when Paige came over to watch TV.

Finally Suzanne spotted the Spanish Manchego—a sheep cheese—hiding on the lower shelf inside a plastic crisper.

"Manchego's perfect with your cab." She told Sam, now on her knees as she kept digging through the bottom crisper, inching her way to the sheep's cheese.

"And I have ripe figs, too. *Perfecto!*"

Delighted, but still with her head inside the lower part of the fridge grabbing the cheese and figs, Suzanne felt a coolness on her hands at the lower crisper level and strong heat from Sam's body on her face at the mid-shelf level.

"Yes Suzanne, it will be perfect." Sam said leaning down as he handed her the glass of wine.

Suzanne turned toward him to accept the Cakebread.

OhmyGod!" Suzanne's eyeballs *popped.* Her body froze.

Sam was up close and naked. His huge *penis* projected straight out, slightly fluctuating like a diving board at mid-shelf—mouth level—a direct hit.

Suzanne had always been afraid of the fat belly coming at her, but in this case she had second thoughts!

Shocked, she stared at the penis. She had never seen or heard of a penis with such enormous proportions. As Suzanne slowly regained a standing position, Sam began prancing around the kitchen like a wild stallion. Large amounts of fat, loose, sagging skin shook on his body. Where did all the muscle go? His arms flapped like wings.

"I got whacked in a football game," Sam said still waving his private part around, "...it wouldn't work after that. Modern medicine changed that. Isn't it beautiful?" He leaned back pointing his penis toward heaven to prove his point.

"Oh*myGod*!" Suzanne was certain Sam had not arrived with that. Anyone would have noticed.

And then Suzanne burst out laughing, "It's a *joke*!"

Sam was not embarrassed or offended. Nope. He was excited and proud. "Don't understand why those guys take Viagra. I took Cialis yesterday! And it'll be good for days. Hey, there's no rush."

"You get a two day hard-on?" she asked, but could not stop staring at his body part…so huge its weight alone could cause it to snap off.

"They guarantee thirty-six hours!" Sam was dead serious.

Suzanne turned away she couldn't look at him. Everything about it was so *not* normal. "How can you walk? How do you sit?" And then she had to ask, "Where do you hide it?"

Not only was it gross, there was something else besides this body part making her uncomfortable. She couldn't put her finger on it, but it stuck in her mind.

"Can't get any better!" Boasted this naked man in her kitchen.

Sam poured more wine and ambled his way toward the living room. Suzanne panicked as this naked man started to *sit* on the white linen, shabby-chic sofa. That's it!

"*Wait*!" she screamed.

"I won't spill the wine," Sam assured her.

"It's not the wine!"

Sam motioned for her to join him on the sofa.

Yes. Suzanne invited him into her house, but this naked parade was not part of the deal.

"Sam, I'm flattered you stopped by. But…I want to finish painting the fence before the sun goes down. Unless you have work clothes, you and your penis will have to make a date."

Suzanne couldn't tell if he was listening, or just in love with his body extension.

Sam stepped closer, leaning over to kiss her pulled her down to sit next to him on the sofa.

Suzanne pushed him away.

"No, Sam. You must leave. You must leave *now*."

In an obsessed passion, the big guy grabbed her, pushing her down into the pillows on the sofa. Trying with all her 125 pound might, she couldn't lift the hunk off.

"Get off me! That's it. *Get out of my house!*" Suzanne was livid and meant it.

There was a loud *crash*. The wine glass shattered. Now, Suzanne was even more pissed.

But then Sam's facial expression froze.

"Sam. Sam? Stop playing games. Get the fuck off me!" Suzanne suspected this to be another one of his attention getting tricks. Sam's dead weight, all two hundred and seventy pounds was stuck on top of Suzanne. She tried to lift his motionless body, but it wouldn't budge. Wiggling, she slid out from under his naked flesh…thanks to Pilates… managed to roll this dead weight from the sofa, down onto the floor.

"Oh no! *Ohmygod!*" Not allowing herself to panic, Suzanne quickly put her hand on his neck and felt a pulse. He was barely breathing.

"Thank God!" Immediately she dialed 9-1-1.

She pressed on his chest with both hands, following the operators dirctions. She wasn't sure if she was doing it right, but his breathing got deeper. Color came back to his face.

She grabbed the cashmere throw from the sofa to keep him warm while waiting for the ambulance. In the distance she heard the ambulance sirens; it would be any minute now. She noticed under the throw, Sam still had an erection—pointing straight to heaven.

All emotions came over Suzanne. She started uncontrollably laughing, so hard there were tears in her eyes, and yet she was raging mad and angry.

She seized the moment *screaming*, "There's no way I want you or your sperm!"

Suzanne whacked the extended penis.

CHAPTER 40

Teresa

———

Following the ambulance emergency technician into the ER admissions at Marin General, Suzanne hustled after the stretcher. The EMT guy continued into emergency with Sam hooked up to an IV and respirator.

"He's going to be fine," the paramedic assured her.

The admissions nurse was overwhelmed. She made Suzanne's morning multitasking look like child's play. Painful screams were unnerving. Suzanne didn't want to look. And if you didn't look, you were ignoring them as if they didn't matter. You can't win. She felt helpless.

The nurse finally got around to questioning Suzanne. With all the chaos she found it hard to concentrate…the blood on the floor didn't help. But Suzanne didn't panic—good news. She was anxious to get out of there. The waiting, the strong smell of alcohol—the anti-infection kind—didn't sit well with her, but a martini would work.

"His name?"

"Samuel Sandburg.

"Is that b-_e_-r-g or b-_u_-r-g?

"I don't know."

The nurse checked all the boxes on the computer.

"Date of birth?"

"I don't know."

"Your relationship to the patient?"

"We are not in a relationship…he's an acquaintance!"

The nurse looked up at Suzanne with a smirk on her face that convicted her—you are lying! And then confronted her directly, "Don't you at least know how to spell your friend's name?"

"He's a very *new* friend. I only met him last night at the comedy show in Mill Valley. You know…Tuesday Night Stand-up at the Throckmorton? He happened to be sitting next to me. I did nothing…."

Suzanne noticed her picture ID tag—Teresa.

Teresa pecked away on the computer. "There's not enough space for a romantic novel. I just need the correct spelling of his name, date of birth, address, basic stuff."

"Didn't he have a wallet? You guys have his clothes. The paramedics said he would be all right."

The nurse held up a clear plastic bag—small tin of mints, lip balm, and an unopened large-size condom.

"That size would never work!" Then Suzanne remembered, "Oh! His wallet is on the table at my house…I'll be right back!"

"*Whoa!* Not so fast. I need your name…contact number. You are the responsible person."

"What? I'm *not* the responsible person, Teresa. He is! I don't even know this person…he came on to me! He dropped by uninvited. He did this to himself!"

"Your name, please?"

"I didn't do anything! He's just…*fat!*"

Suzanne gave the nurse her info and left making her way back through all the hectic, ER traffic. She worried sick, not about Sam… about herself. What if the newspapers got wind of her being here with this guy? Was there the possibility the paparazzi would sell her out?

Then Suzanne dropped the high-ego thoughts and headed home.

It took an hour to get back to Teresa at the reception desk. She put Sam's shoes and tie on the counter. His iPhone rang. She ignored it handing his wallet to the Teresa. The nurse removed his driver's license and looked at his picture.

"Sandburg…b-**u**-r-g, thought so…not bad for sixty-nine."

"Sixty-nine?"

Suzanne could have cheated and looked herself. But actually didn't care one shit about this guy. Especially now that he was OK.

Sam's iPhone rang, again. This time she watched it go to voicemail... noticed the last dozen calls were from the same person—Brianna. Suzanne reached over and grabbed a Post-it from the desk and wrote the address...across the street where Sam's car was parked...attached it to his keys. The iPhone rang *again*. This time, she handed the phone to Teresa.

"I think you need to talk to Brianna."

"Where'd you find this guy?" Teresa had that smirk again.

"On the street where I live."

"OK, OK, I'll talk to the wife, girlfriend...whoever."

Suzanne handed the car keys with the Post-it to the nurse. —*Can I leave now?*

"OK, you were walking the dog...yada-yada-yada." Teresa took the cell phone keeping one eye on Suzanne.

"I didn't do anything!" Suzanne declared her innocence.

———

The whole day was more than Suzanne ever wanted to repeat. Finally home completely exhausted, she was even more irritated as she had to get up early. Her brain was stuck. She now knew what those car and tunnel people stuck in traffic must feel like—helpless.

With mental paralysis...Sam's image didn't go away...so she took a hot shower.

Under the electric blanket, Suzanne finally fell asleep.

But Suzanne's brain didn't get the message and kept ruminating on the day's horrific events—The Sam Sandburg Nightmare.

She got up to open the window for some cold fresh air, and it hit her...what seemed so weird was not the enormous penis so extended, as she had thought.

"Sam shaved his balls!" Suzanne announced to the outside world.

CHAPTER 41

Giving Back

"**I**'ll get kudos from Markowitz, I'm sure."
Suzanne felt as if she were acting, impersonating some other person wrapped in a volunteer apron dishing up food to a long line of homeless people at St. Anthony's Kitchen. She was more the type to let other people do it. If it weren't the obit making her feel guilty, she would not be here on her own.

Paige thought differently. Without hesitation, she got into it. And like Harrison, believed part of life's duties was to give back. Paige's love of charity events and expertise at hitting the phone lines, contacted restaurants for mega donations. Suzanne was ecstatic at the number of whole roasted turkeys she delivered to the church. The old Volvo smelled delicious. After turkeys, came pies...even more delicious.

Over the years Suzanne visited friends' homes for dinner. Even before Lucy went off to her internship, she didn't want to cook a holiday meal for just the two of them...more depressing than fun. Making a dinner reservation meant Suzanne would eat while Lucy text. Suzanne's family lived in New York and with traffic and plane delays, it was more of a horror than a holiday. The ex-husband had long-since disappeared with only an occasional email to Lucy—Suzanne kept waiting for the email, he was on his deathbed. So she tried to stress on this occasion all they had to be thankful for, and not what was missing in their lives.

There were times when Suzanne prepared the holiday meal and opened the house to friends who didn't want to cook or be alone.

Instincts lead her to believe she'd have a happy houseful. It worked… cannot say she enjoyed being tied to the various dishes in and out of the oven all day. But looking back it was worth it. When it was time for guests to go home, she couldn't bear to look at any more food, happily giving the leftovers…sometimes the best part of the meal…to the guests. Suzanne's biggest memory of the day was a lot of dirty dishes.

This year recruiting Paige to volunteer at St. Anthony's turned out to be a winner. She knew Lucy would be away, and suspected Paige would be alone. Suzanne was not going to cook and Paige? She can boil water—yes. Cook—no.

"When was the last time we did anything like this?" she asked heaping a big spoonful of mashed potatoes onto an empty plate, then added buttered corn as a child's eyes followed every move. Taking off her scarf, Suzanne dressed it around the girl's neck letting her know it's now hers.

Joking, Suzanne answered her own question, "We do this every morning. The traffic and weather report!"

"OK, OK! So what happened to Sam?" Paige was not one to let gossip escape her. Multitasking, she pumped for details.

"Sam and some woman in a small, cream-colored Fiat picked up his car from across the street. Sam must be fine because he had no trouble wiggling out of that toy vehicle to go start his car. Then, guess what!"

"What?"

"The woman hustled up to the house where his car was parked, pounded on the door shouting four-letter words until Mrs. O'Brian came out. That's when the woman screamed at her, 'Leave my husband alone!'…so now we know…it's Sam's wife. Mrs. O'Brian of course had no clue who this person…standing at her door…was and yelled back, 'I'm calling 9-1-1 if you don't get off my property!' The two women went at it. I got away from the window…didn't want Sam to come banging on my door."

"Why would Sam come over?"

"To thank me for saving his life?"

"Right." Paige agreed. "I bet the *wife* was pissed…"

"I didn't do anything. I am not the responsible person!" Suzanne pleaded innocent.

"…she's pissed because you saved him."

"What?"

"Now she can't collect his life insurance! …If I had a husband who cheated on me, I'd want him dead, too."

Paige had the ability to see things from other points of view.

Suzanne's iPhone rang. Still serving, answered. "Lucy, Happy Thanksgiving. Paige's with me…we're having dinner with the homeless."

Suzanne turned to Paige, "Lucy almost fell off her stool."

Then back with Lucy, "You have rice and mutton? Sounds good…I'll check the e-mail. We're doing something for others today. Got photos? Good….Yes, I wear it all the time. See you at Christmas." Getting in, "*Love* you!" before loosing the connection.

Pulling on the medical alert tag—Suzanne's good luck charm— she checked that the battery was still good.

"Aren't you worried about Lucy being in Greece?"

"There's a time you need to let go…she's on the boat most of the time." Suzanne took a deep breath, "…yes, I am worried…" The crack in her voice gave her away. "…I miss her."

The corner of Paige's eye captured Sasha. Leaning in she whispered to Suzanne, "Sasha!" Completely surprised, they both watched Sasha sneak in and duck behind the serving table. She tied an apron around her waist before sliding in between them. She reached into a tray and grabbed a pair of tongs. When the next plate was in front of them, she rolled the corn in melted butter and placed it carefully on the waiting plate.

Sasha didn't look at any one but the line of homeless families. Suzanne and Paige served with military precision, yet letting her know they were happy she was there.

Suzanne sneaked a crack of a smile, relieved knowing how Paige left dozens of messages over the past weeks. Even with no response, Paige refused to give up terrified she might lose Sasha.

Suzanne pretended not to listen as Sasha, with her eyes down spoke softly in Paige's direction while she continued to serve the line.

"You're a great Dad. Whatever you decide to do is OK. I will miss *that* Dad, but I can handle it."

Tears rolled down Sasha's cheeks as she rolled the corn in butter. "I'm ready for two Moms now."

Paige turned to her only child and gave her the biggest squeeze. "I love you so much. I will always be there for you."

As Suzanne listened tears cascaded down her cheeks. She had tiptoed around this tenuous relationship for years. At least when you divorce, the kids get it…they had two sets of everything—one at mom's place and one at dad's. If dad didn't buy the car, mom would. They'd be a routine and somehow the kids would feel secure and flourished. This was a whole new ball game!

"Smells good! Can I stay for dinner?" Sasha asked Paige.

"Be my guest, I *cooked* all this myself!"

Emotions exploded into uncontrollable laugher with weeping uncontrollable tears.

———

Later, sitting at one of the long metal tables alongside a homeless family…no fancy china just paper and plastic…they enjoyed every bite of the humble Thanksgiving meal. The donated food from upscale San Francisco restaurants was more delicious than Suzanne could have ever prepared and besides, there were far more trimmings. Suzanne felt good spending the day this way.

Paige pulled a bottle of Pellegrino from her Louis Vuitton bag, unscrewing the tight top Suzanne smelled—Prosecco. Paige poured it into her paper cup.

Sasha scored a can of whipping cream and a whole pumpkin pie. Delighted with her prize, she swirled cream on top, cut and served a piece to everyone.

"Today was not the day to worry about carbs!" Paige proclaimed, spying Suzanne's look of horror.

That's what Suzanne liked about Paige...she was real!

A shy girl, maybe five or six, wearing oversized shoes and tattered clothes inched her way along the bench to be beside Sasha—a perfect scene from *Oliver*. Sasha cut her a piece of pie and after topping the piece with the cream, playfully squirted whipping cream on her tongue and on her hands. The little girl rubbed its gooeyness onto the tips of her fingers, licked it and then tackled the pie with her fingers. With whipped cream dotting her face, pointed to Paige.

The girl cupping her hands, whispered in Sash's ear. "That lady is pretty. She your mom?"

"Yes." Sasha trumpeted, "She's my Mom."

CHAPTER 42

The Best Investment Is In Yourself

"Dinner is for you…but this is for me," Paige said lifting the martini off the bed tray. "And in a couple of days, you'll be driving."

"I dunno." Suzanne shook her head.

"Just look at those perky mounds."

"I dunno."

Tightly wrapped in an ace bandage, Suzanne wiggled closer to the bedside table, s-l-o-w-l-y. Without lifting her elbows reached for a glass of water. With her new swollen boobs, she was not going anywhere. The more she moved, the faster the blood flowed through the plastic tubes attached to the dressing.

Paige brought her chicken soup on a beautifully prepared bed tray—take-out from Mollie Stone's. She didn't let on it was restaurant fare and yet she knew, Suzanne knew.

"One good thing about plastic surgery, do it when you're healthy, you'll heal quickly. Yep! Next week, dancing in front of the mirror!"

"What about that Cat Lady who had all those procedures? What was she thinking?"

"It's too bad she gives plastic surgery a bad rap. Body upgrades are not going to change who you are. It's really a confidence booster, a shot of self-esteem. I'm a perfect plastic surgery *junkie*! Without surgical help…I'd look like a guy in drag, but I'm still me…just matching my outside appearance to my inner feelings. Look what it's doing for you."

Suzanne nodded, "It'll be better when I can move."

"As long as you are mentally healthy…" Paige assured her, "…you'll be happy with the results."

"No way could I look like Kate Hudson. I'm not kidding myself!"

Paige's plastic surgeon agreed to do Suzanne. Of course she was overjoyed and felt comfortable in his skilled hands. This trust went a long way…soft spoken, without a pushy sales talk, a natural look…herself, only better.

"Psychologists say looking good boosting self-esteem and downsizing depression are connected."

"I feel the shot of self-esteem. Sure is cheaper than therapy!"

"Definitely, faster. If you let yourself go it's much harder. Like your house…once that paint peels, it's more work." Paige lectured from personal experience.

"That's exactly what Rosenfeld said, 'look at it as an investment in yourself.'"

"Well…you surprised me. Thought you were going to put on a new roof." She smiled as she sipped her martini.

"My man will do that."

"Who?"

"The man who will be sitting in that leather club chair you gave me, remember?"

"Oh, I get it! Boobs get the man. Man gets the roof." Paige joked.

"Paige, I'm doing this for *me*. If I never find a man, at least I will feel good about myself knowing Rosemary won't have to stuff my bra!"

"Think how good you're going to look in that hot pink dress!"

"It's *magenta!*"

Paige served large glass bowls of chocolate mousse.

"It's to keep your energy level up."

"You see? Who needs a man…you have me."

"True. And I can always call the pizza guy for extra service."

"That's it! You need a practice *fuck*. You know, sex with someone you're not interested in but could get it on with anyway. Younger guy? Married, maybe? Someone a tad…edgy? Definitely a hot body!"

Trying to hide a mischievous grin, Paige read Suzanne's guilty look.

"Italy? You did it with…Giovanni? Perfect! And you can't get hung up on him because he's six-thousand miles away!"

Acting like a mother, Paige fed Suzanne the chocolate mousse, stealing bites.

"Next time, *you* pick a guy for a pleasure *fuck*!"

"You mean…I ask him?" Suzanne laughed.

"Yep!"

"I'd forgotten what it's like…no way, I can get hung up on Giovanni. But the *sex* was incredible."

"The mousse is melting," Paige said as her mood shifted.

"Oh Paige, I'm sorry. You will feel something won't you?"

Paige poured the last few drops from the martini shaker into her glass. "I don't know, Suzanne. I don't know what it will be like. Then again, that's only part of being a woman. There's so much more. Womenness is powerful!"

"That's why you're my coach!!!"

Paige held up her glass, "To boobs and to meeting Richard."

"*Richard?* The name alone turns me off."

Paige opened her iPhone and scrolled down to a photo of a handsome, Richard Burton type. "I know your ex-husband is a shithead, get over it! You haven't seen him in years for God's sake. You don't even know what he looks like anymore or have a *clue* to what he's doing, except for tidbits he feeds Lucy. Get over it! Just look at this guy. He's classic, successful. His name is *Richard.*"

"Good hair." Suzanne admitted finding something nice about him.

"And then there's Josef. Now, he's cool, and I'm working on Matthew—creative, quiet, smart-techie type…designed an award-winning skateboard when he was in high school. Sold millions. He might be your type…not so sure. Never been married and has no kids…timing might just be right. Unless you put yourself out there, you'll never know."

"Paige, what if none of these guys work?"

"Why are you seeing only the negative?

"Just want to know what options are left."

"If you let your extroverted real-self, take over your introverted unreal-self, you'll be just fine…wear stilettos! Hey! If it gets really bad, well…there's always Match."

"Ouch! Rather not go there."

Then Suzanne handed Paige her iPod with her obituary.

"Still doing this? With all these bloody drains you aren't hot or sweaty?"

"I have no idea if I'm cured."

Paige read the iPod, "A seasoned traveler…OK, I guess one trip makes you seasoned. An avid sportswoman?"

"I'm thinking of going river-rafting with Harrison."

"Don't you need to go first?" she laughed and put down the iPod. "Have you had any panic attacks?"

"Well," Suzanne paused, "…not since I got back from Italy, but I still have blood in the fridge…not taking any chances. And I'm hanging onto the crash cart. It's in the laundry room."

"Crash cart? Did Markowitz tell you to get one? You know how it works?"

"No. But it's comforting." Suzanne picked up the obituary section of the newspaper, "Paige, listen to this, 'Evelyn left this world while in the arms of her husband. Every morning he would tell her—I fall in love with you every day, still do…and always will.'"

Paige took the newspaper and reread the words, "…and always will?"

"How do I find a man like that, Paige?"

CHAPTER 43

Richard

The air was cool, traffic calm, and parking was easy. Richard waited at the bar.

Strutting in her stilettos, Suzanne spotted Richard a mile away.

This cool San Francisco evening the fog rolled in...magical...like London. Kokkari was the classic upscale foodie hangout serving Greek food and one of the most expensive restaurants in the city. And like Bix, the bar scene was the place to be after 4:30 p.m. But unlike Bix, a particular hangout for sophisticated men—successful and suited—not a trendy crowd.

Suzanne was disappointed they weren't sitting at the bar. She found bars...thanks to Paige's insistence...are the place to be. Almost everyone there had a drink or two and the conversation was rich. Bars were addictive. But, that was not tonight.

Richard Porter was the grandson of a very well known local poet, twice divorced. Each commitment was the perfect partner,...so he thought...ending up in therapy. This time he planned not to rush and wrote a twelve-point manifesto. In reality it was a checklist for the next woman. His shrink told him a manifesto would keep his mind on the goals. This time, he'd insist on including a couple's therapy before he popped the question.

But Richard admitted he did not given up on marriage, having the advantage of being male. Having worked in London for several years as a young law clerk, he maintained a slight English accent keeping his clock ticking.

Paige considered him a possible candidate. Not super-athletic, but in good shape considering he had a desk job...very little belly fat and good shoulders from his rowing days on the Charles River in Boston.

Yes, he got points for being a Harvard Law grad and a lover of the theater. Paige ran into Richard at a Marin Shakespeare Festival, when she was on the Founder's Board. Somehow the touch of an accent coupled with his classic appeal made the grade for Paige's list of appropriate men. Especially being a guy with interests outside his work. But Paige feared Suzanne would not go out with a man named *Richard*. So she played the name down and all his other unique qualities up.

"Richard's done the trophy wife thing twice, he's a grownup now," Paige reassured a skeptical Suzanne.

Suzanne liked the idea he was serious and not a player. Being more aware than ever of the *getting-my-life-together-ticking clock*, she asked herself how bad could a dinner at Kokkari be? Besides, she was finally getting into this dating game and God knows how many men were left before she'd have to go into the senior bracket—remember Sam?

"Those younger, hot female bodies are not going away." Paige reminded her—daily.

———

Suzanne and Richard scored a quiet corner in a lovely booth. Suzanne was upbeat. With Pilates her body came together, definitely attitude building. Suzanne chuckled when she saw him with a neatly trimmed beard and longish curly hair.

Getting a reservation after seven and before nine at Kokkari was a miracle. Suzanne was impressed with the 7:30 time, but right from the start sensed he was a man on a mission. Or maybe she needed a drink to take the edge off. Even so, Suzanne liked his voice and the fact he had interests. She could go for guy like this.

"How about a red?" Richard asked, "Don't know Greek wines…" (Suzanne thought 'humble') "…but I know Italian reds, I'm sure I can find something." (Suzanne thought 'smart')

Richard selected a Chianti Classico from the town of Vince. The town Giovanni and Suzanne tasted grapes, but she wasn't going there now. She needed to remind herself it was a once in a lifetime experience. —*Don't go backwards and stop dreaming! Maybe Richard has a point, look at a relationship as a business.*

In perfect rhythm, they made a toast and let the wine savor their tongue.

"Nice."

"Nice." Suzanne agreed. "Excellent choice!" She sensed chemistry.

"Italian cooking classes sharpen my taste buds." Suzanne casually mentioned, comfortable with anything about food as an opener.

Breaking the ice was difficult for her. Premeditated on her part, but she took advantage of his love of foreign travel. When she told him about the mistaken identity at Marco's in Florence, they both laughed. He thought she was humorous. Quickly they were comfortable, even smitten with each other. —*It doesn't matter how we get there, as long as we do.*

Suzanne had the urge to text Paige. She'll have plenty to say later. She appreciated this introduction, and found this Richard was not at all like her ex.

"Grilled lamb ribs? Sound perfect?" He asked as he studied the menu.

"The meatballs are fantastic, too." Suzanne suggested.

Obviously, she loved Kokkari's food. Richard delighted in the fact he selected the restaurant. Suzanne had a feeling he was picky. She actually liked that, itching to tease him—*I'll bet you sneak in a Big Mac every now and then?* But she didn't; she knew it.

Nervous! The wine helped. Suzanne needed something to settle down—the crust on the bread? It gave her something to do with her hands. Besides it tasted fabulous.

"So how long have you known Paige?" Richard asked.

"We've been friends for... maybe eighteen years? We're a team at the radio station. She does weather. I do traffic."

"Oh! I *know* now who you are." Richard broke into an enlightened smile with expressional brows. With the waiter now standing over them, his brows turned back to the menu.

"Suzanne, the small plates are wonderful, how about one of each? Could be dinner. What do you say?" Richard asked her as he looked up at the waiter.

"Great idea!"

"The small plates, everything you've got."

The waiter smiled, happy to see them make a quick choice.

"Radio? Isn't there more money in TV?" he asked curious about her job.

"Absolutely." Suzanne nodded.

Suzanne got tiresome of people awestruck about her job, and then telling her it was second best to TV. She didn't need to feel famous or special, it was a job. And she particularly liked the fact she was not on screen. She moved the conversation back to food as it arrived almost immediately. The table couldn't handle one more plate, knife or fork. They began to savor each morsel.

"Richard, did you try this meatball sauce? ... A subtle taste of a red wine, fresh squeezed tomatoes, slivers of fresh basil and a pinch of crushed garlic...oh my God, delicious!"

"And the prawns!" He joined in, "These...here, you must try." Richard put one on Suzanne's plate and dribbled the butter and garlic sauce. Then passed more bread. He watched the waiter pour more wine and seemed pleased Suzanne was enjoying the meal. And even more important, he seemed to be into her.

Suzanne began having second thoughts. —*I wonder if he knows we're close in age? Maybe I'm too old for him?*

"They make...millions?" Richard interrupted her thought.

"Yes. They do. But...that's New York. This is San Francisco a different game."

"I like New York. I'd like to retire there…I hear you in the mornings. You've got this…quirky-feisty humor. You'd be hard to replace. You have a great reputation. That makes you valuable…very valuable."

Suzanne dipped her bread into the Greek olive oil, quietly tasting. Slowly a subtle smile showed approval of both the bread and the oil. "Here, try this. They use *olio d'oliva* with everything in Italy." She passed a bite-size piece of the fresh bread dipped in oil to his lips. He licks the drops from her fingers as he ate the delicious, crusty, soaked morsel of sourdough bread. Was this not a seduction ploy learned from Giovanni? Suzanne felt playful.

Then Suzanne feared she was too cute, so she changed the subject. Dating books recommended centering the conversation on the male. Men like talking about their favorite subject—*themselves.*

"What's your specialty?"

"Patent, Trademark and Copyright law. It's really boring. I want to retire at sixty and do something else."

As crazy as she was about the food, the conversation interested Suzanne.

"Thinking about going into television?" she asked.

"No. Not me. I think *you* should. ZANNA." His hands raised into the air as if to frame a billboard sign. "You already have a local audience. You could brand—ZANNA…you'd *have* to tweak the name a bit and drop the last. Do a website. Go national. Get great photos on Facebook. It's all about the branding, getting your face and ZANNA (imaginary billboard framing) out there. *You* can do that. Blog every day! You can do these midnight comic 'tweets' (he made finger quotes). Get sponsors! Design a fashion line and sell the ZANNA career woman's look…don't forget the speaking tours at ladies' luncheons for your new *book.* You'll need help—PR person, stylist—but that's easy. And with Photoshop and airbrushing, you might even get ZANNA a million dollar cosmetic con-tract…mature women are hot."

Richard paused to take a breath, but wasn't done. "Audiences look for working women they can identify with. *You* can do that. Think *Oprah.*

She can sell anything. Mature women look up to her. You're perfect! I bet they'd love to have you on television…"

Suzanne squirmed sensing her insecurities. She didn't want to mislead him and needed to explain her concerns before he got so into this bubble. Surprises could destroy a relationship.

"I'm not so sure I'd be as *comedic* live. Richard…I like radio…it gives me the freedom to say anything. If I'm being watched, I don't think I would be as flip? Or take the chances I do. Then there's the competition…competition in my field is fierce…." Suzanne smiled and shook her head. "Thanks for the compliment, and you are so great to think of me that way…but…I don't *think* that's me."

"…how about a 'cooking show'? (He made finger quotes) You'd be perfect."

"Hmmmm…a cooking show?" Suzanne was caught by surprise.

He mentioned a cooking show and she got excited seeing a different picture. Never in her wildest dreams had she pictured herself in front of the camera cooking. She could do that. She'd *love* to do a cooking show…maybe add an organic garden. It was not like the TV audience would be watching her. Their eyes would be on the food. Still, Suzanne didn't want to be too anxious—it might scare him away. —*Was this a match made in heaven or what?*

Then it reality hit her, a cooking show? It's a lot of work.

Richard opened up and confessed, "Suzanne, I don't like dating. I'm looking for a relationship—long-term. I'm not into being single."

Whoa! Did Suzanne really hear that? He must have run through his twelve-point manifesto pretty fast.

"You're looking for a commitment?"

"ZANNA, I know you could do this." He used his hands for the billboard framing again. "You don't realize how good you are. And the pay is great. So good we could live in Westchester County and hire a maid. I'm into having a nice lifestyle with travel, theater in London and maybe a cruise on the new Queen Mary II…or was it III? Think about it…

Suzanne, men desire the same things as women…love, affection, attention, financial security.…"

"I'd love a big house in Westchester…a big old brick two story. I like snow!" Suzanne was so smitten, by now. He got her believing she was superwoman.

"…life flies by so quickly. I'm sixty. Paige said I'd like you and she's right. I've been with enough women to know in five minutes if I want to see someone again. Sometimes, it's painful just getting though a meal. Suzanne, I'm enjoying every bit of our dinner. This is a good sign.…"

Suzanne's left and right brains clicked. —*Cooking show, maybe?*

Then he paused, shared the last of the wine…in no hurry to leave.

"…dessert? Coffee?" He asked.

"No thanks."

"Sure?"

"I'm good."

Richard asked the waiter for the bill and turned back to Suzanne. "When a guy gets to be sixty, if he hasn't made it to the top 1% it's not going to happen. But, with the wife in a career, he can. Together is better! Suzanne, you'd be great. Audiences love *you. You* can do this.

Richard picked up the bill.

"He—the man—cannot afford to make a mistake again. Playing games is over."

"Games are trouble," Suzanne agreed.

"Life is too short for games.… I know what's important now…" Richard rambled on.

Suzanne realized Richard had this set picture in his mind and although they were talking, they were not actually communicating.

"…so, this time…the man is smart. He becomes very selective.…"

Richard didn't glance at the bill, instead handed his Visa to the waiter.

Suzanne took the break in his monologue to inch in, "TV has crossed my mind! But I'm not sure it's my thing…" Not wanting to turn his idea and excitement completely down, Suzanne thought—compromise. "…I never thought of branding myself. Yes. It would change my life for sure. Maybe you're right. I need to think about this."

Before Richard pressed on, Suzanne had to ask, "Richard...what would *you* be doing, while I'm writing books, doing TV interviews, designing clothes...branding myself?"

"Playing golf."

"That *sucks!*" Suzanne interrupted.

Out of the corner of her eye, Suzanne saw heads turn and conversations came to a dead stop. But she didn't give a damn if everyone in the entire place was listening. She gathered her things, and as she slid on her Ralph Lauren leather jacket she saved for such a special night addressed Richard and the Kokkari audience who were now tuned into her oratory.

"I was married...a working mom with a beautiful daughter. My husband—Richard—who was called *DICK*," Suzanne made the same billboard framing, "...had a doctorate I paid for. The man was a genius, capable of doing great things that could change the world. Instead he liked to get high and race his motorcycle. He slips on sand and slams into a brick wall or something...at seventy miles an hour. It was very serious. I care for him. I work two jobs while he self-medicates on his drug du jour. I keep up the home—cook, do laundry, pay bills, wash the car, cut the lawn—while *Dick* hobbles around in a cast. Yet, guess what? While I'm working, he's screwing the babysitter! But...I was better looking." Suzanne had to add that! "The judge, a Richard—another *dick*—awards him alimony! To top that, my attorney—also named Richard—charged me a fortune because I wouldn't sleep with him. Another *dick*! ...Oops! Wait! I'm not done yet! My first love—Rick, only a letter away from *Dick*, was screwing me but married my best friend. Another *dick*!!!"

Suzanne guzzled the last drop of wine and stood on her feet. Looking down at Richard, announced, "I'm not supporting a man again...*NOPE*! That ain't gonna happen, *Dick*."

Now she realized people were getting anxious and uncomfortable with the verbiage, probably destroyed their nice evening. Leaving the table rather than being asked, Suzanne was boiling.

"Where're you going?" Richard asked, not ready to give up.

"I'm going to pee...*dick.*

Heading to the ladies room, Suzanne gave Paige a call, putting her on speaker while she washed her hands...as if she was washing this man out of her life. Refreshing her makeup she shared her feelings, "I thought he was the *one*! He sucked me in. Then he goes into this...I should brand myself as ZANNA ..." she made the billboard frame with her fingers "...telling me, I should go into TV, do the lecture tours, write a book! I could make lots of money so he can play *golf*!" Putting the makeup back into her purse, and still rattled concluded, "Golf my eye!"

Paige loses it, laughing!

"He's just a *dick*!"

"So sorry, Suzanne. This is just too funny. I'm so sorry."

Suzanne cracked up, too. Finally the steam was out. "Yeah...maybe I'm better off single. Why go through all this?"

"Suzanne be careful, don't pop your breast sutures!" Paige got serious. "Look, men don't know what they want until they see it. They have their list of must-haves. Look at the online dating profiles. When you read what they're looking for, it's a joke! These guys have so much baggage, and they created it all themselves. They can blame who they want and think what they want, but bottom line...they need to look at themselves first."

"I thought...there was a spark of chemistry. He's up to a commitment! I got sucked in. It's all about him."

"Throw him into the shoebox. Time to move on."

"Oh God, my shoebox is filled with rejections!" They both burst into laughter.

"The right guy is out there, Suzanne. Sometimes they're wearing polyester and you have to teach them how to wear cashmere."

"Well, Richard is shrink wrapped. Let him live in his own bubble."

CHAPTER 44

"A Dulce?"

Disappointed? Yes. Suzanne left the restroom and passed the empty bar except for a guy at the end. She put her purse down giving it an affectionate pat, settled onto a barstool. She smiled at Raj, the dark-skinned, dark eyes, handsome bartender who spoke with an East Indian/British accent—charming and sophisticated. Seems strange to find him in a Greek restaurant, but in such a frenzy, Suzanne wasn't ready to go home. She needed something.

"A *dulce?*" Raj smiled. He must have heard her ranting, probably nothing he hadn't heard before.

The dessert menu looked inviting.

Out of the corner of her eye, Suzanne glanced back at the tables where couples were dining. She was sure they heard her. How could they not? She studied one couple, as they waited for their main course. They sat without conversation, but mimicked each other. He ate the bread. She ate the bread. He added butter. She added butter. He took a sip of wine. Ditto with her. Their faces even looked alike. Suzanne bet their personalities had zero individuality.

Was this what happens to couples over the years? Why do they even bother to go out? Oh, they can't stand each other at home.

Another couple, animated with hand gestures seemed to be in deep opinionated conversation. They had no problem asking for more bread and the delicious olive oil...sucking it in. What could be better...food, wine, conversation...but were they listening or having a conversation? As

Suzanne watched, she wasn't sure she could have dinner with a guy who shoveled in his food. This eating behavior really turned her off.

People watching and creating imaginary stories was a distraction Suzanne found fascinating.

The third couple interested her. They appeared her age, something seemed to be going on…talking, laughing, enjoying food…definitely acted as a couple. The well-dressed woman wore a wedding ring, as well as a second ring with a nice size diamond…Suzanne caught the light… she was jealous. The guy was also wearing a wedding ring, and seemed to be having a real conversation. Suzanne smiled at the thought.

Raj noticed Suzanne's obsession.

Suzanne nodded in the direction of the couple. "See those two. I bet they're married…but not to each other. They're having an affair. I can tell by the way they talk to each other…look at the body language."

By looking into the mirror behind the bar, Suzanne watched them out of the corner of her eye.

"She's dressed trendy, too expensive for dinner with hubby." She confided in Raj, again.

Raj looks amused at her assumptions.

"*Oops!* I'm so wrong." Suddenly, Suzanne changed her mind. "They're married."

"How can you be sure?" Raj studied them in the mirror.

"He's multitasking! Watch him…he's eating and drinking, a lot."

"Maybe he's hungry?" Raj looked disappointed in her amateurish conclusion.

"Watch now! He's eating, drinking *and* talking to her, *but…*" She stopped to whisper,

"…he's watching the ball game on the big TV set here…in the bar."

Raj squinted to study him more closely. "You're right! He's watching the game in the mirror!"

"See? They're married."

They chuckled holding in the laugher.

Raj refreshed the older man's Tanqueray.

When Suzanne glanced over, she could see tears in his eyes. "Is he OK?"

Raj returned to her end of the bar and nodded.

"Don't tell me, his Medicare card arrived. The young, beautiful, trophy wife filed for divorce saying he's too old. Or maybe he cheated on her? Now he's sorry. Twenty-five percent of married men cheat. He'll get over it."

Taking the wine menu, Suzanne thought about Raj's suggestion.

"I don't get men." She mumbled.

The dessert menu looked awesome. "I could go for a *dulce*—the *panna cotta*. I'll pair that with a glass of sparkling French rosé. Why not?"

Suzanne took one last look at the couples, and turned to Raj who had become her new BFF.

"You can be married and still be totally alone."

"That can be." Raj agreed in his beautiful accent. He poured the sparkling rosé, and then placed the lovely *panna cotta,* surrounded with chopped pistachios, dribbled with a thick raspberry sauce and crowned in a mint leaf in front of her. Suzanne beamed at the lovely presentation.

"Yes, what you say is true. But I like being married." Raj confessed.

"Why?"

"It's comfortable."

"I'm comfortable. I'm single."

"You are happy then." Raj surmised.

"Are you happy?"

"She knows how I like my eggs."

CHAPTER 45

Matthew

———

"Short is short. No such thing as a *little* short." Suzanne quoted Paige. "You can dress a man. Get him to the gym. You can change the way he speaks. But, you are stuck if he's short."

Matthew was short. But Paige emphasized other assets…good-looks, late-fifties and never married—no baggage. Suzanne wasn't sure about his never being married…a little baggage was good. Paige heard through the grapevine he had an attraction to full breasted women—especially blondes. This peeked her interest. The guy deserved an introduction and Suzanne needed to broaden her field.

Well aware of the short man's aggressive behaviors…the Napoleon complex…Suzanne knew millions of successful men were short. Many male film stars were shorter than they appeared. Male models were not necessarily big…it was all in the proportions. In Hollywood unlike the corporate world, big men were not always chosen. Tom Cruise was not tall. Paul Newman was not tall. In real life, some leaders won't have tall bodyguards stand near them. Paige defended the short male, "They work hard to prove themselves, and when they do ride the wave." Matthew fell into this category as he had a beautiful $150,000 Tesla he drives to the supermarket.

A plaid Polo blanket covered the wild grass. Suzanne was impressed. A rare tech type with a touch of creativity, Matthew designed an award-winning skateboard in high school and with the same precision planned this picnic—bamboo containers, chopsticks, napkins, wine.

He may be short, but generous when it came to food, especially Chinese. And after her disastrous evening with Richard, Suzanne anxiously wanted to start again.

Suzanne Googled Matthew and found his named popped up as a very successful tech guy with hands in many of the Silicon Valley start-ups. GoPro and Apple were his buddies. Knowing that made this romantic picnic a pleasant surprise.

Maybe having never married was a good thing? Suzanne thought single women were more interesting than married women. Stay at home women maintain a household, carpool kids and when possible, spend time on Facebook. Single working, women don't have as much family responsibilities can develop outside interests…hike, travel, and get involved in fundraising. Why not the same for single men?

Comfortably reclining on the blanket, Matt—Matthew seemed too formal—poured a nice chilled white wine he had packed in a high-tech stainless wine cooler, an eclectic pairing with the white take-out containers. This for Suzanne was a perfect icebreaker. She also filed the idea in the back of her mind.

"This is lovely…the view spectacular. I bet you programmed this perfect day, too." Suzanne played with a coy smile.

Matt smiled back. "Paige tells me you're the other voice. You funny, too."

Thank God, he didn't call Suzanne, 'Sue', as so many of her high school boy friends did. She never understood why they found that so funny, and worse, 'Suzy'. She always had a sense of humor, but it didn't come out until college in her writing class. She was afraid to be edgy back then. Suzanne felt people would avoid her for fear she'd embarrass them, so she kept it light. Which was why being on radio was perfect. There were times a problem developed at dinner parties…the host would be disappointed, expecting her comedic slide to be the entertainment for the evening. But this seemed to fly over Matt's head.

Matt seemed sweet retaining some of his Asian accent having emigrated as a young boy from Hong Kong added a touch of charm. Even though they spoke English in Hong Kong, his mother was traditional Chinese. Possibly why he didn't dive into conversation. Suzanne sensed this and wasn't letting it spoil the delicious lunch. That is, once she got the hang of the chopsticks.

Eyeing the loose blonde strands dangling on Suzanne's back, Matt fingered them. His touch was light and affectionate…something she needed right now. He took several strands, twirled them around his finger and made finger curls playing with her hair.

"Don't know why I have such an appetite," she said leaning back. "It's amazing how beautiful the city is, especially this time of day. I can see Sausalito and Angel Island from here!" Matt stayed quiet listening. He smiled, sensually licking his fingers as he continued to gently twirl the strands of her hair.

Suzanne thought his shyness was attractive. Refreshing.

Struggling with the chopsticks, she unintentionally pulled away thinking she had her hair caught on something. When she turned around, she laughed realizing what Matt doing. He laughed, too. Suzanne ignored this. —*He's simply trying to be friendly.*

Still struggling with the chopsticks, Suzanne searched for conversation. "I'm not into Chinese, but this is tasty. Where did you get it?"

"Mother. She likes to cook."

Matt said he lived at home. He told Suzanne it was not because his seventy-three year old mother was in need of care, or that he didn't have the money for his own place. He liked his mother's cooking and she's a build-in housekeeper. Although he could easily afford it, Matt didn't hesitate to share the fact that he believed women—a wife—costs money to maintain.

Suzanne sized him up—he's cheap.

Matt didn't offer much. Using her extroverted real-self Suzanne got him to talk about his family and discovered interesting stuff.

"If you are fifty-nine and your mother is seventy-three, that means she was a young mother?" Suzanne couldn't help but question this piece of information. She figured this man's mother was only fourteen when she gave birth, and probably thirteen when she had sex. Suzanne felt uncomfortable with this. Now if Matt talked more, maybe she wouldn't be concentrating on all this.

"I watch a lot of movies with mother." He offered, still a bit shy.

Matt preferred staying home and being with his mother than out on a date. He never knew his father, who Matt said was a French sailor. In fact his parents were never married. Suzanne could see he was Eurasian, once he mentioned it.

"Mother is very strong woman. She had to manage early in life." Matt seemed sensitive, quiet as he stroke Suzanne's hair. This seemed to calm him. Only now he had a larger lock of hair playing with it between his fingers, tasting it as if it were a delicacy. —*Was this a Chinese thing?*

Matt's small talk was non-existent. If only Suzanne knew more about computers or how to start a blog they might have more to talk about. But somehow Suzanne felt obligated to keep a conversion going. It was only fair to Paige who searched so hard to find the right match. At fifty-nine + days, it wasn't the same as when you were in your twenties and hooked up with a guy who paid for your drink. That was never Suzanne's game, anyway.

Suzanne needed to give this man a chance. She gazed at the incredible picnic, even if it was his mother's cooking...so what if he forgot the forks. No big deal!

"Matt, what do you do for fun?"

She continued to be challenged by the chopsticks, but at least it gave her something to do with her hands and the silence didn't bother her.

"I help at the cat shelter in Marin."

"*Really?*" Now, Suzanne got excited.

"I play with the kittens...hold them and pet them so they become friendly with people. Otherwise, they'll scratch and bite...children can't adopt them."

Now, this was very interesting stuff, but not interesting enough. Suzanne liked cats. She liked them because they have a sense of independence...perhaps what attracted Matt as well. She found it hard to visualize him—skateboard jock—petting kittens. If it were dogs, it might be more her thing. Suzanne had Bob stories to fill a library, but she didn't know a soul who had a cat.

"Does your mother have a restaurant?" she asked, still hoping to find a topic of mutual interest at least food was a passion they shared.

"Yeah. In Chinatown."

"You must give me the name…station crew would love this food." But that thread didn't go too far either. "You like movies. What films do you and your mom watch?" Suzanne picked up on his earlier conversation. "Nature films? PBS? Documentaries? Westerns?" She read somewhere the Chinese liked to watch old cowboy films.

"Oh, we like to watch real life as it happens."

Suzanne thought, what an unusual way of putting it and asked, "Nature films…animals, people?"

"Yes, people…men and women together." Matt's eyes lit up.

In Bob's words, *Bingo!*

"Oh, you mean romantic comedies! Boy meets girl." She could picture him and his mother in front of the TV with a bag of hot, salted American popcorn watching, *Must Love Dogs.*

"No. Men and women having sex!"

"You mean…porn flicks?"

"Oh, yeah! All the time."

"You and your *mother.*"

Suzanne became uncomfortable with this turn in the conversation. She didn't like the fact this guy watched porn with his mother. In her head she got this image of Matt as a little boy and his prostitute mother in Hong Kong on their seedy sofa watching nude men and women having sex. This really turned her off. And then there was the kitten thing.

At the same time Suzanne kept feeling this weird tugging at her hair, yet each time she reached back, it stopped. Realizing if she wanted to eat, she'd have to learn how to use the two sticks. And by now she actually had enough of Matt, and text Uber for a ride back to the radio station.

"Are you blonde all over?"

"What do you mean?" Annoyed at this crass question…it was definitely time to leave.

"*Ouch!*" Something pulled on Suzanne's hair again.

Looking back, she saw Matt had his fist completely wrapped around her blonde strands.

"What the hell are you doing?"

As she pulled her head away, his expandable watchband became caught in a wad of her hair.

Suzanne couldn't get up. Her hair was tangled around Matt's wrist. She tried twisting and rolling her body on the blanket to untangle her hair from his watchband only making it worse. Strands of hair were caught. Matt sat there with blonde hair in his mouth.

"Eating my hair? Is this some fetish?"

Confused Suzanne couldn't figure out which way to turn to get free. Rolling her body didn't work. Finally, Matt took off his watch. The expandable band dangled breaking her hair.

Grabbing her things with one hand, Suzanne held the tangled watchband in the other. She headed toward the street fortunately catching the eye of a taxi. Waving like crazy, hailed it over to her side of the street…she couldn't wait for Uber.

————

"You again?"

"This is unbelievable!" Suzanne said to the cab driver. "And this may not be the last time!"

She called Paige, but it went directly to voicemail.

"Where did you meet this jerk? It was like a scene from a dumb movie! I've lost a huge chunk of hair! Three strikes and I'm out! I've had it, Paige. I mean it! I'm going nowhere."

Then Suzanne opened the taxi window.

"I *suck* at dating!" she screamed to the city of San Francisco.

CHAPTER 46

The Fixer

———

Dianne chewing gum inconspicuously...a habit she'll never out grow...waved Suzanne to her chair.

Sitting in the empty salon chair Suzanne waited for Dianne to untangle her hair. It was the usual scene with Patti and Margie under the dryer and Joyce reading *People* magazine while Holly did her toes. Sydney, the new gorgeous client with the awesome long, incredible blonde hair, got highlights...a typical day in the salon except for Suzanne's situation.

"Thinner? Taller? You look good. Can't put my finger on it...what's up?" Then she whispered, "You got laid?"

Dianne didn't notice Suzanne's new boobs. Suzanne would have told her, but not now.

"Can you fix this?"

Working mineral oil with her fingers rubbed blonde hairs out from the clutches of the metal band. Dianne laughed as Suzanne recanted the lunch date.

"What's with Asian men? Are they really obsessed by blondes? I thought it was just a myth." Suzanne asked, not daring to move her head for fear of breakage.

She tried to keep a low profile, but sensed the question coming.

"Been dating, Suzanne?" Patti asked.

"Don't have much to report."

"Maybe you're not getting out enough?" Patti suggested.

"Maybe her expectations are too high?" Margie chirped.

"Don't even go there, Suzanne," Dianne diverted the conversation. "They're just jealous!"

"You need attitude," said Patti. "Men like *edgy* girls."

"What do you mean...attitude?" Suzanne asked. —*What good would attitude have done in a situation like today's picnic?*

"When you're on stage you feel your character *oozing* from every pore." Patti gestured in her dramatic style.

"Boy! Does Paige have attitude!" affirmed Harrison.

"Harrison, we know you're *hot* for Paige," Dianne teased.

The Golden Gate Girls gathered their stuff to leave for happy hour.

"I'm so discouraged," Suzanne said whining to Dianne.

"Die alone!" Harrison countered tired of her same old story.

"I'm free on Tuesday. We can pick out a casket." Patti offered.

"Got your plot?" asked Margie. "South-facing? Ocean view?"

"A funeral! What are you serving? Easy chews...champagne!" Joyce shouted.

"Girls, happy hour has started!" Dianne urged them along.

The Golden Gate Girls had all but one foot out the door, when Margie turned, "Be sure to hire the Tombstone Butler!"

"Who?"

"You know...the guy who delivers fresh flowers to your grave every week for ten years. People will think you have lots of friends." Margie said, as if Suzanne was supposed to know all this.

"Don't forget, you need to be specific about your music...make it clear, who gets to speak and who *doesn't.*" Patti chimed, but was serious.

"Better leave detailed instructions, or someone will fuck it up!" Margie wasn't ready to let the subject drop. "Everything's in my computer file—THE END."

"They talk so blatantly about death." Suzanne was surprised she wasn't sweating. Even the mention of music hadn't made her nauseous.

Dianne shooed the girls out.

Neat Harrison organized his side of the salon. "Suzanne, I think you're hot…you just don't know it."

"OK, Harrison," warned Dianne.

"And is Paige ever *hot*! And does she know it!" He lipped.

"*Harrison,* you're out of here!" Dianne yelled back, "You're so hung-up on Paige, why don't you call her?"

Harrison ignored Dianne's remark. Grabbing his Bay Club workout bag on his way out gave Suzanne and Dianne a big wave as he closed the door.

Sydney, who had been under the dryer squeezing her hair as it dried giving her natural curls, paid her bill. But Sidney had heard the conversation. She put on her jacket, folded the office papers she'd been working on and came over to Suzanne, "Have you been on line?"

"Isn't that scary?"

"A bar can be scary! The supermarket can be scary. Any stranger is scary. You have to read between the lines, get a current photo and Google him."

"Full body, not just a head shot," laughed Dianne.

"It's worth a try! I joined Match." Sydney said waving her new diamond as she walked out the door.

Finally the salon was quiet.

"Nice watch." Dianne handed Suzanne the item that caused the damage. Then went ahead and twisted a few curls to her untangled hair.

"WOW! Rolex! Treats himself well…guess I have to return it."

"Feel like Chinese?" Dianne teased as she locked the door and gave the floor its final sweep.

"Could Sydney be right? Join Match?"

"There are jerks on Match!" Suzanne whined again.

"Suzanne, there are jerks—everywhere—at bars, the gym, single cruises, ski clubs, country clubs. You just had lunch with a millionaire jerk!" She pointed to the watch. "There're cool guys out there in the same boat as you. Sydney found a non-jerk and look, she's engaged…I'm back on Match."

Dianne turned up the rock station. Using the large mirror as her audience, she moved her body with the beat. "What about me, Suzanne? Don't I have attitude?"

"Yes, Dianne. You have *great* attitude."

———

Sitting inside her car in the parking structure across from the salon, Suzanne started the Volvo and as usual, the NPR news came on. She switched the FM radio to the same rock-'n'-roll station as Dianne, and turned the volume up. Backing out, moving with the beat, she *slammed* on the brakes stopping inches from hitting the same battered Jeep she almost backed into weeks before. The same man with the same faded baseball cap was driving with one hand on the *h-o-r-n.*

Suzanne couldn't believe…with all the parking spaces in this ten-level parking structure…she ran into the *same* guy. Then again, today was just that sort of day.

Leaning out his window, he flipped her the *finger.* Was Suzanne surprised? Nothing surprised her! She rolled down her window and flipped him *the finger,* back.

"*BEEN FUCKED…LIKED IT! THANK YOU!*"

The Photo

After polling her single friends, Suzanne realized many had been on a dating site for years…not continuously…but on and off as they meandered through relationships. These women were attractive, smart, humorous, and successful.

Suzanne dragged her feet. She feared the photo. Everyone confirmed, the picture sparked the fire and every woman knows men were by nature extremely visual. This brought to mind a breakfast date as a new divorcée. The guy stopped at a red traffic light, but when it turned green, they sat there. When Suzanne turned and looked at him, his eyes were on this chick swinging across the street with her long blonde tresses, four-inch stilettos, tight mini showing every muscle in her butt, and Jackie O sunglasses. It was only 7:30 a.m. "Can't wait until noon?" she asked her date. At thirty-nine Suzanne felt old seeing that young thing with all that energy so early in the day.

"There's always going to be someone younger," Paige lectured. "So what are you going to do about it? Are you going to just sit there? No. Think Photoshop!"

"Photoshop needs something to start with, like sun-kissed color." Suzanne laughed.

The friends Suzanne polled, both male and female, complained the photo fooled them. Even women were just as disappointed—men posted college yearbook pictures. But a photo surprised one friend because his Match date had just come back from Maui.

"You can't just run off to Hawaii before every date!" Suzanne grumbled.

"No. But you can go to a tanning spa and look as if you have been to Maui...and you can do it for a lot less than airfare to Hawaii." Paige offered to treat Suzanne to a tanning session. Since the session was less than ten minutes they decided to do lunch at Bar Bocce afterwards. The day was too nice to eat in and Bar Bocce had a waterside patio.

Walking into the private tanning room with island music in the background and tropical pumped in floral scents, Suzanne studied the tanning bed. About 3' x 6' it had a metal lid that came completely down. Thus, you get a 360-degree tan all at once leaving no bathing suit lines. Of course you'd go in nude.

But this claustrophobic coffin-like setup scared Suzanne. No panic attack, just panic. Suzanne could not do this.

So instead of tanning, Suzanne and Paige headed straight to Bar Bocce.

"I still have thanatophobia. I'm just going to die with it."

"Are you planning to die this week?" asked Paige.

"No."

"Then there's time to check out Match."

CHAPTER 48

What Is A Soul Mate?

When it came to Match, Suzanne feared the worst—competing with younger women. It freaked her out. Why rub it in?

Her brain's self-dialogue played self-analysis, "It's impossible to go to a restaurant alone, but I can hide behind my computer. But then, I'm putting myself out there for the whole world to see how *desperate* I am!" Like a light bulb moment, Sydney's diamond opened Suzanne's opinionated mind. Dianne's words—"Sydney was gorgeous and successful! She went on Match."

Maybe it was just curiosity, but Suzanne decided not to leave Match as the last resort. Better to check it out before the desperate vibes bled through her photos and profile. This social media stuff was taking over the world. "Takes so much time, why?" She realized emails were about all she could handle. But even with the horror stories, millions were on dating sites. Even Paige eyed Match. *Research* she called it.

"How do you navigate a dating site? I'm so behind the times with all this social media stuff." She confessed to Paige.

Paige didn't waste time. She arrived with a bottle of wine. "It's scary, but time to give it a try," Paige convinced her. "There are men who search the profiles every minute they get. One guy I followed…boy, did I feel like a silent stalker…was on seven hours a day for weeks! Assuming he works full time, sleeps for seven, only gives him two hours a day to shower, cook, eat, walk the dog and then drive to work and back. He can't possibly have a life."

"What is he thinking?"

Paige laughed and opened her MacBook. They bantered back and forth.

"No matter how you look at it, the bottom line is—What are you selling? Getting two people together without ever being introduced, you have to sell *yourself*."

"Right!" Suzanne said. "You're not going to say anything negative about yourself!"

"Of course not! You want to hook them and *reel* them in. It's up to each person, to find out more…the good, the bad, and the ugly."

"It works both ways!"

"Yep! It does. We'll just cruise a few pages…you'll get the idea."

Paige walked Suzanne through the maze of filling out the profile.

"It's really a simple concept and ingenious. You complete the check-list of what you're looking for, the computer matches up as many of the checked boxes as it can…maybe thousands of possibilities…leaving you to spend hours going through each photo and profile. It helps if you can narrow it down with your most desired qualities. After you've dated every male in the first search who might be athletic and toned, that is if they did not lie—check out the next batch calling themselves aver-age…*a*fter average comes heavyset, then a few extra pounds and finally stocky. The only body type they omit…which should be listed…is just plain *fat*."

"Each search gets you less of what you're looking for." She got it. "Life's a compromise, you have to start somewhere."

"And God help you if you're over *fifty-nine*!" Paige teased. "Age is the first set of choices and it's at the top of the profile. Some men think age is a magic number. If you are successful, educated, fit and gorgeous with kids out of the house, but still over the age limit in his search—you might as well be dead."

"OhmyGod! I'm dead!"

The wine was down to the bottom of the bottle.

"First time I tried Match, I got 1047 possible matches," Paige said cheerfully. "I checked everything from agnostic to zookeeper within three thousand miles. Nothing worse than—*zero*—matches."

"I'm going to *have* to check everything!"

Paige got Suzanne hooked. Perhaps she'd find her soul mate—the most popular word in the profiles.

What is a soul mate anyway?

CHAPTER 49

A Full Time Job

"This sucks, already," she whined. "It's another full time job." Suzanne joined Match. No one ever mentions how tedious it is to search through these dating profiles. Her strategy was to review other people's profiles giving her ideas, like the obit copying.

"Let's do your profile, that way we'll have a better idea who to look for." Paige suggested.

With another bottle of wine and Paige's help, Suzanne kicked-off her profile...the first thing people read after they look at the *photo*. She struggled with every word. She didn't want to sound like everyone else, and not sound like a quirky oddball either.

"Don't use your real name!" Paige warned.

"How about...*Blondie?*"

"Well now, that's original!" Paige razzed.

"THE SHADOW? It's a radio show."

"They'll think you're 90!"

"SSR?"

"Who?"

"Suzanne Sophia Robins."

"OK, Blondie it is!" Paige sensed this could take forever.

Suzanne's negative fears rose to the surface, "How many guys want a woman who gets up at 4:00 a.m.? Didn't like parties, *hates* the cold, camping, RVs, hunting and fishing. Has no hobbies or crafts and gardens for fun. Politically goes with the flow..." and she was not finished,

"...picky about her music, goes to church to study funerals, shops to eat and only wants to travel her way! *And* can't go hiking because she's always tired, or go to concerts because she goes to bed early!" Suzanne rattled that off in one breath.

"How about EXPLORING NEW AREAS?" Paige searched for something positive.

"Of course not! I'd get a panic attack!"

"FOR FUN stuff?" Paige wasn't giving up.

"Yes—going to bed! Don't think that would give the right impression." Suzanne moaned, "Paige, I'm just wasting time."

"You're scared, Suzanne."

"OK. OK. One month. By then, I'll be sixty and over the hill."

"That's no problem! Just *lie* about your age."

"*Lie?*"

"Hey, it's understood. Men do it, too." Paige knew the ropes. "They not only lie about age, they lie about their height!"

"So you think Mathew says he's six feet on Match?"

"I'm sure of it!"

"OK...let's just write a generic profile. Short and sweet! Edit later." Suzanne ceded.

"Think of it as a sales pitch," Paige beamed. "There are thousands of single woman, same mileage, same damage, same color, same size, same everything. The competition is fierce."

"Sounds like some used car! So how do I cut the odds?" Suzanne's desperate tone wailed on the verge of giving up.

"It's the *photo!*"

"We're back to the photo? You've got to be kidding!" Suzanne bounced back. "How shallow can men be?"

"Match men don't read. They've never outgrown picture books!" Paige summed it up perfectly.

"My photos suck."

"Back to—Photoshop!"

"I just want to look like me."

"Not sure we want that!" teased Paige.

"Paige, please! I'm a loser!"

"*NO*! You're not!"

"You're right...lie about my age, body type, height, name, doctor up my photo, fake my FAVORITE THINGS and INTERESTS...I'm the *perfect* match!"

"Hey, you won't be a complete fraud—you do like dogs."

––––––––

Along with more wine, they read Match profiles. Suzanne anted up to the cause making a checklist thinking she'd find some great discovery about men. Besides, it kept her awake.

Her plan was to print out interesting profiles. The computer was impersonal, one-dimensional. She needed a hard copy in her hands to make notes, circle words that might give her a hint into the profile's personality, like studying the obituaries. This could take Suzanne days.

Paige came up with the usual WHO YOU'RE LOOKING FOR basics—attractive, affectionate, cultured, emotionally stable, loyal, optimistic, humorous, slim, interesting, fun, generous, charming, honest, adventurous, smart, classy, romantic and financially secure...the must-haves—chemistry and passion.

"If I read another profile saying how he's looking for a slim, gorgeous woman to walk on the beach, watch a sunset or drink wine by the fire...I'm going to puke!"

"Then he meets a cute butter-ball who works at the bakery, hates the beach, is afraid of fire and he marries her cause she reminds him of his mother." Paige laughed, "This is not a joke."

"Yeah. What that's all about, coach?"

"Men don't know what they want. Take divorced guys...they hate their ex, go through a humongous settlement or child-custody battle and swear they will never go there again, but turn around and marry the same type of woman?"

"*New wife* is physically a younger clone of *old wife!*" Suzanne agreed.

"We're stereotyping, we can't get hung up on the negative. Let's check these profiles and see if anyone is worth a contact...besides, maybe there's someone for me." Paige set up her MacBook. "With two computers we should cover a lot of profiles."

"I'm searching profiles ages fifty-nine to sixty-five."

"I'm searching profiles thirty-five to forty-five. Ten years younger is totally acceptable." Paige said.

"I'm not comfortable with younger men. Besides, I'd be a jealous wreck every time we went out!"

"Hey, age is just a number. Get out there, Suzanne. Flaunt it! It's all attitude."

"I get it. *Fucking fake* it and it will become real!"

Paige's mantra elicited hopeful truth. It was strong and graphic!

What's wrong with him?

"**O**K, I got BLUEYES1977, 59, never married! No kids."

"OK, what's wrong with him?"

"He's 6'3". Photo isn't bad...if he'd smile. Maybe it's the fact that 'his father died when he was three years old'. Now why does he need to mention that fact in a dating profile? Isn't that a little too much info? Oh, here it is...maybe he's never been married, because he's a dentist...I hate dentists."

"Because you feel they enjoy inflicting pain?" Suzanne shook her head.

Paige nods. "BLUEYES1977! We wish him luck. *DELETE*."

"How about a San Francisco architect, 61...claims he 'has *no* baggage'."

"You know what they say, Big Ego...small dick." Paige chuckled. "No one has *no* baggage...*DELETE*."

"Here we go, 59! No photo. Currently separated...looking for the usual—affection, fun, bright, fit, financially secure...he wants 'debate without being argumentative.' Whoa! Suzanne, what does that mean?"

"Sounds like he's been through some heated *discussions*."

"Separated. No photo. Red flags...*NEXT!*"

Paige cruised more profiles reading silently, but verbalized occasionally when she found someone interesting.

Suzanne set up a plate with leftover cheeses—Costello Blue and Spanish Manchego— ripe nectarines, leftover paté and the very end of a loaf of raisin-walnut, whole-grain bread sliced thin.

"We need carbs!" Paige approved when she eyed the food.

"We're settling in for a long night."

"*NEXT!*" Cheered Suzanne and anxious to keep going.

"*WOW!*" said Paige, "Look at this photo! He's really good looking. Why is *he* on Match? Great smile. 59 again! I'm getting a picture here. I think, if they're over sixty, they say they're fifty-nine. Sounds younger. Check him out! A Santa Cruz man is looking for a woman, 40-55. Suzanne, you're perfect."

"Of course, now that I'm five years younger. What's his profile say?"

"He likes warm places. So do you! Likes small groups or just two-some. So do you! Loves Italian food. So do you! OK, here it comes— 'looking for a woman who has a great sense of humor, is sexy, *senuous,* and loves men'. Well, he did spell *sensuous* wrong, but we'll ignore that. Possibilities here, Suzanne!" Paige looked really excited, but then groaned. "OK. Wait, there's more! 'My match must love experimenting… prostitution and drugs should be legal'." Paige deleted him. "Sorry, false alarm."

Suzanne's disappointment was short lived. She scrolled down for more profiles as if she'd been playing a game with Paige—Who can find Mr. Right first? There has got to be a winner. The wine definitely helped.

"How about Ethan? Widower, says he's 61, but look at this photo. He's got to be 70, or he's had a very hard life." Suzanne was about to delete Ethan and move on, but got stuck on his photos. There was something to this photo/chemistry thing dating researchers talked about.

"How can I get excited by a photo of a guy who's pants are too big, and belted above his belly with a shirt that's neither in nor out? Why waste your time reading his profile? Why even go there. He might be the nicest guy in the world. Yet, if he didn't think enough about himself to take a decent photo, how is he going to treat you?"

"Is he a widower?" asked Paige. "Somehow they seem to be either needy or spoiled and feel entitled. If one is a widow, then finding a widower might work. Each understands their role as a partner. Being alone is something they can't handle. They need time to become independent again. Together is better. The never married Matthews who can't leave mother or spoil themselves with big toys? Best leave those Peter Pan types to grow up. The divorced man is usually happy to be unattached, or if he was kicked out…his faults have surfaced. Either way, a divorced man has learned from his mistakes…even slow learners eventually catch up…"

Paige having experienced life from both sides had Suzanne's full attention.

Oops, Paige was not done.

"…they like being single after a divorce and get back into the dating scene…like me—playgirl—who use Match for social dating."

"And finally there's the super sub-category—those who don't know what they want." Suzanne cracked up with her own joke.

"Your photos from Thanksgiving and of Italy…the one where you're laughing and a little…skin is showing? I can crop it for the headshot. Let's download them to Match and get you up and running." Paige was convinced the time was right.

"Let's be honest, Paige. Was there anyone in these matches who comes close?"

"Wait! This is only the first hundred. We're not done yet," she reassured Suzanne. "We can speed it up by eliminating any profile that listed *camping*. That's one less computer category." Paige sparked hope.

"Not one guy on Match has promised to put the toilet seat down!"

"Suzanne…you can mention it in your profile and see who responds!"

Back to the computers with the wine and cheese, they made it dinner and entertainment.

"Check this guy, another 59, globetrotter. Trying to find a female 30-39…good looking! But in all sixteen photos he's wearing a baseball cap. Does that mean…."

"Yep! He's bald!"

"I like bald men," Suzanne muttered to herself.

"I don't."

"So much is about the age thing. This is my last chance. It's now or never."

"Hey! You still have it. Look at Christie Brinkley…follow her lead… paste her photo on your bathroom mirror! Check out the internet… women into their 70's are having great sex…Susan

Sarandon? Suzanne Sommers? Jane Fonda—80! And they are Tweeting about it. Suzanne you are thirty years from being close to old…get over it."

"Got it!" Suzanne's renewed spirit searched through more profiles. "I found one for *you*, Paige…lives in San Francisco…professional musician…married three times: twice to women and once to a man. Claims he's sensitive, intuitive and bisexual!"

"*WOW*! Has he put it out there. What's he looking for?" Paige's interest peeked.

"'I'm a person who is androgynous and willing to co-exist with a loving, charismatic eccentric'….a single father." Suzanne gave Paige her computer so she could see his photo. "…Oh, look…he's into 'designer clothes, likes to meet new people and loves a good conversation'."

Paige printed a copy of the profile.

———

Into the night Suzanne still struggled. "Better hit the jackpot soon, this is putting me to sleep." And the disappointments were getting greater. But Paige was still going strong.

"RSNewToBerkeley, 66."

"You found one?"

"I'll put money on it!"

"Let's see the profile…location is good…" Suzanne read from Paige's computer—"…looking for new and interesting people, to build a special friendship leading to intimacy and a long term relationship…someone, emotionally stable who wants a man to make life complete. Attracted to women who have energy and a sense of humor…admire creativity, individualism, independence…eager to go into the future with such a woman.…"

"*Future*, not funerals! Look, no misspelled words." Paige cut in.

"I like the words: individualism, independence. Get this…he's looking for a 'sense of humor'. *WOW.*"

Paige turned the computer back towards her. "Did not check *camping*! Comes from the East Coast, said his ancestors arrived in the early sixteen hundreds, which means he's good, classic stock. Has a doctorate and teaches. It's got your name on it! He's perfect! A professor! Suzanne, I think he's your man! Email him!"

"What if he's a dentist?"

"Sounds too verbal—he teaches."

"'Loves bookstores…I love bookstores. Let me see his photo…" Across the top read: Looking for a woman 55-65.

"Age appropriate! Classic-looking, a full beard…you like facial hair." Paige then repeated—loves bookstores.

She pressed PRINT.

"…he has a dog."

CHAPTER 51

Ten days Before B'Day

*A*m *I jumping off a cliff?*
Suzanne's inner dialogue bounced between her right and left-brains holding her back from composing the email. Feeling tense she struggled over every word for fear of accidently giving the wrong impression or possibly having a double meaning. On the radio she loved doing just that, especially if there was a sexual under tone. *—Can you do a one-liner? Can you write three words—Check me out! Or do you present yourself like a business inquiry? —read your requirements, feel I'm perfect for you. No, that won't do either.*

Paige was spot on. You have to sell yourself. Yet, bragging could be a turn off, being understated emits poor self-confidence. Honesty? Not so hot either. *—Why would I go into my high millage and all the repairs I've had or needed?*

Dating books recommended picking something from his profile to catch his interest. At least RS was searching for someone in Suzanne's real age range, even though she cut off five years, it was a good start.

Paige claimed Suzanne would throw off everyone's true age calculation each member concocted. If she gave her true age it would screw up the end of the equation...the usual plus five years was added back by men for the lie factor.

"In real computer dating terms, you have to lie about your age. Otherwise, I'd be 65." Suzanne told Bob, who had no clue...along with most of the world...what she was talking about.

Suzanne's internal dialogue anted up. — *Maybe there is something psychological to it. I felt five years younger the moment I pressed the APPLY box to my online profile. Maybe you are what you say you are, works like a kind of a placebo effect. From now on, I'm going to think of myself as 55. Tell anyone who asks. And be a 55-year-old person. Once engrained in my brain, I'll become transformed.*

Suzanne saw her real-self fucking faking it actually working.

Suzanne decided to make it short and sweet:

Hi RS,
I'd love to know more about your dog.

"Was that dumb or what?" she questioned herself. Then tagged:

Maybe my dog can meet your dog?

"That's stupid!" Suzanne verbalized with the computer confident she'd get no feedback. Reading it over, she deleted the first line making the second line the first line of the email. Chuckling, she thought it might give him a laugh.

Then signed it—*Blondie*—and pressed SEND.

RS emailed back. He suggested a lunch date with the dogs.

Suzanne was ecstatic. —*How innocent can that be!*

———

"You can't go waltzing out with Bob to meet some man!" Paige snapped the next morning in the studio. "You've got to hear his voice. Get his phone number. Start a conversation." Paige made it very clear to Suzanne...at the radio station the next day, "You need to know more about him."

"I'm not good at small talk."

"You can tell a lot about a person from his voice. Think about it, why do you think we have our job?"

"Oh, good point." Suzanne admitted. "But how long do I wait before I tell the truth?"

"Don't worry! At least get through the first round. Remember, take off five…add five to your college graduation. Don't get into discussions about your kid or you'll have to make her younger."

"And then?"

"If there's chemistry and passion, and you respect and like each other, that's so much more important than a few years off your age or a few pounds off your butt. You're not a real blonde. Who is? It's rare to find someone you want to be with. A few years makes a difference when you are six…not when you are sixty." Paige was on a soapbox. "In fact, tell me how many men have you found that you had a passion for, respected and actually liked in your whole lifetime? To find a relationship is far more important. It's very rare. Age is only a number!" Paige paused, then sucked in a deep breath before she blasted, "*GET OVER IT*!"

Paige played the grown-up, taking her coaching job very seriously, afraid Suzanne would return to her old lifestyle or get discouraged as she was stepping out into a new life.

"Ask about what he teaches. Ask him anything you think might open him up to you. How long has he lived in Berkeley? Where did he come from? What's his dog's name? Want a list?"

"No, no, I get it."

"Look, he could be a jerk…then you saved yourself from a boring lunch."

"The food will be good! I'll pick some place nice."

"Be careful. You don't want him to know who you really are—just yet. He could become an irate caller to the station…we already have enough of those."

"OK, I'll ask for his number…call him on my land line. It's a blocked number."

"If you decide to use your personal email and not go through Match, be sure to open a new email address without your real name, something cute—you're good at that. Use that address for Match guys who want to communicate with after a few chats."

"This all seems so sneaky."

"No, Suzanne, you're just protecting your identity. You can't take this lightly."

———

Later that night an email replied with RS's cell number. Suzanne thought it was a sincere gesture, telling herself he probably goes by RS. It sounded a bit formal. Then again, old high school buddies were TJ and BB. And there's JP Morgan, splashed all over the *Wall Street Journal*. Suzanne figured if he was in his sixties from the East Coast, he probably was a Rexford Schmitt or Rutherford Strauss or had some similarly embarrassing birth name. And RS saved him from being teased in the locker room all the way from middle school through college. She recalled classmates who named Lauren, Jamie, Andrea, Dana, Taylor even a Sidney getting teased as being a girl.

Suzanne's high school boy friend was Terry. She had thought to Google him to see if he was single. Old boyfriends were one of the first places to search when older and single. Never know what heat might be left in an old relationship. Checking out old boyfriends went through Suzanne's mind. Maybe they were available? Who knows, rekindle an old flame. Suzanne ditched that idea! —*If they were duds then, they're duds now.*

Still hung up on RS's name, Suzanne considered that it was hip now to have a non-traditional name like Apple, Blue Ivy, or ICE-T. She shared the thought with Paige and could have saved herself a full day of anxiety. Paige had *the* perfect answer, "He could be a Robert Smith, hating to be one of a million Bob Smiths in the world."

"Don't know why I got so worked up about his name! That's it...I'm not going to push it. He'll know I'm going to Google him. Besides, I'll know soon enough. I want to discover him for herself and keep Google out of it." Suzanne decided.

So began an email conversation. Suzanne did want a real conversation, but decided that she'd be more comfortable with the distance one has with emails, at least at first. Emails flew back and forth easily.

And Suzanne learned about his backstory. He started teaching at Berkeley after he moved from New York. He didn't say exactly what he taught and since she didn't want him to ask her what she did, she didn't ask. She liked the fact he had his own place...not a Matthew—still living with his mother. Suzanne didn't hesitate and jumped into family questions.

RS offered a quick bio of his life:

"I was born on the East Coast, moved back there after graduate school in Southern California...marriage of twenty-six years just ended. My ex is a lot younger. The kids are bigger now...so I feel I can move on."

He also mentioned a daughter by his first marriage, which made Suzanne think, he was not into having more kids.

"But, he checked: WANT KIDS box. What is he thinking?" she asked Paige in a quick call.

"Men like to feel fertile, having babies with every partner." Paige answered her question.

Suzanne was not going to go there. She felt somewhat connected already as she discovered both shared they were married in college, and their first car was a VW. She also learned they both had daughters close in age...at least he thought so...he couldn't quite remember the year his oldest child had been born. Suzanne laughed. There were times when she couldn't remember Lucy's age either. They grow up so fast the years become blurred.

He mentioned joining a government sponsored volunteer group over seas. It was a way of running away and RS admitted he milked his way into educational positions by taking advantage of extracurricular activities. RS did not detail what they were, offered no information or specifics, but wrote:

"My second wife kept me on a short leash."

"What a funny thing to say." Suzanne filed it in the back of her mind. They emailed photos of the dogs. RS mentioned how he was crazy about German shepherds and explained how his present dog, Siggy, was actually Siggy III...third generation of puppies. How great was that! Suzanne loved the fact he was into dogs.

"There is nothing traumatic about this." Suzanne assured herself. "In fact, this is fun." And constantly checked her iPhone for emails, hoping RS had left a message.

Already the ice was broken. There were enough similar things in their backgrounds lunch would be easy. For once, Suzanne felt hopeful at turning sixty—oops! She meant, fifty-five!

———

Emails kept coming. One mentioned the book, *The Girl With The Dragon Tattoo*. RS loved the novel and saw both the Swedish and the English film versions. When RS got quite graphic comparing the sex scenes from one to the other, it didn't sit well with Suzanne, but she waved it off as a man's film.

"Do you have any bad memories of your marriage?" RS asked.

Suzanne laughed and responded:

"I have stored my baggage. Only take carry-on these days."

Again, Suzanne waved it off thinking it was his way of asking if she's been in therapy. Didn't most people go into therapy after a divorce these days? She saw this as a red flag sending her back to his profile, "looking for an *emotionally stable* woman". Suzanne thought she was emotionally stable, no panic attacks in weeks and put it on the back burner. She'd find out more, later.

"I'm not going to psych herself out, I'm anxious enough." She told Paige.

Then Paige warned, "Don't make him into an email pen pal. Those guys just love to chat via computer and never meet." She reminded her, "It's time to make this happen. Call him."

So Suzanne pushed it. With a short phone conversation, they set a date.

Tomorrow

———

The night before the date Suzanne texted.

"Hi! Just wanted to confirm tomorrow."
"So looking forward to it," RS answered.
"See you then…noon, at Le Garage."

CHAPTER 53

Beginner's Luck

———

Waiting alone didn't appeal to Suzanne. But being a little late suited her.

Days before she pre-selected her outfit, so as not to change her mind as she dressed…a habit when nervous. Bob smelled nice thanks to yesterday's trip to the doggie spa.

Driving to Le Garage Suzanne took the back road, a better mood stabilizer. She chuckled remembering the *YouTube/Ted Talk* Amy Webb did about her first online dating experience. A video Harrison told her to check out before going on Match—Amy had a dinner date that took her to an upscale restaurant. He ordered quite a few expensive menu items along with the wine pairing. After excusing himself to go to the restroom, never came back. When the waiter brought the bill—$1314.37—Amy almost had a heart attack. Well, Suzanne guessed if you had two bottles of a $500 wine and every entree on the menu that could happen. Or maybe they had two $300 bottles of wine and Amy took home an enormous doggie bag…she didn't go into details.

This video resurrected the Jason Katz date. When do you bring up a discussion on who's paying? If you do it in the beginning, which seemed the right time, it clouds the date. Maybe men only go Dutch when they didn't like the date?

In this case, Suzanne decided to offer to split the bill and avoid any last minute embarrassment. A millennial wouldn't even think about it making this a generational thing. Anyway, if he offered to pay at least she'd leave the tip…Suzanne got small bills at the market yesterday after Bob's spa visit.

Parking across the street from the restaurant gave Bob a few private moments before meeting Siggy. God forbid he'd pee on the patio overcome with excitement.

"You smell delightful!" she whispered in his ear.

Bob responded by wagging his tail. She wondered if RS talked to Siggy? Of course he did! Suzanne stuck to her theory, all people talked to their dogs as if they were people.

Suzanne wore jeans. It was Le Garage—lunch. The impression of a clotheshorse or impersonating a teenager, wouldn't win her points. Besides, she hoped they would amble around downtown Sausalito and she wanted to be comfortable. Well really, Suzanne wanted to at least appear low-maintenance.

Her brain jumped straight to her profile photo…no shock there. "Thank God the photo is actually looks like the real me." She told Bob. "I've heard of men leaving the table when the woman arrives looking years older than her posted photo." She informed him…incase he didn't know. "Yep, Bob, that's the truth."

Suzanne's body felt tight looking good in the skinny jeans and the wedge espadrilles. It was obvious she worked out. Fingering her jacket, recalling how glad she was Paige made her purchase the soft-leather biker jacket…feminine and inviting—smaller softer zippers. The Italian sunglasses gave Suzanne an extra boost of confidence, as well as the blonde. "Letting my hair stay mousy was a dreadful idea!".

And now Suzanne looked back and appreciated those terrible blind dates! Yes, Paige's *real-self fucking-faking it* therapy definitely pushed her confidence up a notch. Suzanne saw herself as a neat package.

From across the street Suzanne had a straight on view of Le Garage, the patio and RS. She watched him pick a table facing the entrance of the patio. The waitress handed him the menu and she observed his thank you followed by a lingering flirtatious smile. How come men got away with those forms of charming seduction? If they are tall, handsome with dark glasses and a full beard, Suzanne guessed they just did. Suzanne left those thoughts when she spied the tweed jacket—very Polo, East Coast and collegiate.

But then Suzanne saw Siggy. "Now how classic is that!" Chatting with Bob, still watched from a distance.

RS was reading the lunch menu…Suzanne knew it by heart.

Bob took his last leak, but Suzanne liked watching. — *Just a little longer.*

All night she twisted and turned feeling anxious. Her first Match date—of course she was chicken. Was she over estimating herself? She wrapped the leash around her hand, tightening it as if Bob were her security blanket. Ready to cross and get closer to the patio, she wanted a better look at this RSNewToBerkeley man. She was sure he would like her and there was no question in her mind—she was attracted to him.

"Bob, it's Match.com beginner's luck, *BINGO!*" Bob wagged his tail like crazy.

Stretching her neck and rolling her shoulders back, she was ready to meet the man of her dreams. She tugged Bob's leash to get his attention, but her eyes were on the handsome, bearded RS who stood up to adjust the umbrella from the noon sun. A good six feet plus, just as his profile said! With perfect posture coming from a youth filled with a parent obsessively reminding him to stand straight. He traded sunglasses for reading glasses giving her a perfect view of his face.

Suzanne stared as he read the menu…an uncomfortable feeling flowed through her body like a hot flash but cold…ice cold. A red flag?

Suzanne ran back to the car tugging Bob, a one confused canine.

Something RS wrote in his emails bothered her. She couldn't put her finger on it, but something to do with his infatuation with the *Girl With The Dragon Tattoo*. Was it her being uncomfortable with his opinion on the subject of rape? Why would he even mention something personal in an email? The fact he didn't have a close relationship with his first daughter didn't sit well either. He didn't remember her birthday? She sensed a red flag. Most of all there was a weird familiarity about him,

Suzanne couldn't immediately place it. Was it something in the *Chronicle* lately? Not good news—someone flying under the radar? She thought she recognized the face—maybe? His manner? Where? Was it on TV?

Sitting in the car, she gulped down water and took a deep breath—stress reduction. Suzanne's brain whirled hunting for the answer—it was right on the tip of her tongue. She could taste it.

"Isn't he that author who was on Good Morning America, last year?" She asked Bob. "A book...*yes*, that's it. He wrote a book!"

Suzanne now realized, she was wrong. It made all the sense in the world—he was famous. Edgy writers got TV appearances. No wonder he didn't give his full name. The man was a celebrity! These guys taught at these big universities, branded themselves and wrote books. Then they would go on the TV talk show circuit and do book tours.

"Bob, I'm going to meet a *famous* man!"

Suzanne ushered Bob out of the back seat, again.

"Let's do lunch!"

Bob doubly confused, had to pee. Confident and more excited, Suzanne gave Bob another minute at the curb before crossing.

"Bob, you're going to like Siggy. I just know it."

Ten minutes late—good. But fifteen minutes late—not good. Suzanne hustled Bob along, but being dog-like Bob discovered a wonderful scent and was not giving it up. Suzanne let him sniff. Watching RS from this distance her mind pin-balled searching to put the author's name to the face.

"I know his name. It'll come to me. Once he speaks, it'll come to me." She promised Bob.

Bob was ready!

They crossed the street.

Suzanne's brain began to drag, questioning, holding back. Her intuition was on high alert—a red flag? Again, she couldn't quite to put her finger on it.

"It's not the face." She assured Bob. "It's something else."

That perfect posture, witnessing that seductive smile, covetous eyes, and his tongue as it wet his lips when he spoke to the young waitress—this subtle body language caused Suzanne to shiver. Her hands became clammy. Acid swirled in her stomach.

Grabbing Bob off the sidewalk retreated back to the safety of the car.

"*OhmyGod*! Paige!" Suzanne gasped as she recounted her deflating non-encounter to Paige.

"I couldn't sleep last night. Too many things felt familiar—Siggy is short for Sigmund, his infatuation with sex in his emails. Then when I saw him…his perfect posture and that smile! I recognized his lecherous smile. Paige…RS is Richard Sherman! This guy is my *ex-husband*!" Suzanne had to take a deep breath or she was going to choke. "*I'm sure of it.*"

"*Richard-the-ex*! What are those chances! Oh! Sh**! His profile is so great, so good-looking." Paige hesitates. "…maybe you should give him a second chance?"

"Paige! If I've learned anything—men don't change!"

CHAPTER 54

Waterlilies

———

Paige stopped at Waterlilies on Sacramento Avenue just around the corner from her townhouse in Pacific Heights. Looking for her credit card to put into the meter, Paige wondered if she would ever find just the right guy. Needing a distraction, she shopped.

Once inside the swimsuit shop, she tried a one-piece. Looking at herself, Paige was careful not to speak to the pretty woman she saw at in the dressing room's mirror. —*It will be only days before I can actually walk out into the shop to look at myself in the big mirror in front of everyone.*

The swimsuit was black, made in Germany with a beautiful high-cut leg. Someone like Paige looked stunning in it...you have to be tall and slender. Paige took one last look admiring her body in the bathing suit, the body she worked so hard to achieve and will be complete in a matter of hours. This was a treat to herself. Every morning she told her image in the bathroom mirror—*"Be true to yourself and the world will accept you."* This aspiration kept her going.

Still, hiding deep inside was the big question—When do you cough up the truth? Saying little white lies was one thing, but Paige knew the day would come when she'd have to reveal her past and confess the truth about life as Peter. She shivered thinking about it, knowing the possibility of finding a man who'd accept her past was next to impossible. No matter how gorgeous she appeared, to most of the world she was a freak. One day the truth would have to be told.

After paying for the swimsuit, Paige called Suzanne.

"I wish it were only about age and a Photoshop picture." Paige sobbed, choking up.

Suzanne realized for the last few months their conversations had been all about her—planning her funeral, the search for Mr. Right, her trip to Italy, her thanatophobia—and more. Paige had been secretly hurting. She feared falling in love and when she'd be honest about her past, she'd get tossed out—rejected. Paige did not want to be alone either. It was a haunting fear. "When will it be safe to cough up *my* baggage?" she asked.

––––––––––

"Got everything you need?" Suzanne questioned Paige, driving to her townhouse in Pacific Heights. "Can't believe tomorrow's the day. Eat tonight, but nothing after midnight. Uber is set up. Call Sasha as soon as you're done. You're sure the doctor knows what to do? This is not a nose job."

"You're more nervous than I am," Paige commented without a drop of anxiety.

Suzanne pulled up in front of Paige's townhouse.

"I'll feed the cat tomorrow, go to the farmer's market and stuff the fridge so you won't need to worry about shopping. I want you to call me, if for any reason you change your mind. OK? You have the right to change your mind at the last minute." Suzanne paused. "Sure you don't want company tonight?"

"Thanks Suzanne, I'm fine. I mean it. I've waited for this for years. Tomorrow at six I'll be knocked out! At eleven, I'll be a woman. L-o-v-e those drugs."

"I'll be there when you get out of recovery."

"Don't worry about me. I'm not having heart surgery! You have better things to do tonight. Go meet Josef. Have fun. You have to kiss a hundred frogs before…."

"I know, I know…if he wears polyester, dress him in cashmere!"
Paige stepped of the car, long legs first and climbed the front steps.
"Love you, coach!"
"Love you, too! Wear the black leather pants!" Paige shouted back.

CHAPTER 55

Farley's Bar

Farley's Bar was an incredible success from the first night it opened its doors. You sit on the porch to watch the fog as it drifted under the Golden Gate Bridge...sometimes cavorting and sometimes angry, as if it was having an emotional experience. Either way the view was fantastic. The resort was sheltered by the Marin Headlands and nestled inside the old Fort Baker Presidio Officers Club, minutes from Sausalito and close to Pacific Heights. The location, view, and savories attracted upscale clientele from Palo Alto to Napa. Unlike Le Garage, Farley's Bar liked the splash it got from *Conde Nast* and travel magazines...promoted themselves throughout the expensive international foodie and travel networks. It was not a local hangout.

Paige encouraged Suzanne to get out more. "New people with fresh ideas helped to create an interesting Suzanne with an interesting persona." Paige lectured threatening to paste it on her bathroom mirror instead of the obit clippings.

Still, going out *alone* was not easy for Suzanne. Walking into a restaurant or bar, even after work was foreign to her nature. Going home and staying in with her favorite glass of wine and a good DVD was far more comfortable...of course this led exactly to where Suzanne has been—stuck in her life.

So it took Suzanne awhile, but gradually she found going to a bar—alone—became addictive. Paige was right, if you go alone you talk to people. Meeting new people can be far more interesting than hearing the same old girlfriend stories and listening to the same old ex-wife monologues...both got monotonous.

Paige believed—if you can walk thru the door and over to the bar, the evening will deliver a good time.

————

Josef Jourard, from his name you know he was gorgeous. This young French-African descendant reeked of sex—his skin color is called *brunette* in his native West Indies. Josef tarried at the bar...hard to miss this male model. While living in Paris and New York after attending the San Francisco Art University to be a fashion photographer, he quickly found himself on the other side of the camera—successfully. Paige met Josef at a SF gallery opening, an avid art lover and theatergoer.

Black, gorgeous, young...Suzanne pegged him. —*Gay can be good.* They're into gossip, up on celebrity outings, keep politically advised and know the best shops, bars, and food. Yes, gay always promised to be an interesting evening.

Suzanne sauntered up to the bar appearing thinner wearing the tight, butter-soft black leather pants with classic stilettos. She felt attractive, feisty—sexy. Paige was seldom wrong.

Josef beckoned Suzanne to join him. His manner and style confirmed her suspicion—the guy was gay. His face, body and everything about him were absolutely perfect.

Josef ordered for them, "Tequila, purple perilla, lemon balm... shaken over crushed ice."

Suzanne read the bartender's facial expression—Where's this guy from?

"When Paige told me about you...the *other* voice. I had to meet you," he confessed.

Josef was *hot*! London hot! New York hot!

Flattered, Suzanne sipped the tequila studying him. Magnetic. No chemistry, pure sex. She hungered to touch his face—chocolate, chiseled. She longed to run her hand down his ponytail. Just the thought turned her on the triggers of attraction turned upside down. —*Paige, what are you thinking?*

Suzanne was lost for words. Cooking school her safely net for a comfortable icebreaker was out of the question and pleased when he stepped in.

"You have this quirky sense of humor…you go for *espresso*! What are you guys really drinking?" Josef asked with this innocent child-like and yet dangerous animal smile. But, Suzanne knew damn well he was anything but innocent.

Suzanne laughed. It was a nervous laugh. She could hardly handle vodka, let alone tequila. She sensed she needed to be up front, to get things straight before the drink headed to her brain making it foggy. Yet Suzanne was truly curious about this exceptional guy. She pegged him a male escort, otherwise how could he afford those expensive *rags* clinging to his sculptured body? She guessed, Armani.

"So Josef, what do you do between shoots?"

"I'm a caregiver."

"Boy, they must fight over you at the nursing home." She couldn't help it! In her head she imagined the scene—this hunk of a guy pushing some little old lady around in a wheelchair. Her brain was already fogging up.

"Well, I don't go that far."

"You mean, they have to be ambulatory?" she teased.

"Actually, I like to live in and get a couple of years out of it."

Is he serious?

"Exactly what kind of caregiver are you?" she questioned, looking for specifics.

Oops! I wonder if he can hear my brain thinking out loud? Or, did I really say that to him?

"I'm not into short term. I like to be with someone, who can benefit from my talents," Josef said with a touch of a Brit accent. "I cook, I drive. I'm a personal companion…I service emotional needs, as well."

I'll bet he's paid well. Suzanne's tongue was careful not to ask.

"You have an age bracket?" she asked instead.

"Just no kids living at home."

"How about the basement?" she teased again, this time with a giggle.

"Don't want any parenting responsibility. Don't carpool. I like... being the kid."

Suzanne was light headed now, but realized this guy was serious.

"A Peter Pan, perhaps?" Suzanne tried to keep it together.

Josef said nothing. He smiled quietly.

Suzanne thought she lost him.

But he picked up the pace, "I'm particular about what part of town they live in."

"Really? Sausalito, OK?" she joked.

"Absolutely!" he was not joking.

Bursting with laughter thanks to the Tequila, Suzanne had to be up front and needed to clarify her position, "Josef! You're a gorgeous man, but you're too young for me. Did you turn twenty-five yesterday?"

A shy smile appeared as he sipped his drink. "Twenty-one...last month."

"*Oh my God!*" she gasped under her breath. Suzanne's body turned red...the blushing worked its way up her cheeks.

"Cougars can be sexy. I draw it out of them." Josef said in all seriousness.

What an interesting answer for a gay guy. —Suzanne's inner self clicked. But she offered a different response, "You are a boy-toy, totally out of my price range!"

Josef opened his arms and gave her a big hug. "Maybe we can just hang out?"

This secretive, shy, boyish guy turned Suzanne on.

"What makes you think I can just hang out with you...and your sensual body? Your young...sensual body...." She repeated words. The tequila and her heightened animal attraction turned her on to his worldly shyness. He was right. He drew sex out.

Josef lifted her hair and kissed the back of Suzanne's neck.

It was just the first ten minutes. Suzanne never saw the second tequila arrive. Josef touched her inner thigh. —*Isn't this way too friendly for a gay guy?*

"It's so addictive. Not the drink—you," She responded. But Suzanne knew better. Even with the tequila she was aware if she had a fling with a boy-toy like Josef, it would postpone the reality of finding the right man.

"Having sex for only sex? No strings attached? That's not me, Josef." She was not even sure whether this guy was gay, bisexual, trans or what. She couldn't handle getting involved in an uncomfortable relationship.

"Once a week? Pick the night. We can make dinner, do a movie."

"Thanks, but...no." Suzanne shook her head. —*I've got to leave.*

"Can you call me a taxi?" she asked the bartender. "I'm only a few blocks from home, but I'd better not drive."

Suzanne finished the last drop of the second delicious, tequila and whatever else was in it. Yet, the heat in Josef's hidden smile, the unsaid words in his dark eyes stuck with her. Leaving was painful.

Josef took her face into his hands and kissed her. Then with a big hug reached down to the back of Suzanne's thigh pressing her to him. It left an imprint of his hand in the soft leather.

"*Taxi!*" The call came from somewhere.

———

Suzanne looked back at Farley's Bar. She felt frustrated. She had a flashback to her first visit with Jessica—she called Dr. Markowitz by her first name now. She remembered her *slip* when Markowitz asked her about her fantasy. It just came out...her subconscious talking.

Suzanne had been the good girl. In college she was the last to have sex at twenty-one. Except for Giovanni, she never lived in the moment. For Suzanne it was about saving it for the right man.

What if there is no right man? What if I die tomorrow?

"Stop! Please! I forgot something." Suzanne pleaded with the taxi driver.

The driver waited in front of Farley's while Suzanne went back into the restaurant. She scanned the room. Empty glasses and money were lying on the bar.

Josef was gone.

"Damn!"

She returned to the front steps.

Josef with his jacket thrown over his shoulder, leaned up against the taxi.

Suzanne's heart was beating, "You're straight?"

"Straight."

As the taxi pulled away, Josef handed the driver two crisp one hundred dollar bills.

The taxi driver turned up the music.

Suzanne had never made love in the back seat of any car, let alone a taxi with a stranger driving. She blamed it on the tequila. The space was tight, his body big, the heat incredible. Her hair dripped, her skin slippery wet. Josef peeled off his white T-shirt and unbuttoned Suzanne's black silk Blumarine blouse.

Hot...steamy hot. Josef cracked the back window before unzipping the tight leather pants, pulling them to her knees. There weren't panties—Suzanne didn't wear any. Josef unzipped his jeans. Suzanne couldn't wait. Foreplay happened at the bar. No touching. No teasing. None needed. Josef's tongue deep into Suzanne's accepting mouth, all else fell rhythmically into place. The windows steamed, dripping with condensation.

Josef's savvy tongue and hands moved beautifully down to Suzanne's breasts. He gently pulled each one out from her bra, tasting and licking her perfumed sweat. At first titillation...but then, in one thrust he was inside her fuming with pleasure, absorbing every drop of wetness and used it to advance more satisfaction. Suzanne's legs wrapped around his body kept him close. Each forward motion and luscious moan, stayed in sync with the hum of the engine and mesmerizing movement of the taxi traveling along the concrete pavement.

Suzanne saw his beautiful face as headlights from on coming cars filled the taxi. Josef was totally lost in pleasure. Suzanne had no clue where the taxi was going, except they were driving over the magnificent Golden Gate Bridge with Josef tight inside her going deep and deeper. Suzanne accepted the amazing orgasm. Her body in rhythm with Josef's continuous thrusts turned him on even more until he came.

Should I tell Paige I just had my first pleasure fuck?

CHAPTER 56

Full Circle

My left and right brains are splitting into an alcohol headache. My inner self's right brain spun—first a man, a second chance at love, then you won't die alone. The left brain moaned back—is there a guarantee with that? Repeating Paige's words, so as not to forget.

Now midnight, Suzanne hopelessly confused, downed two aspirins. She lifted the lid off the shoebox.

She printed in large letters:

I'M GOING AROUND IN CIRCLES.

Then she added:

IS THAT TO SEE ALL SIDES?

Suzanne wanted answers.

"There were days I float between the radio station and Sausalito… nothing's happening. I can't count on Paige to be my savior every time I get hung up. Or Markowitz…the answer is not going to come from her big leather chair."

Suzanne shook the shoebox when it didn't answer back.

"The answer is about writing the obituary, isn't it?" she asked the shoebox. "I've got to bury the old baggage, get my act together and start living. I need to move on with my life. Markowitz is right. I need to become *visible*."

The aspirin must be working, as the dialogue with the shoebox seemed clear. She searched the bottom of the shoebox for her pen and pad.

"I've got to figure it out," Suzanne said aloud reaffirming her thoughts.

On the pad in caps, she wrote:

I'M JUST TOO GOOD FOR A MAN?
DO I REALLY NEED A MAN?
MAYBE I JUST LIKE HAVING SEX?
AM I TOO SET IN MY WAYS?

"Oh, God! It's all of the above!" she yelled for both brains to hear the truth.

Folding the paper, she put it into the shoebox returning it to the closet. Waiting for the aspirin to completely kick in, she flipped on the TV wondering if *Dr. Phil* was up at that hour. She hoped so.

Half asleep, Suzanne woke to the house rumbling and shaking.

"*WHOA!*"

The house was moving!

Suzanne instinctively jumped into the doorway. She held onto both doorjambs and felt the house sway.

Lights flickered. The TV turned to snow. The bedroom lights dimmed and then everything turned dark. The shoebox badly shaken, fell to the floor. Finally the security alarm triggered.

The rolling motion came to a stop.

A weird silence lingered except for the tinkling of glass, but she heard no breakage. Pictures settled in a slight tilt. The lights returned and the TV was fuzzy. The clock blinked and the security alarm kept beeping.

BOB! BOB! OH MY GOD, BOB WHERE ARE YOU?

Frantically searching Suzanne rushed downstairs, but immediately raced back up. The last she remembered in her foggy state, Bob was upstairs. Instinct again, Suzanne pulled Bob out from under the bed, hugging put him on top of the bed. Then she shut the TV off and reset the security alarm. Spotting the mess on the closet floor, she collected the notes throwing them back into the shoebox, and replaced its lid.

"Don't want old *baggage* to escape," she explained to Bob.

Suzanne knew she should take a tour of the downstairs to see if any cracks had developed from the movement, but she couldn't deal with it now. —*Tomorrow will be soon enough.*

Strangely, her iPhone ring tone began playing posting an unrecognizable number.

"H-e-l-l-o?"

"Suzanne, it's Luca."

Who the hell is Luca? Why do I know that name?

It was a wrong number? The earthquake must have caused a crossed connection. In Marin there's been rumored, when a strong wind hits the Golden Gate Bridge, the Wi-Fi in the area goes crazy. With an earthquake, Suzanne wasn't surprised if the tower was down.

"You all right? It was pretty bad downtown." He said, in a caring tone.

"Luca?" Suzanne now recognized the Italian accent as the voice of the irate bridge caller.

What does he want? How did he get my cell number? It's after midnight?

"I called to see if you were OK?" Luca said sweetly.

"I'm fine. Thanks. Shook-up, but I'm OK…I've been through this before, but never so strong. It was weird, it had a long rolling movement…." Suzanne climbed back into bed next to Bob. "…there was a lot of tinkling, but no broken glass. And you?"

"My condo is in the financial district. *Emozionante!* Lots of movement, *ondeggiante*…swaying…twenty-six floors up…"

"Oh my God, must have been awful. Were you frightened?"

" …to tell you the truth…I felt helpless. I have to admit, I'm amazed how the building handled it…flew in from Milano this afternoon. What a California welcome!" There was a pause. "Do you think the bridge is OK? You know, I need to drive over it in the morning. By the way…you looked *fantastico* at the airport."

Then there was a silence.

Wait! This is the Milano guy? The man I drenched in coffee at the airport?

This wonderful Italian accent pulled at Suzanne's heart. She collected herself. She got it! This Luca and the Italian businessman were the same person. There was no question both her brains were alive and well.

"Luca, thank you. Yes, it's a tough bridge. I owe you for that coffee stain…how was Milano?"

"Too little time, as always! And the food! Never can find authentic, Italian cooking in the states…not even in San Francisco. Have you been through one of these…earthquakes before?"

"Oh, yes…."

The clock continued to blink, the conversation continued, as did the laughter. Suzanne had no clue Luca—the irate caller—had such a great sense of humor. Nor would she have ever guessed from that Starbuck's scene at the airport he ever a laughed. They ended the call slowly, neither wanting to say goodbye.

Dazed from the tequila, shaken by the earthquake, and surprised by the late night phone call, Suzanne grabbed Bob and pulled him closer. "OK Bob, what was that all about?"

It's after midnight, but Suzanne called Paige.

"Are you OK? Did you feel it? Don't think it's a *sign*?"

"Hell, no! It's just a reminder we need to live our lives. All signs are a *go*. Doctor even called to confirm."

"Paige, you're never going to guess who just called…. Remember my telling you how I smashed into a well dressed Italian at the airport and spilled coffee all over his expensive suit?"

"Of course, the traveling Italian."

"The traveling Italian and the bridge-caller, Luca, are one and the same guy!"

"You've got to be kidding…the same guy?" Paige laughed, "Don't tell me, Luca calls you at home and wants to know if the bridge is safe?"

"Yep!"

"Ask you out?"

"Nope."

"What then?"

"We talked, mainly about Italy."

"Was he…nice?"

"Yes, he is really nice."

"Maybe he's just not a morning person?"

CHAPTER 57

"Did you steal it?"

"It's mine. I'm not going to let them trash my body part," Paige responded in her defense.

Suzanne and Paige kneel digging in the dirt. Next to a small mound were two shoeboxes tied with pink ribbons. Suzanne found the perfect spot in her garden. As if these boxes would bloom, she made sure the depth was right, but not too deep. They each lowered their shoebox into the hole. Then on the count of three, shoved dirt on top with one big push. Paige didn't even mind getting her white GUESS jeans dirty while she planted a yellow gerbera to mark the spot. Suzanne posted markers:

SUZANNE ROBINS	OCTOBER 2017: BAGGAGE
PETER MILLER	OCTOBER 2017: PENIS

To mark the occasion, Suzanne prepared a nice little celebration spread—grilled eggplant, Italian prosciutto, figs and roasted peppers. For something sweet—a warm, walnut and raisin bread spread with a French brie drizzled with a local rhubarb preserve.

Paige opened the pate crock as she watched Suzanne pop the cork of a very chilled bottle of Perrier-Jouet.

"Suzanne, you look great—sexy," she said.

"Thank you Paige *and* Aunt Blanche!" Suzanne toasted Paige and lifted her glass to the sunset. "Aunt Blanche, I know you are up there."

"It's sunset, the perfect time to mark the end of an old, haunting lifestyle for both of us." Paige said holding her glass to the sun as it lowered in the sky.

Sitting on the patio in old Adirondack chairs, the mood was somber. Neither Suzanne nor Paige felt uncomfortable with the silence. The burial and the expensive champagne sealed this once-in-a-lifetime occasion.

Mellowed by the bubbly, Suzanne asked Paige a few aching, personal questions. Paige has been her encyclopedia of relationships. After all, who else has had a firsthand experience dealing with both the physical and emotional aspects of being male and female? And Suzanne trusted Paige. Suzanne also sensed there was a time and place to ask such questions. And that time and place was now.

"Do you have any regrets?"

"Only that I wasn't strong enough to address my gender earlier," Paige replied.

"Like maybe not having a kid?"

"No. I'd never want to change that. It's being a father that makes me realize I would not want my kid to have her sexual orientation discouraged at an early age...a child is only being honest. It's not the child. It's what parents project onto the child. Now, it's so much harder...I've caused enormous emotional trauma to my daughter and my wife. My doing—or undoing, depends on how you look at it—will affect them the rest of their lives. Rebecca will be OK, but Sasha. I only wish it could be easier for her..."

Suzanne poured more champagne. A chill filled the air as the sun disappeared.

Paige looked reflective. "...how is she going to explain *me* to her friends? Her future husband?" Paige shrugged. "I guess we'll deal with it as the issues come up. Sasha won't be alone. We'll do it together. And then...it's not just Sasha I worry about...it's this fear I have...one day other teenagers out there, walking around with *my* genetic material will be looking for their biological father."

"*What?*"

"With the internet and DNA testing, they can find you. Will they be pissed off?"

"So, how many other kids do you have?"

"A dozen…or so."

"Here, I thought I knew everything about you?"

"When I was in college…for fifty bucks you could…."

"Sell your sperm!" Suzanne interrupted. "You're right. They might be pissed."

"Not going there now." Paige made a second toast to the glow of the sunset.

Suzanne knew a girl from college who couldn't get pregnant. She searched the sperm banks, looking at pictures and reading the bio of the young men. Peter Miller was a very good-looking, well-built young man. And he was highly educated. Why not pick his sperm? It was easy. And after twenty years, you put it all in your memory bank. That is, until some of those births became curious eighteen-year-olds. Then, they become parents themselves and want to know more about their biological father.

"Just when you think all is sailing, something else pops to rock the boat," Suzanne uttered.

"That's life," Paige replied. "Hopefully, you only have to deal with one thing at a time."

"Do you really believe we enjoy life *more* if we have someone to enjoy life with?" Suzanne asked.

"I do. It's that partner thing. It's nice to have someone to share life with."

"*But* will they stick around for the bad days?" she questioned in a serious tone.

"You're asking the million-dollar question," Paige conceded. "Why do so many bail when the times get rough? Are they spoiled used to having it all? Many don't want to participate in working it out when the shit hits the fan. They walk if they can't have it their way. If it works for both to move on in different directions, I can buy that. But leaving a committed relationship? I have a hard time with accepting those who abandon ship."

"Didn't you…bail on Rebecca?" Suzanne was sorry she asked, afraid she was treading in dangerous waters.

"It's one of the reasons it's so hard for me. It wasn't an affair or about money. We talked. And we still talk. We had a small child.

And fortunately, we're very open with each other. She knew I was unhappy…made her unhappy. We still love each other, only differently now. It's not easy to destroy a family and then put the pieces back together to make another kind of family. But we have a family of sorts…it's different. But we truly care for each other, and that's what's important."

Paige sipped champagne as she gathered her thoughts. "I'm looking for love just like you, Suzanne…a sensual body-touching, heart-touching love. One that's deep with long lasting feelings."

"A man?"

"A man!" Paige does not hesitate to express her desire.

"Does it have to be the *same* man?"

"No. There are no rules, but…" Paige was quiet. "…I truly believe…" she continued in her reflective mood, "…that in the beginning, it should not be the same man. How do you figure out what's important to you, unless you go through all the garbage you're going through? All the profiles on Match, blind dates, younger men, old belly-fat guys…."

Suzanne immediately thought about the taxi ride with Josef. She wasn't going to there now. Paige's words were more important. "…it's how you learn about *yourself.* You are not learning about him as much as you are learning about you," Paige said.

"When do you know he's the one? Does he even exist?" Suzanne wondered.

"Oh! The million-dollar questions!"

"Paige, you know it from both sides."

"It's simple, Suzanne. Men want the same things as women—respect, love, affection, companionship, honesty and admiration. Men want to laugh…want sex. They don't want to be in an unhappy relationship, either."

"It's going to take me forever!" Suzanne's discouraging tone said it all.

"When you meet the right guy, you'll click. It will be right."

Paige lights up a cigarette. Suzanne watches her slow pleasurable breaths, following the smoke stream as it jogged a quick Z before resuming its smooth upward drift. She didn't nag her. Paige only smoked on special times, a personal treat. Today was such a day and Suzanne let her get away with it.

"I guess it's all about compromises," Suzanne said.

"You've had your wake-up call. Your must-haves are not so important anymore. Your priorities take a new place on your checklist," Paige reminded her.

"*Remembers to put the toilet seat down* is still top of my list." Suzanne cracked up laughing.

"I think that one can be worked out!" Paige joined in, "Automatic seat return?" Laughing so hard she could hardly get the words out.

"Marriage is such a tenuous commitment."

"Sometimes, I think *marriage* is overrated," Paige nods. "You need marriage…a legal paper, so you can get divorced! It's the commitment that's the important element. Two committed people can put together their own marriage paper."

"When *shit* happens? What then?" Suzanne wanted clarification.

"Like an affair or wanting an updated model?" Paige laughed.

"I guess I'm old-fashioned, but I want that signed paper. When you sign something, you're more committed."

"If you l-o-v-e each other and the two of you *talk*, nothing bad is going to happen," Paige answered with the conviction of a true believer.

"I want to wake up with that special man. Hold hands, have picnics on my front lawn."

"Have trust, it will happen."

"So, you're saying…when you find the *right* guy the important pieces will fall into place, even stuff like having another baby?"

"You work *stuff* out."

Paige was convinced.

For a moment there was silence. They made another toast as the late afternoon light totally disappeared and the fog rolled in. The city lights turned on.

"Just don't wait for perfection!" Paige smiled. "You might have to accept that toilet seat wherever it lands!"

"Paige, are you going to get married again?"

"Me? ...a perfect marriage for me is when my man lives next door."

CHAPTER 58

One Day Before B'Day

———

The afternoon sun filled the bathroom making skin look healthy and young—a tint of color. Suzanne loved to take her bath at this time of day. It was the perfect *me* time.

Adele amplified through out the house.

With the bleaching tray out of her mouth, she brushed her teeth. Immediate results pearled in the mirror. Suzanne tossed the saved piece of dental floss hanging on the towel rod into the trash and tore off a new piece. After flossing, she threw the piece away—without giving it a second thought. The bath water pounded. She loved the sound of the water as it filled the tub.

Standing nude, she couldn't remember the last time she looked at her body in a full-length mirror. She smiled owing it to Pilates and the no-carbs-no-sugar diet. She guessed her soft spot for wine didn't help, but she counted on the Pilates to make up for it. Paige's rant, "*It's not a diet but a lifestyle*"—was, if not glued to her mirror, glued to her fridge.

"Maybe I can keep the lamp on the next time I have sex!" Suzanne dialogued with the image in the mirror chuckling at what she saw.

Suzanne reached for the pair of sharp scissors in the draw, with her other hand twisted a clump of hair and snipped away. Dianne would be horrified, but Suzanne wasn't going to wait, she couldn't stand it any longer. Why does every single woman have long hair whether it looks good on her or not?

"*Men like long hair.*"— She mimicked Dianne's words.

Blonde clumps of hair fall to the floor. Suzanne watched Dianne so many times…she was sure she could do this. She ran her fingers through snipping a few more ends, going even shorter. The shorter hair felt healthy and thick…the longer locks have been wearing her down.

"Searching for short. Searching for sassy!" Suzanne told the mirror image.

Satisfied the claw-foot tub was filled high enough, she sprinkled bath crystals. She remembered buying those crystals years ago and saving them for just the right time. Now was that time. She soaked letting the water get as hot. The windows steamed. It had been way too long. It felt wonderful—the warmth, the lavender aroma and *Adele* made it perfect—her mind was empty.

What an enormous treat for Suzanne to just be free of thought.

She dribbled the lavender gel on her chest and massaged her breasts, playing with her nipples. She took a pink sponge and gently scrubbed her tummy and between her legs. She reached down to touch her coitus. The response was immediate and she continued to gently massage this delicate spot. She arched her body. A magnetic seductiveness ran through her body—wanting more. It was addictive.

Reluctantly, she pulled the rubber plug and watched the suds swirl down the drain.

After toweling, she rubbed in lavender oil—finding it hard to get enough. Wrapped in her terry robe, She opened the windows and watched the seagulls over the bay as she relaxed on the bed with a glass of Valdobbiadene Prosecco and a piece of dark Swiss chocolate. Yes, Suzanne was feeling like a princess.

But she also felt mischievous and scrolled through the iPhone until she stared at his number. She text:

FAME? CUCINARE SCAMPI!
QUESTA SERA? He responded.
YES @7:00
SI! FANTASTICO! @7:00 *CIAO!*

CHAPTER 59

Night Before B'Day

———

"Shall we start with a Bloody Mary?" he asked.

"I thought I'd save the blood for a red sauce!"

Luca examined Suzanne's kitchen. He noticed the obituary clippings when he opened the refrigerator. He moved the six pints of blood to make room for the Chianti he smuggled into the States.

Luca spotted the IV pole, "Breakfast?"

Their eyes met and in perfect synchronization burst into uncontrollable laugher.

"I can explain!"

"American Women! No need to explain!"

If having the blood and IV fluid hadn't been of any other benefit during the last sixty days, they came in handy now. Awkwardness was the dread of all first dates. Suzanne felt the change in mood immediately, the laughter let out the tension—the tension it took to gin up the courage to make the call.

Is it that I like the way I look…the slim body…the shorter hair…going blonde? Or, was it Paige throwing me to the wolves? Giovanni? Josef? It certainly isn't the clothes…my worn jeans and a tattered men's T-shirt. I look good in these jeans and T-shirt—soft from years of washing. Maybe it's the investment I received from Aunt Blanche—the boobs! Whatever the reason, I'll deal with it later with Markowitz. Is it possible I don't even need Markowitz anymore? I'm going to live in this moment and I know she'd approve.

Suzanne prepared the scampi just as she had been taught at cooking school. Luca brought some spicy dried coppa and a bottle of olive oil from his family's farm outside Milan.

"Sometimes, even a red needs a slight chill," he said. Feeling the wine bottle as he took it from the fridge, "*Perfecto.*"

Luca put the coppa onto a plate and searched for a fork.

"*Mi piace cucinare!*" Suzanne smiled, chopping away.

"*Adoro da mangiare!*" Luca stole samples from the chopping board.

Maybe Paige had a point—he's just not a morning person. Those words stuck in Suzanne's head as she watched Luca, not the least bit shy around the kitchen. She was embarrassed as she caught herself admiring how good he looked in his jeans and a white dress shirt. So unexpected. He seemed to always be perfectly dressed for every occasion. In essence, he was.

Suzanne could see him in a white T-shirt, which she thought he'd look even better. But, she didn't say it and stopped herself from going there. She wanted to accept the man as is. She did not want to start thinking how to would she change him. For once, Suzanne only wanted to get to know this man, have absolutely no expectations and absolutely no plan to remodel his behavior or the way he ate or the shirts he wore.

So much about him she liked…his accent, his ability to be laid back and yet feisty. He reeked of fun. Could she have sex with a guy who shaved his head? Suzanne was not going there! But on second thought, yes she could—it was sexy!

Suzanne sauté the scampi in fresh chopped garlic, dash of red chili pepper flakes and Luca's olive oil to just the exact touch of high heat and covered it for a second or two with a heavy lid to create stream. The fresh pasta purchased from the Italian deli was exactly al dente. She figured he couldn't possibly expect her to make the pasta, so she didn't feel one bit guilty. She had pulled out her one and only white tablecloth. Most times she held back and didn't use it for fear the stains would never come out. But this night she wasn't going there, or thinking of traffic or

Markowitz. Or obituaries. If anything her inner self reminded her brain, the old baggage was buried in the shoebox.

This night was all about the moment. Luca lit the candles and poured the wine. Suzanne liked a man who showed he could be romantic—without having to hint at it. She put everything on the table using the pans from the stove as serving dishes...something she noted in Italy...it kept the food warm. *Andrea Bocelli*—Luca's gift played. He also brought her a *Botti* CD and they laughed when Suzanne showed him hers.

Suzanne discovered how garrulous he was, revealing his passion for wines, foods Italian, superbly designed fast cars and the exquisite beauty of the Golden Gate Bridge. "You must be driving a convertible, there's no way you can enjoy the incredible design and structure of that bridge in a hardtop. You will never understand its symmetrical beauty! You will never *feel* its *magnificenz!*"

Luca revealed his past in Italian using emotional hand gestures. Suzanne actually enjoyed watching him be so expressive, as he related how as a young engineer he designed and built nuclear power plants both in Europe and California. He had huge global responsibilities and although never experienced one then, lived in constant fear of earthquakes. This tension destroyed his marriage. Now, he wanted to start all over. His life changed when his Italian sports car needed repair, and discovered his mechanic in downtown San Francisco planned to retire. Seeing an opportunity for a career change, he bought the shop. He always had a love restoring Italian sports cars. Now, having expanded to building powerful racing engines, Luca did test runs on the #280 at four in the morning—Suzanne wasn't sure that was less dangerous!

"If I crash, I'm not creating a huge humanitarian disaster. My conscience would never forgive myself." Luca answered her look.

Luca had a passion for life, Italian food, family and all things Italian making him real and a down home guy even if his clients held 1% of the wealth. Inside this Italian persona, he was a genuine caring, unselfish, family man.

And Bob liked him, too—Luca gave him nibbles under the table!

Suzanne chitchatted about cooking school and her excitement for Italian food, clothes and incredible art feeling like a schoolgirl who returned from her first field trip. As the night passed, Suzanne and Luca discovered they had more in common than a thirst for Chianti, a love of Bocelli and Botti and the taste for scampi.

Luca touched Suzanne drawing her to him as he kissed the back of her neck. It sent a hot flash down her spine. She felt the sensation of her breasts swelling. She wanted to be in his arms, but held back. Luca liked to be affectionate. Suzanne liked it, too. Still, she sensed a slight panic as thoughts spun in her head. —*I don't want this to be about sex and then never see him again. I don't want him to think that's why I asked him here.*

Suzanne listened to her brain talking. —*It's unwise to have sex on the first date.*

Then the heated spell was broken with laughter when Suzanne told Luca about the misunderstanding at Marco's in Florence. They indulged in more pasta, more wine, more scampi, more music, until graceful dining gave way to using their fingers to peel and eat the scampi. Suzanne totally accepted that there would be multiple stains on the white linen cloth. It was so unimportant!

Suzanne untied her apron and kicked off her bunny slippers.

Lucas sang along with Bocelli.

"*Fantastico voce!*" Suzanne delighted in using the Italian words she mastered.

Luca reached out for Suzanne's hand and pulled her close. They danced in the kitchen.

Finally, Suzanne couldn't retain it in any longer, bursting she asked as they danced, "The morning *frustrations?*" She hated to use that word, "…they don't seem like you, Luca?"

"*Frustrazione sessuali!*" Luca whispered in her ear.

Suzanne laughed at his honesty.

———

Later that evening, the full moon beamed through mists of fog. Suzanne's bedroom window was open and the candles flickered from the gentle air currents. She hid the medical alert tag under the bed pillow.

The night air was chilly, but it felt good.

Luca's nude body displayed shadows on the wall. Fog rolled into the room and hovered over the fresh-cut flowers. The moist air collected the distant scent of jasmine and it filled the room.

Suzanne's satin and lace nightie followed her curves. Its wide, delicate lace trim reminiscent of the negligees of the twenties...cupped her breasts. The demure gown was delicate, yet sexy. She knew Luca to be the kind of man who enjoyed the sensual touch of delicate silk fabrics and fragile lace.

The candles flickered faster as the breeze got stronger...the light illuminated...allowing Suzanne to enjoy the excitement of his body—a masculine structure—well tended and healthy with wonderful shoulders and sexy dark hairs on his chest. Everything about Luca was age appropriate, adding to the comfort and ease of him being in her bed. She especially liked the beginning lines on his face and around his eyes created by squinting when he laughed, and he laughed a lot—a contagious laugh.

Although he was an experienced lover, Suzanne sensed no pressure, being instinctively free and open, yet hesitated.

She had this hunch that she had known him for ages, yet he was still a mystery.

"Luca, why do I sense we have some sort of history?"

"*Si*, we do. We've had two dates and several phone conversations."

"Really? Two dates?"

"*Numero uno*, you crashed into me with your coffee—*terribile. Numero due*, we met in the airport corridor on my trip back to Milano—*molto meglio*." He recanted.

"So, this is our third date?"

"Si! And don't forget our many phone conversations. We are old friends."

"Oh, yes, I remember those *intenso* conversations."

"*Prego perdonami*," he asked for forgiveness. They laugh.

Suzanne realized she unearthed a man with a great sense of humor and passion. His laugh was real, honest coming from the depths of his soul. A laugh that said, he understood...he'd been there. Life was to be lived. Life was richer together.

Suzanne never understood how much she needed someone who saw life as a great experience. His touch was passionate and sensitive. He's prepared to love. This man was different from the others. He cared and accepted responsibility, not into loving lightly.

Maybe we will make love, maybe not. It didn't matter. I'm savoring the closeness.

Luca held Suzanne's face in his hands and gently kissed her lips. Lifting her nightie he caressed her breast. He massaged her neck.

She nibbled his ear. He let her know it turns him on, too.

Luca slid down Suzanne's body kissing her belly button—having fun. It tickled and Suzanne couldn't help, but laugh.

Suzanne gently stroke him, "I want this," she told him, sending a signal she was freeing her body for him. She gave permission.

"And I you." He whispered in her ear as he kissed her neck.

Luca slipped off her nightie and moved his way down from her neck, kissing her breasts, relishing her body with his tongue...sensually tasting her. She smelled wonderful.

Excited by the intensity of his gentle touch and the feeling of his tight body against hers, Suzanne unexpectedly noticed his body was tan all over. She gave in to a chuckle. —*He's so Italian.*

Suzanne's wetness was beyond belief...a spontaneous reaction to body heat and the cool breeze scouting for sweat. They moved slowly delighted with every touch—playfully exploring, teasing, teaching. Luca sensed when the hunger peeked and deftly slid into her body. Their contact was perfect and wonderfully satisfying. His thrusts were deep and intense. He felt Suzanne as she responded joining his body's rhythm. He wanted her there. The fit was perfect. These two bodies were made to belong. Suzanne didn't want him to stop—ever.

They exhilarated in the luscious sharing of two people savoring a perfect pairing.

"*BEEP. BEEP. BEEP.*" Under the pillow, the medical alert tag accidently triggered. Suzanne and Luca went completely to pieces laughing! But the magical moment was not broken. Luca held tight fighting. Gently the two bodies slipped away.

Luca grabbed the down quilt from the foot of the bed and sliding under, pulled Suzanne's naked body next to him. She snuggled into his body as Bob discovered a warm spot at their feet.

"I need to get up early," he whispered.

"How early? Five?"

"Four?" He said apologetically.

"Oh, you have a hot date?"

"*Si.* With a blonde Lamborghini."

"Taking her out for a drive, are you?"

"I am going to rev her engine until she screams."

"Aren't you afraid of getting a ticket?"

"They have to catch me first." Laughing, he sounded like a teenager.

"With all the wine you've had, it'll be a DUI. They'll throw you in jail," Suzanne teased.

"Will you bail me out?"

"Of course, Luca. Of course!"

Luca blew out the last candle and snuggled even closer, which seemed impossible. As Suzanne fell asleep, she realized how much she had learned about this man. And how much she discovered about herself. It was a good feeling, organic and dynamic at the same time.

"I like you," he confided softly, "...molto," tussling Suzanne's short tresses and kissing the back of her bare neck.

"I like you, too." Suzanne whispered giving him a kiss on his shaved head.

NOTE: He put the toilet seat down! Class act.

CHAPTER 60

B'Day

Cold. Dark. Foggy. Suzanne backed down the driveway, blasted the heat and popped in a Taylor Swift CD. At 4:25 she needed to make one stop—the New York Bagel shop. It wasn't open, but if she banged on the back door, Danny unlocked it. They had these routine, fresh still-warm bagels for cash.

Suzanne had plenty of time when she arrived at the broadcast booth...maybe two or three minutes to spare. She definitely shocked the engineer—not by the dripping cream cheese from the bagel in her mouth—but by the Jimmy Choo stilettos, Calvin Klein skinny jeans, GUESS tank top and the two wine glasses she dangled. He eyed the clock: 4:56 as Suzanne pulled out a bottle of Perrier-Jouet from her new Balenciaga bag.

Paige chuckled as she watched Suzanne empty the leather bag as if a grocery sack, and was especially surprised by the sealed bag of ice cubes, which she threw into the empty trash container. With two minutes to go, Paige carefully untwisted the wire on the champagne and aiming away from the glass panel, popped the cork. Grabbing the glasses caught the bubbles, licked the overflow. It tasted nice and cold...the ice will keep it that way. Paige grinned approvingly at Suzanne's haircut.

With sixty seconds to go, Suzanne ripped open the brown bakery bag, spread out the bagels and cream cheese, thin slices of fresh-cut prosciutto, melon, lox, and a farm box of beautiful, organic blueberries!

It's only when you deal with minutes you find just how much you can get done in a second. Suzanne knew this drove the engineer who dealt in precision, absolutely nuts.

Suzanne clamped on the headphone.

The clock read: 5:00.

The blinking red warning light turned to solid green.

"Last night's full moon sneaking between the puffs of fog looked incredible," Suzanne began the traffic report to the early morning bridge and tunnel listeners.

"If it kept you up, it was worth it. Just grab an extra cup of Joe this morning. Better yet, stop by Starbuck's espresso bar and get a Chocolate Cookie Crumble Frappuccino latte. Yes, folks, take time and enjoy the moment. Sorry for the chill, drizzle and black ice, but that's what we love about San Francisco! Could be worse! We could be living in tornado country. Then again, we won't talk about last week's little surprise jolt…."

Paige smeared more cream cheese on her bagel, and sipped champagne all the while shaking her head at Suzanne's running commentary.

She mouthed—*Traffic?*

"North #101 moving well. Bay Bridge meters just turned on, no problems there, yet. The #880 is moving nicely. Looking at the #580 and #80 interchange…no hiccups. Is today a holiday? Then again, folks…it's only 5:02 a.m."

The assistant pressed a note against the glass: GG Bridge Luca.

"Thank goodness, we can wake up now. Luca, you're up early! Did you see the moon last night? How's the Golden Gate Bridge? Stuck in traffic?"

"The moon…incredible, the night pure pleasure. A night I'd like to repeat. The traffic?…smooth as silk. By the way, Ms. Robins, I love this bridge."

"Yes, Luca, I know you do. You are a very passionate man. I know how you…*feel.* I love the bridge, too. Drive safely, Luca. Yes…drive safe."

Suzanne took a sip of the champagne before she cut back to the monitor.

"…*hot* news from Pacifica, potholes are gone. See what happens when life is good? The pothole fairy works all night. Let us know about those 'jams'—*traffic,* not the fruit! You're on your way to work and I'm sitting here with my…" Suzanne held up her glass of champagne, "…espresso! Ciao!" And then just before commercial, "KABC RADIO, YOUR TRAFFIC AND WEATHER, EVERY TEN MINUTES." Quickly she added, "Stuck in traffic? Tell us the *hot* spot."

The blinking green light turned red.

Suzanne and Paige drank champagne, munched on bagels, and tossed blueberries up into the air catching them in their mouths.

"Oops! Missed one!" But, Paige caught the next.

The red blinking light turned solid green. The clock: 5:10.

Paige ignored it…mischievously *grinning* turned off both the mic and the monitor.

Suzanne and Paige slapped a high-five.

The green broadcast light changed to a warning red blinking wildly.

The monitor crashed to snow.

The engineer jumped to fix a power failure, on the other side of the glass panel flipped switches.

"How come, we don't do this more often?" Suzanne teased.

"So? Tell me! Does Suzanne Robins die alone?"

"It doesn't matter. What matters is Suzanne Robins wants to *live!*"

Another high five!

"You're cured!" Paige shouted, ecstatic! She took an elegant box from her Louis Vuitton bag. The tag: HAPPY BIRTHDAY!

Suzanne ripped off the silver ribbon fashioning a doll-like headband. Then like a two year old, tore open the box to find a delicate silk and lace, magenta bra and matching thong—delicate, beautiful, sexy.

Inside the broadcast booth, Suzanne and Paige party. Eating, drinking to the rock music that blasted from Paige's iPod.

Paige took out a cigarette and lit up. When she saw Suzanne's look, she just smiled, "Special occasion!"

Suzanne stripped and tried on the new bra and thong. All the while recanted the past night with Luca—not leaving anything out, especially how the medical alert tag could not have been more perfectly timed. They both laughed so hard it hurt. Tiny tears rolled down Suzanne's cheek.

"Thank God you failed therapy!"

"Thank God you are my coach, Paige."

The bra and thong fit Suzanne perfectly. Feeling sexy, she slipped back into the stilettos and strut out into the middle of the broadcast booth, taking her place as if on stage danced wildly around an imaginary pole.

Turning up the music, Paige stripped down to her thong and bra, joining Suzanne with her bumps and grinds. While dancing, Paige discovered the LOVE tattoo on Suzanne's shoulder, giving a thumbs-up just as she spotted a sparkle.

"Awesome!" Paige approved pointing to Suzanne's newly purchased diamond.

Paige went wild dancing when she got a text. Smiling and without missing a beat, held her iPhone up for Suzanne to read—DRINKS? HARRISON.

It was Suzanne's turn for a thumbs-up.

Suzanne and Paige completely ignored the engineer on the other side of the glass panel who frantically waved and pointed to the ceiling of the sound booth.

First there was warning hissing noise, then the automatic sprinklers sprayed full blast.

Getting soaked, Paige poured more champagne, and tossed more blueberries.

A drenched Suzanne dangled prosciutto into her mouth while sensually swinging her body around the imaginary brass pole.

"Sex makes me so *hungry*!"

ENGINEER'S VOICE CAME OVER THE RADIO: "We apologize for the interruption. The radio tower has lost contact with the station. Stay tuned for KABC TRAFFIC AND WEATHER coming up—sometime.

ABOUT THE AUTHOR

Nola's career as an award-winning writer has been recognized at the Austin Film Festival, The Houston International Film Festival, Hollywood's TOP TEN writing contest and was a finalist at the Nicholl Fellowship. Nola also wrote and directed the film, *WHERE'S MARTY?* with cameo roles by Betty White, George Lopez, Tony Curtis.

Nola is a graduate of the master's program at Loyola Marymount University and attended the UCLA Film program. After her divorce and as a single mom, she taught the gifted program within the L.A. Unified School District. At this time her young students wrote, directed and filmed three incredible short films. Each winning awards at the Children's International Film Festivals.

Nola first wrote for young adults and then discovered writing for her peers. Her blog:excuseimnotdedyet.com offers suggestions and information on issues for the fifty+ woman.